WHY NOT EVERYTHING

Only one life to live, and thousands of
sexual dreams and fantasies to fulfill!

Libby Pepper wants to be erotically
aroused, seduced and passionately possessed.

Libby wants to savor the delicious
joys of infidelity.

Libby lusts after the intricate pleasures of
power, position and money.

Her dream is to zoom to the top, and
to enjoy it all.

Why not everything?

Why not?

WHY NOT EVERYTHING

A NOVEL BY
BURT HIRSCHFELD

BANTAM BOOKS · TORONTO · NEW YORK · LONDON

*This low-priced Bantam Book
has been completely reset in a type face
designed for easy reading, and was printed
from new plates. It contains the complete
text of the original hard-cover edition.*
NOT ONE WORD HAS BEEN OMITTED.

WHY NOT EVERYTHING
A Bantam Book

PRINTING HISTORY
William Morrow edition published June 1978
1st printing .... May 1978
2nd printing .... July 1978
Bantam edition / July 1979

ISBN 0–553–12402–1

Published simultaneously in the United States and Canada

*Bantam Books are published by Bantam Books, Inc. Its trade-
mark, consisting of the words "Bantam Books" and the por-
trayal of a bantam, is Registered in U.S. Patent and Trademark
Office and in other countries. Marca Registrada. Bantam
Books, Inc., 666 Fifth Avenue, New York, New York 10019.*

PRINTED IN THE UNITED STATES OF AMERICA

To Kathleen Hill,
soon to be a
beautiful woman

part one

1972

one

Happy endings are out of style.

So says Walter and Walter knows about such meaningful matters. Walter, my husband, is a man of sober single-mindedness, a trait I greatly admired when first we met.

Walter is a committed literary person. That is to say, he reads a great deal, informing his brain with large chunks of knowledge, common and extraordinary. Walter reads history, biography, novels, whodunits, *Screw* Magazine, memoirs, *Commentary;* whatever comes his way. Walter belongs to seven book clubs, subscribes to twenty-seven periodicals, including the *Times Literary Supplement, The New York Review of Books,* even *Rolling Stone;* and Walter loathes rock music. If those big-money quiz shows were still on TV, Walter could win a fortune. And, boy oh boy, could we use the cash.

Personally I prefer movies. Especially the kind they don't make anymore. Old-fashioned pictures with fadeouts, dissolves, halos of light around the faces of the leading women. I like my movie stars to look like movie stars, special, that is. Larger than life, an aristocracy of beauty and talent. What I enjoy most in movies is plenty of kissing, poetic declarations of love and eternal fealty. Also fireworks going off instead of naked men and women fooling around with each other.

Blue movies put lots of strange and unsettling ideas into my head. That makes me nervous. It becomes hard for me to concentrate, harder still to get to sleep at night. Besides, those old pictures always had happy endings, and that's what the world needs more of these days.

Which brings us back to Walter. Walter is a practical man. He insists sad endings are inevitable and realistic, even if painful. True to life is the way Walter likes his movies, plays and books. "Most people never get what they want," he is fond of saying. I say, "Why shouldn't people get what they want?" Why shouldn't I? Living happily ever after strikes me as a pretty good idea.

Here I am, reasonably pretty. Attractive, at least. Well, I used to be. What I've got is an okay face. My eyes are exotic, sort of. Not exactly Chinese, but heading in that direction. My skin is on the pale side and I have to be careful in the sun and about the kind of makeup I wear. Not that I've been using it often lately. As for my mouth, it doesn't amount to much. Too wide, too much lip. I've always admired girls with thin lips, cool and neat. The kind of mouth Cici Willigan has, a perfect mouth. And then there's my hair, kind of wiry and rebellious. There are times when I let my hair go its own way much of the time. As for my figure, it's good enough. Not what you'd call petite, except in the chest area, but slender, and with a shape. Men used to look at me a lot. Not as much as they looked at Cici, of course, but they looked. Some of them. Some of the time.

I perceived myself as an incomplete puzzle, parts scattered all around. Put them all together and—voilà! key elements still were missing.

Give me back my parts!

Self-deceiving mists beclouded my days. I grew weary of surrender in advance of battle. Ashamed of personal inadequacies and aberrations, real or fancied.

Bored doing bad things to myself. I yearned to put myself back in the picture, to rearrange the puzzle into a more livable reality. A serviceable life.

Be yourself, Libby.

I was trapped in place by a split vision of myself, left weak and relatively incapacitated. Picture this: a faint, reminiscent outline of Libby Pepper as sensitive, courageous, noble. Flip the glass and there is this crazy-house reflection of a deformed and deprived creature, insignificant in deed and in fact.

For too many years I had labored in an arid garden of self-pity that gave up weeds of discouragement in return. A West Side zombie was what I'd become, jailed by bars of my own making. A rising tide of unfocused anger left me flushed, trembling, more and more out of touch with myself and the real world. I wanted desperately to take charge of my life. Change it at least. To get a firm hold on one small segment that would belong only to me. Was that so unreasonable? Was it wrong to do what I wanted to do?

I gave it a great deal of thought and came up with a solution, which I presented to Walter. "I think we should leave the city," I told him one evening.

"Leave the city." Walter had a tendency to repeat what I said.

"Yes. It's awful, living here."

"Where would you like to live?"

"In the suburbs. Long Island, maybe. Or Connecticut. We could buy a house," I ended with an anxious rush.

"Have you forgotten," Walter replied slowly, "I'm out of work?"

I gave that one up and thought about the problem some more. And discovered another answer to my unsettled state and presented it to Walter the following week.

"What would you say if I told you I want to have another baby?" I didn't really mean it. I was all for zero population growth, at least in my own case.

He put aside the book he was reading, assessed me

gravely. He frowned. In horror, I assumed. I noticed Walter was showing more gray at the temples. If anything, he had become better looking as he grew older. Not that Walter was old, far from it. Just sliding without protest into middle age.

"Another baby?" he said. "You don't mean it."

"Stevie is almost five years old. Wouldn't it be nice? . . ."

He shook his head regretfully. "I'm out of work, remember."

Walter's logic was sturdy and unshakable. I needed another, a much sounder plan. It took nearly three weeks of hard thinking before I came up with one.

It was a marvelous idea. Exciting, stimulating, and scared me half to death. I began to quiver and was unable to get warm.

I would get a job. Go to work. Make a career. What an awful idea. I was jumpy, suspicious, exceedingly afraid of the Demanding Demons that I was about to unleash. It was a personalized fear, like the fear of being punished, a night fear trodding heavily into my consciousness. This beast could destroy me.

I found Walter behind the *Collected Poems* of James Wright. I stood erect and cleared my throat, waited for him to pay attention.

"Yes?" he said eventually.

"Suppose I told you I wanted to go back to work?"

'Go back to work.'

'Get a job.'

'Get a job—you?'

A convulsive shock broke over me. I really meant it. Really wanted to find a job, purposeful and productive work, create a special place for myself in this world. I braced myself for Walter's response, afraid he might mock me, even laugh out loud. Not Walter, that wasn't his way. His eyes glinted and his jaw seemed to square itself, like some terrific TV hero.

"Soon," he said evenly, "I'll be back at work."

No matter what I suggested, it seemed to turn Walter's thoughts back to his own employment situation.

Obviously, in his mind, we were inexorably linked up so that any movement at one end of the chain gave off a sour clunking at the other.

Walter had been out of work for nearly a year. We lived off unemployment insurance, food stamps, and had used up almost all of our savings. Not to mention my meager emotional reserves.

"One day runs into another," I said. "It's as if I exist in a fog. What happened to the Libby I once was? I want to do something with my life."

"After six years, of marriage, of not working, one does not simply go into the marketplace and announce one's availability. Times change. Skills once in demand no longer are. A new generation of workers is on the scene."

"It can't hurt if I try."

"Who will take care of our son?"

"A housekeeper."

"A good housekeeper will cost more than you're likely to earn."

That sent a chill through me. "There's always day care."

"Not for my son."

"Lots of working mothers . . ."

"I don't think so."

"We could put Steven back in nursery school. Next fall he'll enter kindergarten and—"

"The afternoons. That leaves the afternoons."

"I'll arrange it, Walter."

"I must be frank, I believe you'd be wasting your time."

Had he given his assent? My hopes rose. "Oh, I really need to go to work, to accomplish something, something that's mine alone." I began to weep.

Walter changed his position. Any overt display of emotion made him uneasy. He assumed a wise expression and delivered his all-purpose explanation for my loss of control. "You must be premenstrual."

I gagged on my resentment. "That's not it."

"Check your calendar."

"I already did."

"Then you must be coming down with something."

You bet. A bad case of depression and defeat. "I'm fine," I lied.

"Take two aspirin."

"I'll be all right."

"People don't cry when they're all right."

He brought me two aspirin, one Valium, and a glass of water. The water had a sickly gray cast to it.

"Would you like me to take your temperature?"

"No, thank you."

He kept insisting until I agreed to a trade-off; I'd get into bed and he'd bring me a cup of hot tea. He sat on the foot of the bed, not wanting to contract my disease, and read to me out of James Wright. Poetry couldn't fix what ailed me. I was tripping along a narrow line searching for dignity, self-respect, tilting crazily toward disaster, at the same time picking at the bare bones of my thoughts. What would it be like to have a job again? To do good work again? To know that somebody depended on me and was willing to pay for what I did, believing that what I contributed was mine alone and special. That made me feel good. Although I knew damn well nobody in his right mind was going to hire me. That's when the shivering started all over again.

two

The next morning Stévie woke me, yelling that his bed was wet. Stevie, beautiful fruit of my womb, my hope for the future, a four-year-old nag. A raucous reminder of my maternal shortcomings. Okay, kid, you peed in your bed, you can lie in it and suck your thumb. Oh, the guilt . . .

Stevie's relationship with his thumb played havoc with Walter's emotional stability. Walter gave no credence to the sucking instinct or other forms of oral gratification.

"You know what it means?" Walter couldn't bear to give the sucking a name.

"What?" I replied with assumed innocence. There was in me, you see, a niggling quality of character which I detested. Oh, I understood Walter's attitude very well. He perceived the pernicious traces of faggotry in every suck in the same way Tailgunner Jo McCarthy used to see Bolsheviks in every federal closet.

"What's wrong with you?" Walter said it mildly, in complete control of his emotions.

Only two things, I almost answered. My fears and my anxieties. Otherwise mark me down as being in tip-top condition. That comes from the eminent Dr. Xavier D.C. Kiernan, M.D., Ph.D. Former seminarian, former authority on urban affairs, former instructor in

Latin at Fordham University. Kiernan, one of the world's foremost dispensers of advice, fancies himself as a laureate among shrinks when what he really is is greatly full of shit. It took many, many painful and expensive sessions for me to discover that Xavier D.C. Kiernan knows very little about human people.

Question: If I'm so smart, why do I feel so bad?

Next to me, Walter stirred grumpily. Why grumpily, you wonder. When it comes to body language, Walter is a linguist. When it comes to verbal communication, however, Walter suffers from emotional lockjaw. All Walter's feelings have been deposited in a well-guarded cerebral vault. Safety first, and very little interest paid.

"Steven is crying."

"I know."

"You should do something about it."

You do something about it, I wanted to say. Just one morning, you get up first. You make the coffee. You squeeze those damned oranges. You go to Stevie, peel off those clammy, smelly pajamas. Instead I said, "I'll take care of it." Which was kind of funny since I didn't feel capable of taking care of anything. But why let on?

I opened the drapes and sneaked a look outside. The bright sunlight made all the pollutants in the air dance and sparkle, and in the distance the skyline seemed to shimmer. On such a fine morning, a right-minded wife and mother should wake up feeling good. Full of the old get-up-and-go. Instead I felt like a lost and lonely little girl. I doubted I could make it all the way through my life and was terrified by the awful possibility that I might.

"Ah." Walter had the covers up to his chin and his eyes were closed. "What a nice day."

I put on an old flannel robe but it didn't help at all. I was still cold.

"A good day to take Steven to the playground."

Playgrounds and playpens. I'm troubled by anything with bars. "I'll see." I went into the bathroom.

Walter opened his eyes when I came back into the bedroom. "You're old enough to shut the door," he said, right on schedule. Walter believes in lofty principles by which to live, beauty in all things, and privacy in the john. The splash of my pee sets Walter on edge, relatively speaking, that is.

"Next time." I gave him my most conciliatory smile and pulled on my old lavender sweater with the big C.C.N.Y. on it. There were holes in the elbows and the cuffs were frayed, but it was strung with good memories and kept me warm. A really nice sweater.

"You didn't flush."

If it weren't for Walter, how could I get along? I went back into the john and flushed. When I reappeared, Walter nodded his approval.

"You really should take Steven to the park."

"I have a very low opinion of Central Park."

"It's becoming a phobia."

"You may be right."

"Of course, I'm right. You're afraid."

"Afraid, yes. I admit it."

"There's nothing to be afraid of."

"Just muggers, purse-snatchers, rapists . . ."

"Don't exaggerate. It's safe enough during the day."

"That's how much you know."

Walter sat up and tugged at his T-shirt, which had gathered under his armpits. "What are you trying to say?"

"Last time out some weirdo flashed his pride-and-joy at me."

"His *what?*"

"His ding-dong."

"His penis?"

"That's the word, Walter."

"Is that your idea of a joke?"

"Aired it out and played rub-a-dub-dub . . ."

"In Central Park?"

"In broad daylight so nobody could miss anything."

"In the playground?"

"That was his game."

"What did you do?"

"Do! I didn't do anything. Did you expect me to lend a hand?"

"You could have left."

"I couldn't move. I was paralyzed with fright. The sonofabitch watched me every minute."

"Watched you?"

"Watched me watching him."

"You watched him do it?"

"There was a certain fascination."

"I don't understand you."

"A thing like that can ruin all your fantasies."

"Fantasies. Are you saying you fantasize about things like that?"

"Well, not exactly like that."

"I don't understand you."

"That's what Dr. Kiernan says."

End of discussion. Walter, the great reader, didn't read Freud. He didn't believe in psychiatry. I wasn't sure I did, either. But what else was there?

It required a massive effort on my part not to respond to Stevie's continuing howls, but I managed it. In the kitchen, I made coffee. It was flavored with mother's guilt. Or was it that I simply made lousy coffee?

I was halfway through that first cup when Walter appeared in the doorway. He wore only his underwear and a look of disapproval.

Walter walked into the kitchen, his Fruit of the Loom ass clenched and hardly moving. There was a time when I believed Walter had the most beautiful ass in the world. Either his ass had changed a lot or I had.

three

Anything to keep warm. I put on the oldest, softest jeans I owned over tights. Also one of Walter's old sweatshirts and two sweaters. None of it did much good. I shivered all the way along Sixty-ninth Street and into the park. Stevie ran for the sandbox in the lower playground and I settled down on one of the railroad ties that framed it, hugging myself for warmth. Stevie attacked the sand as if it were a living enemy. I wanted to bury myself in it.

After a while I began to get annoyed with myself. I was wasting time. Instead of wallowing in self-pity, I should have been mapping strategy, making plans to find a job. If that was what I really wanted to do.

It was, it was.

I could see it all. Libby Pepper, Woman of the Year. Zooming to the top of the human pyramid—title, salary, glory and sex. *Power.* What a beautiful dream. Another super production from L. P. Fantasy Films. Continuous showings going on inside my troubled head.

I should have brought along a book to occupy my mind. Occupy myself constructively, as Walter liked to say. Waste No Time was one of Walter's mottos. Fix Up Your Mind is another. Try this one: Empty Moments Lead to Empty Lives.

Not that Walter's all wrong. It's just that—ah, why complain? After all, Walter's overweening urge to stock his brain with intellectual sweetmeats is what brought us together.

We met in the Global Book Emporium, one of those dusty shops where you can find hard-to-find books. Mostly out-of-print stuff that nobody else wants. Global was on Fourth Avenue, managed by a fat old man with bifocals and a bad case of unwashed armpits.

In those days, I was doing research and campaign development for Lebow, Hineman, Seabury Advertising. Which meant I did whatever had to be done. It was my second or third job after college and I was glad to have it, even though it paid a miserable wage.

Lebow had come up with an idea for a client who was obsessed with patriotism. The campaign was called Little Known Incidents of American Glory. I remarked that all incidents of American glory were well-known. Lebow told me to get my butt into the street and come up with something worthwhile.

"Better than that," Hineman warned me.

"Something fantastic," Seabury added.

"For sixty-seven-fifty a week, before deductions," I replied, "you're lucky I come to work at all." I had a certain feistiness in those days, a product of my youth and inexperience. But even then I never felt as brave as I acted. It was the act that got me by, the mask I wore. After all, everyone wore a mask to conceal his real self, didn't they? It was just that some masks were acceptable and others not, according to society's needs and fantasies.

So there I was, backing through the narrow aisles of the Global when I spotted an old book covered in green leather that looked as if it might be good for a historic gem or two. Just as I reached for it another hand did likewise. A brief struggle ensued and I won. I looked up and there was Walter, looking very good. Pale and intellectual, with a pared-down muscularity.

At once I decided that grabbing the book out of his hand had been a mistake. I directed an encouraging smile in his direction.

"Sorry," I said, offering him the green book.

"My fault," he said.

I noticed that he had a rather noble brow and a square chin. But did he have a wife? Oh, God. One look and I was arranging a wedding party. A wife and mother, that was what life was urging on me. And no matter what else I accomplished, no matter how well I did, the social conventions bore down heavily on me. I shrugged them away.

"Take the book," I said, in what I hoped was a provocative and somewhat lewd manner.

He didn't seem to notice. "Oh, it's yours."

"No, no, you saw it first."

"Not really."

"Yes, really. I just happen to possess excellent reflexes. It's only a book."

An expression of horror crossed his heroic face. Obviously I had committed some terrible faux pas. "It's an original reproduction of a diary kept by one of the common soldiers with Doniphan. That's in the Mexican war, you know."

"I know. I think I could use that." I explained my reason for being in the Global.

"Coincidence," he said. "I, too, am in advertising. Bing, Birnbaum, Berry and Kelly."

"Imagine that!" It seemed to me that every second New Yorker worked in advertising, but I didn't want to chase him away. I liked the way Walter looked from the start. If he'd been an actor, he'd be playing Sensitive Intellectuals in movies. Or quiet, dedicated, brave men, the kind of role Henry Fonda used to get.

"New York," Walter said, giving it a great deal of meaning. I perceived a great deal of meaning in everything Walter said back then, hints of dark cerebral meanderings, suggestions of wisdom and irony, profound convolutions that I was unable to penetrate. I liked Walter a lot from the start. Also, I was lonesome

—I had no steady boyfriend and comparatively few dates. I was also relatively sexy, and beginning to think I might never get married.

"You can say that again." Not very clever, but encouraging to Walter, I hoped.

"Well," he said, edging away. "It was nice talking to you."

I nearly panicked, as if my entire future would soon be forever shattered and scattered in the dusty stacks of the Global. "What do you say to a cup of coffee?" I blurted out. "On me, naturally."

A gleam of terror went on in his eyes. Or was it merely suspicion?

I tried to reassure him. "You've been so helpful in my professional quest," I explained.

He bought it. "There are some more things I could tell you—"

"Gee," I said in awe and hope. "That would be just great."

So we got started. Like a couple of overcautious drivers afraid to burn up their engines. We ate in inexpensive Italian restaurants off heavy blue and white china with mirrors on the walls and loud noises and bad smells coming from the kitchen. The food was uniformly bad. And we talked about Walter.

All he ever wanted to do, he told me, was be a Serious Novelist. Sort of a New York version of Faulkner was what he had in mind. He'd been the best writer in high school and in college and was only marking time in the advertising business until he was ready. He managed to make virtues of his limitations and victories of his defeats. But it all sounded wonderful to me and I made it very clear that I was ready, able and willing to support his noble dream.

Except for one thing. All that bad Italian food was giving me heartburn and eventually I talked Walter into giving another ethnic segment of the society our patronage.

"Like what?" he wanted to know.

"Like Japanese."

He looked me right in the eye. "Raw fish gives me a pain in the belly."

I convinced him it was worth a try, and over a sizzling platter of Japanese vegetables and pork I told him a little about myself. When he learned that I had excelled in mathematics in school, he seemed genuinely impressed.

"You are aware, I'm sure," he said, "that you are among a small minority of women who take up mathematics, let alone get good at it."

That checked out with my observations, but I decided it was smarter not to let on. "Why do you think that's so, Walter?"

He shrugged. "Women who do go to college usually train for the obviously safe careers—teachers, nurses, that sort of thing. Those who do go into the business world do so at the lowest echelons and do not expect to progress very far."

"I hope I can get ahead."

"You seem well-equipped, Libby. You appear analytical, creative and ambitious . . ."

He made me sound like Sammy Glick or some other adventurous, power-mad type. Couldn't he see what a wonderful wife and mother I'd make? I decided I'd have to find ways and means of letting him in on my secret.

Our relationship—it was not exactly a romance, not early on—progressed in sensible, logical, slow stages. That is to say, we didn't jump right into bed. That was not my fault, I was willing. Put slightly on edge by the prospect, but loaded with anticipation and the desire to please. I'd had enough experience—let me state loud and clear that I was not the World's Girl, but neither was my hymen intact. Not by a long shot.

Be that as it may, and despite all the time Walter and I spent together, we didn't seem to be getting any closer to a bed. What we did do was go to concerts, to the theater, to poetry readings at the Public Library and to a Great Books Discussion Group.

Once in a while Walter took me to his apartment,

where he was cool, an anodyne and circumspect character. Oh, we did some kissing, once or twice making it to the tongue-sucking stage. On a few occasions his hand made casual contact with my breast, but hardly long enough for me to begin panting and moaning.

This way of life was giving me stomach cramps. The desire to place the sexual stamp of approval on our dates rose to a red-hot pitch and I began to plot devious schemes to turn Walter on. Maybe I wasn't the wildest number on the block, but as indicated, I was no virgin. That condition had been terminated some years before while I was a student at City College, done in by Professor Felipe Hernandez-Marcano, an Argentine who taught a course in the Latin American Avant-Garde. Hernandez-Marcano suggested that I was falling behind in class and could use a little private tutoring, at his apartment that afternoon at five.

Ten minutes after I arrived, Hernandez-Marcano had me naked and on my back. He kept suggesting a litany of dirty words for me to say in Spanish but since my pronunciation was such an abomination he agreed to accept their English counterparts.

"Fuck me. Pound me. Split me open."

Well, that's what Hernandez-Marcano went for. After a dozen or so encounters with the Latin Lover I discovered I had grown no warts, nor was I suffering from any new psychological deficiencies. My confidence thus reinforced, I launched myself into the Domestic Sweepstakes. Yankee Doodle Dandies came and went —Snap, Crackle, Pop; some Pizazz, but mostly a lot of Fizz. I ended up jittery, disappointed in myself, convinced that sexual satisfaction for a woman was just another popular myth. Clearly sex was designed to excite and please men, a celebration and reinforcement of their manhood. Why then were they in such a damned hurry to get it on and get it over with? It never entered my foolish mind that a woman could find real joy in bed. Or that I could have an orgasm. Or should.

Still I wanted to keep trying. And since, at the time, there was only Walter within reach, I directed all my efforts in his direction. One Sunday afternoon, when most of New York was watching the Giants lose to the Redskins on television, I sat on Walter's Victorian sofa listening to him read out of Stegner's *Angle of Repose*. Unable to restrain myself, I grabbed for Walter's cock. For a long beat, I wasn't sure he even noticed. Until he put Stegner aside.

"Libby," he said in disappointment.

I gave him an extra little squeeze and he rose up in my hand. "That's very nice, Walter."

Walter shifted around. For a moment, I thought he was making himself more available. No way. He lifted my hand away with gentle patience, as if removing the hand of a child from a much-coveted plaything.

"Ah," I said in regret.

"Uh-uh," he said in reproach. "You must understand."

"You don't want me to touch you?"

"Oh, I do."

I grabbed him again. He clucked in disapproval and removed my curled fingers, one by one. "You mustn't think I don't desire you."

"You have a funny way of showing it."

"Just keep in mind that I am a man."

"I can't get it out of my mind. Why don't we fool around a little bit?"

"Libby." He took my face in his hands. "For some time now I've been wanting to speak to you. Seriously. I have developed a great amount of feeling for you, the deepest kind of feeling—love, Libby."

"Love Libby? You love Libby?" I sounded like an idiot.

"I love you. I think we should become engaged."

My spirits perked up considerably. "Married, you mean?" Is that what I wanted, to marry Walter? The question bounced around my head like a red-hot bearing, giving painful shocks, making me wonder if I wasn't severely out of my skull. Did I really *want* to get married? To anybody? Of course I did. That's what I had spent a lifetime preparing for, to become a wife, somebody special's wife. A *special* wife. Super Wife. And then—Super Mother. In return for these exalted and immensely rewarding conditions, I would throw off all the ancient restraints, surrender my dreams of Success in Business, buckle down to the Good Life, the Truth according to what Everybody Said. What a base, buyable creature I was.

I inspected Walter closely. If you were going to marry somebody, Walter seemed like a first-class Husband-To-Be. Good-looking, tall, intelligent as hell, with a bright future assured in the ad game, with a cock that fit my hand. I judged it would fit elsewhere as well. Marriage with Walter seemed like a very good idea at the time.

"Marriage," Walter repeated. "I imagine so, eventually. Everything in its time, a time for everything."

That's what he said and in my unsettled condition it sounded swell.

So we became engaged. That figured to loosen things up a little. Don't you believe it. Kissing, yes. A soupçon of feeling and squeezing. But no serious action. Walter seemed to have unflappable self-control, but not me. I spent many an engaged night with my paw between my thighs.

By the time of our wedding night, I had almost convinced myself that I was still pure. I spent the entire goddamned night holding back. Careful to commit no unspeakable act that might shake Walter's belief in my unspoiled condition. What a meager supply of integrity I possessed.

The next morning I woke charged with affection and anxious to get going on some good sexual experimentation. Walter, already up and dressed, was deep into a new literary experience—would you believe *The Guinness Book of World Records*?

There was my future, and it reads . . .

four

Picture me. Huddled up in the lower playground envying Stevie the sand, and shivering. Asking the same old question—What Is Going to Become of Me?

Take a peek at my past glories. Most Likely to Succeed in my class at the Bronx High School of Science; you have to be pretty bright just to get into that place. Magna Cum Laude at City College; a major in math, a minor in psych. Plus courses here and courses there, taken out of sincere intellectual interest or to fill in empty spots in my social life, which were many.

Beginning in my second year in high school, I held a variety of jobs. At night, on weekends, on holidays, summers, piling up a wide and somewhat disconnected experience. There must have been a hundred jobs. Some paid well and seemed to promise an unlimited future. Others were ordinary and offered nothing beyond a small paycheck.

Taken in total, it all looked good. Even now it looks good. A background that must inevitably lead to Success. Status. Riches, even. Except it didn't work that way. From High Potential, I had slipped steeply down to Emotional Loser, your everyday West Side shlep. What happened? Who did it to me? Where did I go wrong?

She sure looked good. She'd always looked good, of course. But not this good. By some magic trick she'd acquired the face of a *Vogue* model and the body of a Hollywood sex kitten. She looked good enough to eat. At once I felt perverted, grotesque, depressed by the dirtiness of my mind. It occurred to me that I had forgotten to comb my hair.

"Still not wearing makeup," Cici said.

"You're not wearing a bra." I blushed and took in those tight pink hot pants, thigh-high French leather boots, and a lot of flashy rings on her lovely, tapered fingers. Oh, how I envied her those fingers.

"The natural look," she said. "That was always Libby's way."

I felt frumpier than usual.

"The twins," Cici said, with a gesture.

I peered around her. There stood a pair of neat and beautiful miniatures of Cici, watchful, silent, polite. The twins.

"Scottie and Brucie."

One after the other, they offered clean hands in a manly handshake. How Nice to Meet You, each of them said. Mother's Told Us All about You, they said. Compared to the twins, Stevie looked like a savage. "Nice boys," I said, and maneuvered to screen off Stevie from view.

"I," Cici was saying, "am ticketed for lunch with Bella. Do you know Bella? Of course you do. At Tavern on the Green. A series of interviews is what I'm up to. With women who count. The out-front women, breaking new ground for us all, if you know what I mean."

I didn't know what she was talking about, but I wasn't going to say so.

"*Good Housekeeping* is interested," Cici said. "None of your common women's crap shit, these are to be straight-from-the-shoulder pieces. Tell it like it is. Hit 'em where they live. Next week it's Betty, the week after, Gloria. Maybe I can do a story about your career, Libby. From Grand Concourse to Grande Dame.

That has a certain ring, don't you think? We must talk about it. The Movement, the Movement, my true passion. What are we if not sisters in blood, tears and oppression?"

I felt as if I were a couple of paragraphs behind, on a cerebral treadmill with no chance to catch up. I didn't have a career . . .

"Cici . . ."

"Poor Hedda," Cici said.

"Hedda?"

"Hedda is my housekeeper, Hedda Svenson. Beautiful woman but not reliable. Without a sense of time. Do keep an eye on the twins for me, Libby, until Hedda shows. Won't be more than a few minutes. Is that your son over there? Looks a great deal like you, Libby. Darling, you and—what's his name?—your husband, must come to dinner. One night next week, I insist. Let's say seven-thirty on Wednesday. No, that will never do. Next week is a bitch of a week. The week after. Tuesdays are out, all those gallery openings. You must make the rounds with me sometime, all those painters . . . Oh, damn, damn, the week after is a drag, all filled up. Anytime after will do. Tell you what, you call me, sweet? We'll arrange it. You will call? Bye-bye, now . . ."

She swept out of the lower playground and it was as if the sun had suddenly gone out leaving me in a world bare, gray and lifeless. I began to shiver again.

Seeing Cici again brought back all the old hungers, all the thwarted fantasies. The worlds left for others to conquer, the peaks I never attempted to scale. Not trying, that's the Original Sin. Anger and cowardice existed side by side in me, and weirdnesses and shortcomings; giving birth to passivity and inaction. Libby Pepper, a half-person, crippled and incomplete, dealing out duplicity with every breath.

No one observing the ordinary transactions of my life would have reason to be critical. I fulfilled all the requirements, or so it appeared. I did nothing bad. How could I? To be truly bad you had to dip deeply into the unknown, into the danger zone. You had to take chances.

All the old lines of thought, past dreams of glory and achievement came rushing at me. All the victories that were supposed to come my way. None of it had happened.

I had surrendered all my dreams when Walter, the man in my head, became the man in my bed. He had given me what I wanted—a husband, a home of my own, a son. Conflicting inner forces rose up, gave me trouble. Part of me wanted to blame Walter for what had happened to me—or didn't happen. For allowing me to let go of what once I had been, slipping into the soft coma of indecision and inaction. If only Walter were to blame, I could hate him and that might make it easier.

Or was it my mother? Did she encourage me too much to become a wife and a mother, to steer me away from any other kind of life?

Or was it the dream itself that was at fault? Should I have recognized it as empty and false from the start?

Cici had stirred everything up. One look at her said it all loud and clear for me. Cici had all the parts of her life in perfect working order. Husband, children, home, job. She was beautiful. Smart. She had figured life out. She must have all the answers. I would ask for her assistance, sit at her knee and absorb her wisdom. There was only one thing wrong; I didn't even know the questions.

As for me, just a sweet little job would satisfy me. Paying a modest little salary. Nothing pretentious, nothing grand. Some remote corner of the universe where I could lie low and function without much pressure in mild and quiet competence. Something that belonged exclusively to me.

Was that too much to ask for?

I made up my mind to give it a try. When I grow up, I said to myself, I want to be exactly like Cici Willigan.

Fat chance.

five

Thursday was Sybil's day to visit. She arrived, CARE package in hand, smooching Stevie quickly and lightly. Then she delivered an obligatory maternal kiss in my direction, missing by a full ten inches. It flashed into my mind that Sybil and I hadn't actually touched each other in years.

Sybil insisted that the CARE package be opened in her presence. Inside were two jars of beluga caviar, a tin of kippers and one of Twining's breakfast tea, plus a box of English water biscuits. For Stevie, Callard & Bowser's licorice toffee. He stuffed his mouth full and black saliva ran down his chin. Sybil turned away in revulsion.

Sybil was an Anglomaniac. A believer in the future of the Empire, English country weekends and the eternal soundness of the pound, no matter the evidence to the contrary. Sybil viewed the American Revolution as an act of political and social folly bordering madness. Sybil considered George III, Elizabeth and Churchill in a class by themselves. After them, according to Sybil, there is a sharp falloff in quality.

Unlike me, Sybil is birdlike in physique, gesture, and manner of speech; a tidy woman skipping along in time to a beat she alone can hear. Sybil wears clothes from Bloomie's junior department. Or Bergdorf's. Or from some very, very fashionable boutique east of Lexington Avenue.

Sybil lives in an apartment on East Seventy-ninth Street, thanks to a small but correct legacy from Sam Markson. Sam was Sybil's husband, my father, a man undervalued and overinsured during his lifetime.

Sybil looks a dozen years younger than she is. Her skin is like milk, her voice is like honey. Her hands are delicate and her feet are tiny, the ankles exquisitely designed. No matter the time of day, Sybil seems to have just come out of Cinandre, every shining auburn hair in place. She glows with good health, an inner spark, a love of life. The sort of woman who makes it through menopause with hardly a pause.

Sybil likes to talk. Words come out of her in torrents, each one salted with the inflections of upper-class Britain, an accent acquired during the three years the Marksons resided in England. An accent studiously nourished and polished ever since. Sybil was a fantastic woman and slightly unbelievable, in my opinion.

Sybil gazed down at Stevie. "I brought you a gift, my darling."

Stevie shoved more toffee into his mouth. "What's it?"

"Be polite," I said.

Out of her oversized Gucci bag—or was it Pucci?—Sybil brought forth a recording.

"A record," Stevie said in disgust.

"Wipe your chin," I said.

He did so, using his sleeve.

"Music is food for the spirit," Sybil said.

"You always bring me records," Stevie accused my mother. True, true, she always brought him records.

"The Orchestre de Paris," Sybil announced loftily. "A fine selection of French music."

Last time it had been a Verdi opera. "Say 'thank you,' " I suggested.

"Thank you." He made tracks for his room.

"Beautiful child," Sybil said in a voice redolent of Belgravia. "A strong family resemblance. My side, of course."

Translation: Stevie did not look like his mother, for which all thanks. In truth, I am cast in the likeness of Sam Markson, which leaves a little something to be desired. Sybil has described Markson as a Hasidic Abe Lincoln, and that was no compliment.

On those rare occasions when Sybil speaks well of my father, there are always reservations. She points out that he spoke seven languages, each one with a Polish accent. She mentions that Sam was a musician and that she had always been enamored of musicians. She confesses that she saw in Markson the second coming of Heifetz and was rewarded instead with second fiddle in a Meyer Davis dance band. Weddings, bar mitzvahs, debutante balls.

"Who could imagine," went Sybil's smiling lament, "Markson would have a stiff wrist and slow fingers?"

A good question.

Sybil had transformed their apartment into what she hoped would become a Continental salon, full of massive black mahogany furniture and dusty Oriental carpets. Complete with a used Steinway grand. Inevitably second-raters showed up for her Sunday musicales, which drove Sybil wild. She longed to be a winner.

In desperation and despair, Sybil skipped over my older sister, Candace, and landed on me. She prescribed large infusions of musical appreciation until I came to loathe all of it. I received instruction in how to listen. How to interpret. How to understand.

It got worse. One day Sybil noticed I had inherited Markson's long, skinny fingers. She perceived her future in my hands and put me down at the Steinway, a lesson a day for the next three years. Plus practice time. All under the near-sighted gaze of Micha Lipschitz, a rehearsal pianist at the City Center. Lipschitz was plump and sweaty, with fat thighs and bad breath.

He filled my head with sharps and flats and my stomach with nausea. A lot of good it did. A large span does not a great piano player make. "Chopsticks," anyone?

"You look tired," I said to Sybil.

"Mr. Michaels had a performance last night. We were up rather late."

Mr. Michaels was Sybil's beau; her word. Mr. Michaels sold classical recordings at Sam Goody and played cello in a string quartet on the side. He had a tin ear and a lead fist, but otherwise was a pretty nice guy. Sybil's luck with musicians was all bad.

"A little giftie for you, too." She handed over an avocado pit.

Do you laugh or cry? "Mother, how thoughtful."

"I'll get it started for you."

Sybil was more at home in my kitchen than I was, not a very difficult feat. She inserted four toothpicks into the pit, as if at the points of the compass. Filling an old Hellmann's mayonnaise jar with water, she arranged the toothpicks on the lip of the jar in such a way that the pit floated lightly on the water.

"It will grow roots and at the appropriate time I'll pot it for you. It makes a beautiful plant."

"Thanks." But I knew better. Living things did not respond to me. The avocado pit was doomed to end up in my garbage can.

"Shall we go?" Sybil said.

"Go where?"

"Bonwit's, I thought."

"I planned to take Stevie to the playground."

"What playground?"

"In Central Park."

Her brow drew up in revulsion. "Over my dead body."

"Walter says . . ."

"Central Park," snarled Sybil. "Walter," snarled Sybil.

"Walter's all right."

Sybil put things in their proper perspective. " 'All right' has never been good enough for us."

The words came out before I understood what I was saying. "What would you say if I said I was a little fed up with Walter?"

She sniffed optimistically. "What took you so long?"

"The way you talk about Father, I could ask you the same question."

"Rudeness doesn't become you, Libby. I was deceived into thinking your father was a musical genius. Time proved he was a flop at everything he tried."

"Why didn't you walk out on him?"

"You mean divorce! What kind of a woman do you take me for? In my generation, decent women never considered divorce. An ugly word, an ugly idea. Put some lipstick on, fix your hair, and we'll go."

"Being a wife isn't all it's cracked up to be, is it, Mother?"

"There are devils and angels everywhere, my dear, stairways leading to heaven, or to hell. Life can be a mug's game, if you let it. You have to know which way to go."

"I thought it was all pink roses and waltzes by Strauss and living happily ever after. You should have taught us."

"Us?"

"Candy and me."

"Candy has always known everything. It was you I was concerned about. I always believed that marriage was the only answer for your kind of girl."

Ugh. There was no way I was going to ask her what she meant by that.

She went on. "Women are genetically superior to men, you see. Morally, too. Men are defective creatures, full of flaws in their characters and some very disgusting habits."

"Then why did you keep talking marriage up as if it was the Holy Grail?"

"One always hopes one's daughters will improve on one's own performance. Shall we go?"

"Maybe I should get a divorce."

That neat triangular face turned white, still a shade or two darker than my own. She had a marvelous complexion, naturally tinted, healthy-looking, youthful. "What a terrible idea! You have a responsibility to my grandchild."

"Women do get divorced."

"Not in our family."

"Candy's working on her third husband now."

"Her fourth," Sybil corrected coolly. "Anyway, your sister lives in California."

I chose not to pursue the meandering logic of that remark. "I suppose I could have an affair . . ."

"A little respect, please. You are talking to your mother."

"What about you and Mr. Michaels?"

"Young lady, please censor your language."

"Mr. Michaels used to come around Sundays while Daddy was alive. Were you and he making it then?"

"This entire exchange is in extremely bad taste and shocks me. I am going to go to Bonwit's, with you or alone, if necessary."

"Mother, admit it."

"My dear, a lady admits nothing."

"I used to try to imagine you in bed with him, doing all sorts of sexy things."

"Where do you get such ideas? You were raised in a decent home, taught to be respectful of your elders and the accepted social institutions. Anyway, I confess to nothing. I deny nothing."

"It might be nice to have a lover."

Sybil's eyes went round. "Am I to infer that you are having an affair?"

I laughed. "Not recently, Mother. The trouble is nobody wants me."

"Nonsense. You have a very pleasant face. A little lacking in color and you must do something about your hair. Bergdorf's, I think. Bergdorf's will be more appropriate. Bergdorf's has a tranquilizing effect on people."

"Mother, I can't afford to buy anything."

"Use my charge plate."

"I'd rather go to the playground," I lied.

"Those jeans are threadbare, that sweater is awful."

"New clothes won't change anything."

"Be of good cheer, my darling. There is a rather exotic cast to your features. Some makeup, a new hairstyle, a few decent things to wear. People will never guess your father was a Pole."

"I'm not ashamed."

"Tell them you come from Tartar stock. That has a certain aura, a hint of mystery and danger. Mongol warriors, Genghis Khan, all that. Yes, that might work for you. We'll lunch at Serendipity. Stevie will like it . . ."

I gave in. "All right, Mother."

"And please, call me Sybil."

We ended up in Saks Fifth Avenue where Sybil picked out a long black evening skirt with blouse to match. It made me look like the Dragon Lady. I loved it.

"It's not for me," I protested.

Sybil paid no attention. "We'll take it."

"When would I wear it? I never go anyplace."

"If you have it, you'll wear it."

As usual, Sybil had her way. She completed the transaction and we headed for Serendipity. Deprived of the joys of McDonald's, Stevie refused to eat, disappeared under the table. With luck, he'd stay there and attract no attention. I turned to Sybil.

"I've been thinking about getting a job."

She put her fork down and stared at me. "In our family, women do not work."

"That's such an old-fashioned attitude, Mother."

"Media madness," she recited. "Let me remind you, the family still is the glue that keeps civilization together. Men work. Women raise children, spread culture, do other good works. Music is good, stealing is evil."

I wandered off in my head and lost track of what

was going on around me. Was I sliding into madness, due, of course, to an oxygen deficiency in New York's air? At that moment, the waiter brought coffee.

"Anything else, ladies?" Then he screamed and began hopping about, holding his ankle. *"He bit me!"*

Stevie. I dragged him out from under the table. There was a thin glow of victory in his eyes but no blood on his fangs. "What have you done!" I cried, shaking him.

"Mustn't bite the nice man," Sybil said, nibbling her pecan pie. My mother was unflappable.

"Rotten kid," the waiter growled, limping away.

"Faggot!" Stevie yelled after him.

"The park," Sybil said. "That's where he learns those terrible words."

"Never bite anybody," I said.

"It was just a little bite."

"Central Park is not for innocent children," Sybil put in.

"It's this city."

"It's that husband of yours."

"Why blame Walter?"

"He is the one who orders you into that park. Why isn't he working like a normal human being?"

"He's looking."

"He should be finding. A man with slow fingers I understand. That's a tragic disability, nature's terrible curse. But your husband, a college man with three degrees. Why isn't he supporting his family in style? You should live in a decent neighborhood. East of Fifth Avenue, in the upper Sixties. Yes."

I felt obliged to defend Walter. "He does his best, Mother."

"A prima donna."

"He's not like that."

"The world is filled with prima donnas and most of them can't carry a tune."

All those junky combinations of words, made meaningless by distortion and overuse. "Please, Mother," I said in a futile attempt to stop her.

"Call me Sybil. You should never have married that man. I know, I'm an expert on failures."

"What kind of man do you think I ought to have married?"

She gave it serious consideration before replying. "A man like Beethoven, for example . . ."

six

"I have been thinking about going back to work."

Eight of us were seated around a polished round coffee table. Coffee was not served, however, and smoking was forbidden. All eyes shifted my way, examining me as if I was the new girl on the block. Fear flushed all confidence out of me and I felt alone and lonely.

"What's wrong with that?" I said, as if someone had challenged me.

The Family, as my Friday night therapy group liked to call itself, made no response. Their eyes were watchful, their faces impassive, waiting for me to make a fool of myself. From out of the corner of the room came a reassuring drone, the soothing sound of Dr. Xavier D.C. Kiernan.

"Within these walls there is no right or wrong, only what is pragmatic and profitable to the individual."

Kiernan, with his cropped silver hair and goatee to match, gold-rimmed glasses perched high on the bony bridge of his narrow nose, dispatched a remote smile after his words. Talk or smile, smile or talk, never the two at once. That was Kiernan's way. He had separated life into all its various parts, nothing overlapped. All neat and very clean.

"Thinking!" That was Helene, the whore, talking. "You mean your mind's not made up yet?"

Helene made me uneasy. Not that I passed judgment on the way she earned her way. Still, since when was whoring such a terrific way to make a buck?

"Well," I said. "I've practically come to a decision."

Seymour snorted. "Practically." Seymour bore a startling resemblance to Woody Allen, only with thin lips and a predatory nose. Seymour was in television. Directing, he claimed. Repairing, I suspected.

"Almost," I said.

"Almost." Seymour sat back smugly, hands folded protectively over his crotch.

"This sounds like a typical Libby Pepper fantasy," said Mabel Foxx. Mabel was a gilded blond of some forty years who bought girdles for Macy's basement. Her husband, Charley, a New York cop, was also in The Family.

"I mean it," I said.

"What kind?" Seymour said.

Mabel Foxx was there to help. "Seymour wants to know what kind of a job Libby Pepper has in mind."

"A really excellent question," Kiernan said.

Seymour latched on to his balls in pride and pleasure.

They were all looking my way again. Waiting for the magic words that would allow them to assault me once more. Was that an awful thing to think? Didn't The Family have my interests at heart? Everybody said so, Kiernan included.

"It seems to me," Carla said in her syrupy, soothing voice, "that Libby is justified in wanting a job. I think it's a good idea."

Carla had been in therapy for eleven years, in The Family for six years. She had returned to school and intended to become a therapist herself. Carla played the guitar and sang Spanish love ballads whenever The Family had a party, which was about once a month. That's the kind of group it was.

Rodrigo, resident Third Worlder, revolutionary, and professional mugger, swore. "Wantin' is not gettin'."

"Getting," Carter added, "is not doing." Carter was a corporation lawyer.

"I've had jobs."

"Good ones, too, I'm sure," Carla said.

"Tell us about them," Seymour said.

I struggled to make my way through a closing fog. "Lukas Advertising, I worked for Lukas . . ."

Frank Rivers said, "A respectable shop. Small. Not really creative, but——" He had a million-dollar smile.

The rat. No way I'd let him into my pants. Ever. Not even if he tried.

"All of us here love you dearly, Libby Pepper," Mabel said. "What other jobs?" Mabel asked.

"SCS!" I cried in triumph.

"Whatafuckisat?" Good old Rodrigo.

Carter answered. "Standard Communications and Shipping. Good, solid stock. I've owned some shares from time to time."

"I had certain long-range ambitions . . ." I said.

"Enunciate them, if you can, Libby."

I kept my voice low. "What I wanted was to become a member of the board of directors."

There was a lot of laughing after that. Loud noise, clapping and foot stamping, crummy little cracks at my expense. I sat up straighter. But it was hard to do.

"You failed to make it?" Kiernan offered.

"The company was not open to women executives."

"The bastards," Helene griped.

"Women don't know how to give orders," Seymour threw out.

"Was that the last job you held before your marriage, Libby?" asked Kiernan.

"Yes."

"And you haven't worked since?"

"No. But that doesn't mean I can't."

"Of course not. You chose to be a wife, a mother, rather than have a career."

"I . . . guess so."

"That's nowhere," Helene said.

"Did marriage provide what you wanted?"

"I don't know, not entirely. I'm not satisfied, if that's what you mean."

"Dumbness," Rodrigo said. "All dames is dumb."

I was growing desperate. "I accomplished a great deal before my marriage."

"What?"

"Some things cannot be measured exactly."

"And since your marriage?"

"I can't say precisely."

"You have a child?" Mabel said.

"And a husband," Carla pointed out, with envy, I thought.

"A home," Kiernan said.

"Still coasting," Carter said.

He was smiling. Meanly, I was convinced. "Coasting," he said again. "Unable to adjust to the changes that have taken place. Dreaming still of becoming great again, like some great society that has fallen from the heights."

I looked around. "Is it a crime to want a job?"

Mabel said, "You wanted a family, a husband, a home. You got what you wanted, now make the best of it."

"I want to change my life."

"Try stealin', that's hard work," Rodrigo said.

"You can do anything you want," Helene said. "As sensuous as you are. But you must do something about your hair."

"Dyke," Rodrigo said.

"He who calls one is one."

"Cunt."

"Motherhood," Carla crooned dreamily, "is the most valuable and rewarding of human endeavors."

"I've done good things before," I said. "I would like to do good things again."

"About your husband," Kiernan said. "Your son?"

"What I really want——"

"Tell us, Libby Pepper."

"What I need—is a modestly satisfying interval, where nice things happen to me."

"Follow the yellow brick road."

Kiernan gestured, cutting through all the rhetoric. "Who do you think would hire you, Libby?"

Well, what can you expect from a Gentile shrink?

seven

No big deal. Just go out and begin hunting for work. I possessed all the equipment, the necessary experience, the ability to perform on the job. Or so I kept telling myself.

Years before, when in need of work, I had made application at the Harold Schor Agency. This shortly after I was graduated from college. Mr. Schor had placed me as an interviewer with a marketing research company. The pay was low, the work on the dull side, and it offered no chance for advancement. It took me nearly a year to discover all that and work up nerve enough to move on.

Still, I was willing to give Harold Schor a second chance. Susie Lebenthal, herself the mother of two, and living directly across the hall, agreed to take care of Stevie for the morning. I left him in her foyer, kicking and screaming, giving me a severe case of mother's guilt. Ah, to hell with it . . .

I rode the bus down to Forty-second Street, increasingly aware that I was becoming estranged from everything around me. I was a tourist in a familiar landscape, yet unable to connect, unable to identify. All around me was intensifying activity. Crowds of strangers pressing in, giving off rude street noises that made no sense to me. I felt in imminent danger of exposure, of pain and destruction. I longed to shrug away all those overvalued daydreams and turn myself into a fair-trade item. You get what you pay for.

Across from the Public Library, in a solid old building was the Harold Schor Agency. By the time the elevator lifted me to the twenty-second floor my sweat was icy and I was trembling. The American Dream was for me a living nightmare. All I wanted was to be happy. I never knew it could take so much out of you.

I came up to an ancient wooden door with opaque glass in the upper portion and stared at the gilt lettering:

HAROLD SCHOR
Personnel

My palms were damp and I suspected a drop or two had dribbled into my panties. I put my hand on the shiny brass knob. My fingers tightened but the knob wouldn't turn. My wrist refused to function as intended. I was unable to make that knob budge. I could not open the door. I had visions of myself attached forever to that knob, a living doorstop always in the way of those able to proceed bravely through life. I snatched my hand away and ran for the elevator, and the street.

I boarded the M-104 bus and was jolted up Broadway to Sixty-eighth Street. I went into the A&P and bought two cans of Progresso minestrone, one of my all-time favorites, then went home. Relatively secure behind the triple-locked door, I heated a can of soup and spooned it down, along with a couple of dozen Ritz crackers. In time I began to calm down.

My mind wandered and I dreamed I was a movie star. Movie stars were rich and famous on their own terms and so they were free. Or at least they seemed to be. Success, I was convinced, was an effective painkiller.

Success. Always I came back to that. I thrived on

the promise of its rare and fattening nutrients. I wanted very much to be a controlling factor in the world, to make hard deals with reality, to kick ass.

I was enslaved to adolescent fantasies. Chained by rough equations of accomplishment, of pain and power, of gold and glory, of decisive sexual triumphs. So much star-spangled foolishness, I told myself. It was all nothing.

However . . . I couldn't stop. On the following Monday I launched myself out into the asphalt jungle once again. This time, courtesy of the Sunday *Times*.

I studied the columns, page after page. My fingers grew stained with newsprint and poring over that tiny type gave me a headache. Anything to avoid confronting closed doors with resistant doorknobs. The *Times* was excellent emotional insulation against that terrifying world outside.

I blamed it all on Cici. Putting her in my path was Fate's Dirtiest Trick, placing me directly into the line of fire of doom and disaster. A scurvy device, forcing me to compare the promising creature I'd once been with the quivering bunny rabbit I'd turned into. No fair.

Here it was. I would find a job. Do good work, make lots of money, acquire all the ornaments and trophies capitalism could offer. Provide a purpose to my life.

No longer was I going to be satisfied being an incompatible housewife, a tormented mother, just another idiosyncratic female prowling the city's streets and coming up empty.

Make a move now or my future was clear and unappetizing. I'd likely become one of those women you see shuffling along the curb kicking and spitting, cursing at strangers, shopping bags loaded with trashy goods, taking shelter in doorways and spending their nights in the waiting room at Grand Central. Ugh.

Back to the *Times* I went until my eyes began to blink and tear and my head grew mushy. I leaned back, tuned out, drifted aimlessly into space.

There I was, working for the big GM, baby. Gen-

eral Motors. Not just working, but V.P. in charge of
Planning, Creation, Invention, and other Good Things.
Big job.

RESPONSIBILITY: *Enormous.*
SALARY: *Fabulous.*
POWER: *Infinite.*

I stand before the board of directors. All those rich
old men and all those rich young men working so hard
to act like rich old men. They check me out. I stare
them down.

"Sorry," they say in one apologetic voice.

"Just don't do it again, fellas." They shuffle feet,
scratch and snuffle. I give them my best grin. "Forget
it, okay." I put a cigarette between my lips. The young
ones scramble to light me.

"I can't give you men much time . . ."

The chairman understands. He stutters. "We have ob-
served your career in the months since you were
gracious enough to join us, Libby. *Mrs.* Pepper, that
is. Ms., I mean."

"Save the soft soap, Chairman. Say what's on your
corporate mind."

"Just so. Exactly. You've noticed, I'm sure, Chrys-
ler's catching up. Ford's on our tail. VW—those Germans can be tricky."

"I've made a close study of the Hun. Go on."

"There! You see! I told the board your grasp of
these matters was phenomenal. Ms., we require your
imagination. Creativity. Strength, purpose, dedication.
Your unique knowledge of people, finance, the way
the economic system functions."

A week later I'm on the cover of *Time, Newsweek,
Business Week* and *U.S. News and World Report.
Playboy* devotes its centerfold to the first queen of a
major U.S. corporation. Give the boys a thrill—a peek at
my bare bottom and one nipple in profile. But that's all.

Sales of GM cars skyrocket. Pontiac brings out a
new model—the Queen Libby. It sells like crazy.

Hef invites me out to the mansion. The White House wants me for dinner. Warren Beatty pleads for a date, gets his sister, the dancer, to intervene on his behalf. Pack it in, men, Libby's into bigger and better stuff.

I ask you, is that a great fantasy? One of my best. But it had one flaw; it brought me no closer to finding a real job. So I composed a résumé, rewriting it seventeen times. Had it Xeroxed. Next I worked up a letter, four different versions, actually, each tailored to different kinds of ads. Résumés and letters went into the mail and I was left with nothing to do but sit back and wait.

I prepared in advance for my first interview. Lipstick, eye shadow and liner, a touch of rouge. One look in the mirror almost sent me screaming back to bed; I resembled one of Stevie's fright masks.

I worked feverishly on my hair. Nothing did much good. When I was finished it still looked as if it had been seared by a high voltage line gone mad.

Then I discovered I had nothing to wear. Literally. It had been years since I had bought anything new and everything in my closet was worn and frayed and out of style. It took a major effort of will for me to go on; I settled on a black skirt and a ribbed purple turtleneck. I draped a massive brass sunburst on a chain around my neck and went back to the mirror. I hoped to appear conservative, serious, ready to take on large responsibilities. Instead I saw a woman wild of hair and eye, pale, glowering, a creature out of a Greenwich Village dope den.

I decided not to dwell on it. I located Walter comfortably curled up on the couch behind Leslie Fiedler's *Love and Death in the American Novel.* "Is it good?" I said, not giving a damn but trying to attract his attention.

He looked me over. "Where do you think you're going?"

I told him.

He brought Fiedler right back up into reading position.

"Do I look all right?"

"Fine," he lied.

I did not look fine. I did not feel fine. "I'm a little nervous."

"What arrangements have you made about Steven?"

"Stevie? I thought you'd babysit for a few hours, till I get back."

"I've got to go out."

My brain tipped and tilted. There had been no mention of his going anywhere when I told him about my interview. Hadn't we discussed Stevie? Hadn't he agreed to sit while I was away? I couldn't be sure about anything.

"You can do the interview another day."

"Yes," I said reflexively. *No!* No. My nerve quotient was low, would not carry over to another day. Now or never. "I'll take Stevie along."

I found my son drinking water out of the toilet bowl.

"We're going out," I told him.

"Don't wanna go out."

"We're going."

"The playground."

"We don't have much time."

"No."

Somehow I managed to get him dressed and out of the apartment, onto a bus.

Bell Advertising was on the thirty-sixth floor, looking down on Madison Avenue. The reception room was constructed of glass, polished chrome and soft green leather. A carved Chinese rug was on the floor and a skinny palm tree grew out of a glazed white pot in one corner. Some magazines were stacked neatly on a glass coffee table.

The receptionist, who resembled the youthful Ava Gardner, inspected me suspiciously. "May I help you?"

"Mr. Bledsoe is expecting me. I'm Libby Pepper."

She picked up the telephone to announce me, then let out a screech, came sprinting out from behind her desk. Across the room, Stevie was making an earnest effort to topple the palm tree. Young Ava arrived in the nick of time.

"Mustn't break the tree, little boy." Young Ava waggled a finger in Stevie's face. He lunged, teeth snapping. She avoided his charge only barely and retreated quickly to her place behind the desk, pale and shaken. "Very aggressive child."

"It's the times we live in," I said.

She put through the call to Bledsoe's office and said I was to go right in. I admonished Stevie to be good, to be quiet, to obey Young Ava. I left before he could answer.

Bledsoe was a plump man with damp eyes and dry lips. He wore a suit made out of shining Italian silk and a pink shirt and a black tie. He rubbed his hands together and got me into a steel-and-leather chair that looked very expensive and made sitting very uncomfortable.

I crossed my legs and uncrossed them and crossed them again. Bledsoe didn't miss a cross, an experienced crotch-watcher. My nervousness increased and I wished I were someplace else.

"Good of you to come," he said.

I tucked my legs under the chair, hands folded primly in my lap. Bledsoe, enjoying my discomfort, wiped his eyes and wet his lips.

"So you want to join up with Bell Advertising?"

He made it sound as if I intended to enlist in the military.

"You've worked the Street before?"

"It's all in my résumé."

"So it is, so it is. Bell is an extremely creative shop."

Ever met an advertising man who didn't characterize himself as a Creative Person? "I understand," I murmured discreetly.

"The question is, are you equipped to keep up? At Bell we move fast. Think fast. Onward and upward, you might say."

"I used to be quite good . . ."

"Ah, 'used to.' There's the rub."

"I've kept in touch . . ."

"How long since you were active in the profession? Eight, nine years?"

"Six, just six."

"Nothing like being in the swim, though, is there? Mixing it up every day, the bumps, the grinds, the hits, the misses. This is a very impressive résumé, a wide variety of experience. Commendable, commendable. Do you take shorthand?"

"The job is for a copywriter, I thought . . ."

"Oh, yes. But coming off the street this way. Cold, that is. We prefer our people to become part of the team, learn our ways, our winning ways. Then— Ah, the point is, talent always rises here at Bell. Reveals itself rapidly."

"I'm not a secretary."

"You can type?"

"Type?"

"Personnel administers a test."

"A test?"

He was on his feet, moving me toward the door. "Think about what I've said. Consider all the ramifications, the possibilities . . ."

"Possibilities?"

"You can begin in the typing pool, move up . . ."

"I'm not a typist."

"Advancement can be swift. The opportunities limitless."

"Your response to my application said nothing about typing—"

"Let us know."

"What I want—"

"Keep in touch."

"My interest lies in another—"

"Ambition is treasured at Bell."

"I was under the impression—"

"Check back in a month or so."

"Yes."

"Thank you for coming."

"Thank you."

"Thank you."

I found my way back to the reception room and encountered a familiar stench. My Stevie had dumped in his pants. Young Ava was not amused.

eight

Mired in an emotional bog I rattled and rolled around to shake off an extraneous burden. There was always maternal culpability. So I fastened on Stevie and dragged him off to see the dinosaur skeletons at the Museum of Natural History, determined to do my motherly duty, no matter what the poor kid might want.

"Knowledge is ammunition for living," I told him, quoting Walter precisely.

"Bones," he said at the sight of brontosaurus.

"Culture is the joy of life," I responded, and steered him to the large Indian dugout.

"Where's the motor?" he wanted to know.

I guided him through the gallery of gems, laboriously explaining how precious stones came into being, why people prized them. Stevie said he was bored.

Another day, I loaded him onto the subway, rode all the way out to Coney Island and the aquarium. He let me have it right between the eyes. "I hate fish," he announced.

We went to the Bronx Zoo. I had to carry him from cage to cage.

The ballet "Coppelia": I loved it, he sucked his thumb.

Nothing worked. Nothing helped to diminish that awful tear of looking for a job. Even worse, what if my dreams came true and I found a job? I'd be out there in the jungle once again on my own, no handsome prince to defend me. For this Cinderella, it was always midnight. The landscape of my soul was barren and without promise.

I began to question the entire project. It seemed suddenly an exercise in personal futility, the outcome preordained. Win or lose, I would come out of it a loser. I desperately needed someone to talk to, to enlist on my side. I tried Walter once again. He heard me out as I recited a litany of my fears and shortcomings, real and imagined.

"I have a great deal of faith in you."

That came as a surprise. "I wish I did."

"You'll work it all out."

"How?"

"You'll find a way."

His apparent confidence alarmed me even more. I had always believed Walter understood me in ways no one else did. But if he thought I was capable of directing my own destiny, he was wrong. And if he was wrong about that, he was certainly wrong about many other things as well.

I found myself thinking about Mexico. A quick trip to Juárez and a cheap but binding divorce. Goodbye Walter. There, south of the border, I would fall passionately in love with a handsome airline pilot who would fly me to Acapulco where he would perform all manner of aberrant activities on my body, to my edification and delight. He would speak no English and I would speak no Spanish. But how well we'd communicate!

Viva, viva!

With my luck, I'd get a bad case of *turista,* fall prey to bandits, and never be heard of again. I wrote off the perverted pilot and called Cici Willigan.

"I need to talk to someone," I told her.

"Let's have lunch." Now that's a friend. "The Ginger Man all right?"

Burger King would have been all right.

The Ginger Man is one of those restaurants that looks as if it has been in place for a century or more. In fact, it's comparatively new. Carefully designed to appear nostalgic, it has a bar that's always crowded and food that is no better than it should be. Naturally it is overpriced.

Everybody in the place looked as if he or she were famous. Or about to become famous. Lots of French-made blue jeans and blue blazers or Shaggy Dog sweaters from J. Press.

The maître d' greeted me as if I'd come to the wrong place. He looked like an actor who did Alka Seltzer commercials. As soon as I mentioned Cici's name, he warmed up, led me to her table.

She sat with her back to the wall, able to watch the world go by, talking to a beautiful young man.

"Ralph Muir," Cici said, "meet Libby Pepper."

"Libby," he said in a resonant baritone.

"Anybody ever tell you you look like Cary Grant?" I said.

"All the time," he drawled. He shrugged. Great shoulders, like Robert Mitchum. What a dirty dream Ralph Muir would make.

"You may go now, Ralph," Cici said. God, if he had been mine I'd never let him out of my sight.

He blew a kiss and walked away. He had a walk like John Wayne.

"How could you send him away, Cici? He's magnificent."

"He is pretty, I guess."

I got it. Cici and Ralph Muir were engaged in a clandestine affair and she was playing it cool, secret and safe. I was shocked. I was envious. I told her so.

She laughed.

"How do you manage it?" I said.

"Manage what?"

"Doesn't your husband suspect?"

"Dear Libby, couldn't you tell? Ralph is one of the regular New York tutti-fruttis. He dances in the City Ballet."

"You mean he's gay?"

"None gayer. He's handy to know, whenever I need an escort and my husband's too busy . . ."

My mind reached back to high school. "I can remember you saying that when you got married you would never sleep with another man."

"I said that?"

"Do you still feel the same way?"

"Do you? Have you been faithful to—what's his name, Walter?"

"Well, nobody's been pounding at my bedroom door lately."

She assessed me gravely. "Oh, I imagine lots of men would like to make love to you, Libby. You have a vein of sensuality, it's always been there. I have always been a faithful wife," she ended.

I was disappointed. "Really?"

"Never even tempted."

I felt like some kind of weird, crazy lady, full of outlandish sexual cravings, all going unfulfilled.

"Let's face it," Cici was saying, "one teaspoon of seminal fluid isn't worth the trouble. All the arrangements, the sneaking around, a place to do it. So many bothersome details."

"I never thought of it that way."

She nodded. "The marriage vows mean a great deal to me."

"Oh, I agree," I said quickly.

"Sex is not that important, after all."

What could I say? My day dreams and my night dreams frequently shot me off into uncharted sexual orbits, putting an edge on my nerves. It seemed to me I spent more time imagining forbidden things of life than sampling them.

"Are you in some kind of trouble?" Cici said, after

the waiter took our drink order. He reminded me of Steve McQueen.

"I need some advice."

Cici glanced at her watch.

"It won't take long."

"I'm interviewing the mayor at three."

"He's so handsome."

She seemed to take it all in stride, a toss of her fine feline head, a quicksilver show of teeth. "What's your problem, Libby?"

"I want to go to work."

"Of course you do. What intelligent woman is content to stay home and muck around in drudgery? Does he—your husband, Walter, object? Most men do."

"He hasn't said no exactly."

"But he hasn't said yes, either?"

"Walter manages to slip and slide around most issues."

"Don't they all." She patted my hand. "Do whatever you think is best for you, Libby. The women's movement is growing, our time has come. Historical necessity is on our side."

I wasn't sure what she was talking about. "I'm not into group activities."

She smiled, pityingly, I thought. "We're all sisters in the flesh."

"I'm scared, Cici."

"Men, they've done this to us. Turned women into sniveling, helpless creatures dependent on them."

"Maybe you're right."

"Of course I am. Women are designed to be strong, courageous and aggressive."

Sounded good to me. Only why was I so frightened so much of the time? So uncertain and cowardly?

Cici talked through the meal. I may not have understood all that she said but I liked the way it sounded. When the check came, I reached for it. She made no objection.

I was halfway home when it occurred to me that

Ralph Muir was not gay. Not all the time, anyway.
He and Cici almost certainly were sleeping together.
Knowing that Cici felt compelled to lie to me made me
feel much better.

Fifteen minutes later I walked into the apartment
and the phone began to ring. The Executive Placement Service was calling to turn my life inside out.

It took twenty-five minutes of fast, hard talk to
get Sybil to agree.

"But with conditions," she insisted.

"Whatever you say," I said.

"Baby-sitting is not my style."

"Whatever you say, Mother."

"You will deliver Stevie to my apartment in person,
by yourself."

"Yes."

"And retrieve him in like manner."

Couldn't I send UPS instead, I almost said, but
didn't by reason of my great restraint. "Yes, Mother."

"And call me Sybil, for God's sake!" She slammed
down the phone. Our relationship was getting riper if
not richer.

I fulfilled my delivery obligations and hurried down
to the Executive Placement Service. In the elevator I
came under the lecherous scrutiny of a man in dark
glasses, obviously a sex maniac. I kept my gaze averted
and was glad to leave him behind.

This time I had no trouble opening the agency door.
The interviewer who had contacted me was named
Beth Dooley, a very attractive black woman about my
own age. She tried to put me at my ease.

"You prepared an excellent résumé."

"Thank you." My cheeks felt stiff, my tongue clum-
sy, my lips swollen and slow to function. Nobody
had complimented me in a long time and I was immediately suspicious.

Beth Dooley began to read off some of the jobs
I'd held. "Copywriter, researcher, office manager,

computer planning and management . . ." She looked up. "That's a lot?"

There was an unspoken question in her voice. "I've always worked, since high school. Weekends, evenings, part-time, summers. It adds up."

"You've been away from it for a number of years?"

"I got married, had a child. Just sort of slipped into another world. Out of things. Left out, I guess."

"Now you want to get back in?"

"If I can."

"I don't see why not. Your qualifications are first class . . ."

They are?

"You're obviously bright . . ."

Me, Libby Pepper?

". . . and you're attractive, personable."

Aw, shucks.

"You've heard of IFP, of course?"

International Food Products. "Oh, yes."

"There's an opening there."

"Oh."

"A number of jobs, in fact, for the right people. Personnel systems operators . . ."

I put on what I hoped was a confident smile, but said nothing.

"Just your old-fashioned efficiency expert," she explained. "Wearing a contemporary disguise. I think you can handle it. Do you?"

"Oh, yes." Damned if I believed that for a minute. The whole process was an empty charade designed to entertain, to give the illusion of accomplishment without substance.

"IFP is rather thorough. There'll be a number of interviews. They want fifteen people and based on your background I'd have to say your chances are better than good. If you're interested, that is?"

"I'm interested." Also scared. My knees were beating out a fast Latin tempo and I had to pee something fierce.

Beth Dooley placed an official-looking document in front of me. "An agency contract. It includes the fee schedule. Read it and sign if you agree."

I couldn't wait. I scribbled my name. I'd've signed with the devil. And perhaps I had.

"You were supposed to be here fifteen minutes ago!" Sybil made it sound as if I'd betrayed Her Royal Highness the Queen, God and Country in one sweet stroke. Her voice was stretched thin with disdain. "I do not want to listen to excuses."

I persisted. "The interview took longer than I expected."

"You are a mother." I know, I know, I didn't say. "You have responsibilities." There was no way to forget them. "Obligations." Sybil could, under a full head of steam, turn into a world-champion list-maker. "When may I expect you?"

It felt as if my throat was closing down for the day. I forced the words out. "They arranged an interview for me at International Food Products in an hour."

"And you agreed to that?" Oh, the scorn, the glittering edge of pain.

"The job—I had no choice."

"There is always a choice." Sybil was eternally logical if not always rational, I decided. She reached back into history. "Even as a child, you were without a sense of duty, never aware of where your primary responsibilities lay." She summoned up the ghost of Sam Markson and I knew I was beaten. "You were always a source of disappointment to your father and me. Perhaps it was our fault . . ."

The Department of Dirty Parental Tricks. Sybil was a charter member. I suspected I had passed through my apprenticeship, was well on my way to being a full member, too. "All right, Mother. I'll call off the interview."

"And blame me when you don't get the job! You certainly will not. I brought my daughters up to have honor, women of their word. You will participate in the interview as planned. Failures, alibis, dissembling. I've listened to too much of that in my lifetime."

"I really appreciate . . ."

"I will take your son, *your* son, to lunch at the Modern Museum and expose him to some good art. At three o'clock, I shall expect to see you in the lobby. Please be prompt."

"Thank you, Mother."

She exhaled, cool and critical. "You'll never learn . . ."

"What?"

"To call me Sybil."

International Food Products, Inc. They own their own building on Lexington Avenue. Not one of those mirrored erections springing up all over town, but an old, honest-to-architect building made out of solid brick and dependably spread mortar. It had a granite cornerstone and a bronze plaque etched with the company name.

IFP was no fly-by-night outfit, either. A century ago they had wheeled and dealed in places like Nicaragua and Guatemala, pulling out tons of bananas and coffee beans. Still in the fruit business, IFP also ships and packages and processes a variety of foods, not to mention TV dinners. They own a trucking company, a ship line, a half-dozen coal mines and some oil fields in the Gulf of Mexico, among other moneymaking interests. Six advertising agencies are kept busy grinding out material for magazines, newspapers, radio and television. Their commercials are top-drawer, entertaining and selling.

In the ground floor lobby—all Carrara marble with black trim—there were eight armed guards. Back in the Sixties, some political hotshot had planted a bomb in one of the executive rest rooms, taking out four toilets, two urinals and one nonfunctioning air-dryer. IFP never forgets, therefore the guards. I gave my name to a man at the reception desk and he checked me out with someone in personnel before passing me through to the elevators.

On the ninth floor, I was escorted down a narrow, softly lighted corridor to a door marked:

JONATHAN MARRAS
Personnel Manager

A secretary directed me with a polite smile and a gentle word through another door. Jonathan Marras, a soft man with puffy cheeks and gray sideburns, rose to greet me. He had one of those faces that never changed, no matter his expression. He indicated where I was to sit.

"Be comfortable, Mrs. Pepper."

I arranged myself with care. Knees tightly pressed together, skirt modestly in place, hands folded in my lap. I tried not to blink or otherwise reveal how damned scared I was.

"Nice to see you, Mrs. Pepper."

"Nice to see you, Mr. Marras."

He cleared his throat. "Miss Dooley spoke very highly of you."

I searched for a noncontroversial reply. "She was very kind."

"I've studied your résumé."

I let the corners of my mouth lift, but not too much. With no great effort, I could have come undone.

"Interesting background. How much did Beth Dooley tell you about the job?"

"Personnel systems operators . . ."

"Ah." He leaned back. "Some excellent people have come to us via Executive Placement. Dooley is good at what she does. Her competence is high and no criticism is implied or should be inferred."

"Oh, no." I grew worried.

"But the agency does only preliminary screening. Final decision resides in company hands. You understand?"

"Oh, yes." My thighs were damp with perspiration and I was afraid to change my position lest they make unseemly slurping noises.

"Some words about the company," Marras was saying. "As you undoubtedly know, the company owns plants, factories, plantations throughout the free world. Essentially we grow and process foodstuffs. Packaging and marketing takes place everywhere. Branches everywhere. Sales, distribution, shipping, records, the like. Personnel systems operators . . ."

I broke in and that was a mistake. "Miss Dooley said there were fifteen openings."

"Fifteen jobs," he corrected me coldly. "Fourteen of them have been filled with first-rate men, all soon to embark on a special training program. That leaves one *opening.*"

My hopes plummeted. What chance had I against the strong competition that must surely exist? Experienced, trained, emotionally stable men and women. All unburdened by personal doubt or deficiency. I felt like a small child on a large carousel, competing for the last painted horse. No horse, no ride.

"What we do here at IFP," Marras was saying, "is to infuse into the system, so to speak, any new people. There is, I should point out, an IFP way of doing things. Doing *what,* you ask yourself. I will answer. These men, these personnel systems operators of ours, will travel extensively. Didn't Beth Dooley so inform you? Not her fault. No blame attached. Outsiders tend to commit such oversights. Our people will go to our various plants, outlets and so on, helping to tighten up, sharpen, streamline company operations."

That revived some good memories. "I'm very good at . . ."

"You were at IBM?"

"Two summers and—"

"Also World Wide Oil and Transport. Excellent corporate entity. Their training programs are legendary."

"I didn't—"

"Didn't you? Too bad. Your record at the Management Institute was excellent. We know the work done at NYU. Commendable. Dooley did well to send you along."

My hopes rose. "Thank you."

"However . . ."

Down they went.

"It's been some time since you were last employed . . ."

He was looking for a response. I unclenched my fingers, relaxed my sphincter, wiggled the toes of my right foot. "When I got married . . ."

"You gave up working," he supplied. "Admirable."

"But now . . ."

"The family, the family. We at IFP feed the American family, you could say. Children?"

"I have a son."

"Only one?" He seemed disappointed. He examined my résumé. "Six years since? . . . It can be hard to swing back into the world of commerce. Do you sincerely believe? . . ."

"Oh, yes. I'm sure of it."

"You are?"

"Oh, yes."

"Without a great deal of trouble, would you say?"

"No trouble at all."

"You've kept up?"

"Trade magazines, journals, business papers."

"Good, good. Personally, I have no doubts. Do you have any doubts?"

"Doubts? Me? None at all."

"Then you're confident?"

"Oh, very. Very. Very confident." What I didn't tell him was that although there were times when I did feel very confident, I was never *that* sure of myself.

"Confidence is important, Mrs. Pepper."

"I agree."

"I feel confident enough to say you are an outstanding applicant."

My cup overflowed. "You mean I'm hired?"

"Oh, I wouldn't want to go that far. You see, it lies

not within my province to make that statement. Have I given that impression?"

"Oh, no, not you. It's me, not you."

"My recommendation bears a great deal of weight, I'd say. But it is only one step in the sifting process, as I like to call it. Screening out the obviously unfit applicant, which surely you are not."

"Not?"

"Not at all. Final decision must be made by an authority higher than my own."

"A higher authority." The phrase owned a certain solid resonance. "Ah," I said in conclusion.

He nodded sagely. "Our Mr. Emil Lieber."

"The higher authority?"

"Exactly. Vice-president and manager of Systems Development, Executive Personnel Affairs, Internal Company Operations and Expansion."

"I see."

"Mr. Lieber will want to consult with you face-to-face, as we say."

"I see."

"His is the ultimate judgment."

"The final decision."

"As we say. Should you wish to continue the sifting process? . . ." He waited for me to answer.

"Oh, yes. I wish to continue."

"Well, good. I'll arrange an appointment with Mr. Lieber for you, if that is your desire."

A vision of an impatient Sybil flashed into my mind. She looked like an angry Lilli Palmer, caustic, dangerous, and so very lovely. I gave Mr. Marras my absolutely best smile, the one Sybil used to say lit up my face.

"That is my desire . . ."

The question of Higher Authority was also on Walter's mind. Enough so that after hearing my report of the meeting with Mr. Marras, he made no moves in the direction of his book. Instead he made encouraging comments ranging from "I know you'll get the job," to "If not this one, then another. You've got what it takes." Walter had his surprising moments and I told him so. But he wasn't interested in continuing that discussion.

"I've been thinking," he said.

"Oh?"

"About Steven."

"What about Steven?"

"I believe the time has come to introduce Steven to religion."

Now that surprised me. Less than a year ago I had suggested enrolling Stevie in a Bible class at a nearby synagogue, to Walter's considerable annoyance.

He had said, "You know how I feel about organized religion."

Walter was opposed to organized religion. Also unorganized religion. And what he called "the superstition of God." "All those kids with their cults," he liked to say. "Becoming Muslims or Buddhists or Jesus Freaks. It's all a bunch of voodoo, dressed up in chic dialogue. A lot of myths and legends, all proof that religion is a fraud, that God is dead."

It flashed into my mind that it might just be the reverse. All those kids might be proof that God had never died, was alive and thriving in their search for spiritual values. But I wasn't very sure of my position and so I said nothing.

"Yes," Walter said deliberately. "It might be a good thing if Steven were to learn about his religious heritage."

"What made you change your mind?"

Walter answered confidently. "A parent has a responsibility to introduce his child to the realities of this world. Negatively or otherwise, religion is a force in all our lives, don't you agree with me? Let's prepare Steven, give him the strength of knowledge, equip him to make the intelligent and rational choice when he grows up."

I said with some trepidation, "I always thought religion was an irrational belief."

"Nonsense."

"Faith, and all that."

"The human brain is a marvelous instrument. It can comprehend and explain everything. Let's enroll Steven in a Bible class."

"Jewish?"

"Of course."

The idea pleased me. My Jewishness was more of a soft cultural heritage than a religious belief. Neither of my parents was a believer and yet they had quietly insisted on remaining Jews, though it was seldom mentioned in our home. I put it all down to complex feelings about their European experience. Sam Markson had told me once that anti-Semitism was an accepted condition of life in Poland and when the Nazis entered that country many Poles welcomed them with open arms. So in some small and undramatic way, I felt that teaching Stevie what it meant to be a Jew would pay off an unnamed debt to Sam Markson.

"There's a temple on Seventy-first Street," I said to Walter. "It's convenient and—"

"Absolutely not."

"Not? Why not?"

"It's Reform."

"I thought that's what you would want for Stevie."

"Think again. Those Reform Jews might as well be Episcopalians, they're so watered down."

Recognizing a joke when I heard one, I laughed. My mistake.

Walter frowned. "If I wanted my son to study religion with somebody with a drooping mustache who smokes pot I'd turn him over to those Hare Krishna people."

"I think they're against drugs and all the boys shave their heads, don't they?"

"Don't confuse the issue. You want first-rate fruit you go to a first-rate fruit market."

"Conservative," I said brightly.

Walter was patient with me. "If a thing's worth doing at all, it's worth doing well."

"Not Orthodox!"

"Why not Orthodox?"

I searched my memory for an answer. "You always said those Orthodox were crazy, that they tried to stop the Israeli soldiers from fighting during the War of Independence."

"Don't confuse the issue. That had to do with the biblical account of how the nation of Israel would come back into being. First the angel Elijah would appear to herald the coming of the Messiah, then the Messiah himself. Those old Jews in Palestine, they wanted it all by the book, not the Israeli army."

"Thank God for Golda Meir," I said.

"Not so much Golda," Walter said. "Ben Gurion, Dayan, Rabin, men like that. Find an Orthodox synagogue for Steven."

It's not easy to do that in the middle of New York. Manhattan's primary orthodoxy is unorthodoxy. Everybody's hewing to his own line of thought, subject to change without warning, naturally. I made phone calls. Oh, did I make phone calls. To twelve Reforms, seven Conservatives, and one humanist congregation that didn't believe in God. Finally I located Temple Adath Ben-Ezra, between Madison and Lexington, on the Upper East Side. Where else?

I dialed the number and asked to speak to the rabbi. A competent-sounding woman asked for my name, where I lived, and what the purpose of my call was. She sounded exactly like the receptionist in my doctor's office.

"To speak to the rabbi," I said sweetly.

Didn't bother her a bit. "Can you inform me of the gist of your business with Rabbi?"

"I'm in the midst of a spiritual crisis."

That got to her. "A breakdown! Fantastic. Rabbi is trained in the latest psychoanalytic techniques. He is a man who knows how to deal with people . . ."

A hand of blackjack, maybe . . .

"Hang on, will you?"

I hung.

"Shalom." Rabbi's voice had been chipped out of Mosaic Law.

"My name is Libby Pepper," I began.

"You're Jewish?" he interrupted. He was taking no chances on an outsider getting the benefit of his psychoanalytic techniques. A cultural, religious, and undoubtedly genetic hand-me-down, straight from Freud to rabbi. So how come I had a goyish shrink?

"Yes, I'm Jewish." But not much, I felt like adding.

"Ah," he said impressively. "You require my assistance, Mrs. Pepper? Even though you are not a member of our congregation, when a Jew is in trouble . . ."

I told him my problem.

"Oh," he said, clearly disappointed.

I tried to rekindle his enthusiasm. "I believe my husband must be having a spiritual change of life, you see. Otherwise why would he want our child to attend a Bible class?"

"Ah." Recognition dawned. He saw some lost sheep drifting back into the fold. "Religious instruction for the young is vital."

"Walter and I both agree that too many of our people are losing their Jewishness . . ." Walter and I had never even discussed it and I, surely, had never thought it. What a liar I was becoming.

Rabbi intoned heavily. "Pogroms, cultural anti-Semitism, assimilation."

"Yes, yes. Jews everywhere are being devoured."

"You have a way with words, Mrs. Pepper."

"So you can understand why I've come to you. We want our son to receive a sound and superior Jewish education."

"What a pleasure it is to listen to a contemporary mother speak in terms eternal and therefore wise. We must converse about—what's the kid's name?"

"Stevie."

"I'll call him Steve, a little Jewish man. How old is Steve?"

"Four."

"So I'll call him Stevie. Four. The perfect age for my Bible class." He chuckled, a roll of biblical thunder and injunction. I visualized him as a huge man with great powerful shoulders and immensely strong hands, a great flowing beard, speckled with gray. Something out of the Sistine Chapel, but slightly more Jewish. I was in awe of his ancient wisdom, his deeply rooted faith, his unbreakable links to that long-ago past. "We must talk, Mrs. Pepper. You. And . . . I."

"Suppose I bring Stevie to your next class?"

"It is vital that the parent know and comprehend exactly how we at Temple Adath Ben-Ezra perceive ourselves, and what we believe our function to be. Our yeshiva is no ordinary yeshiva, let me tell you. Your place or mine?"

"What?"

"I could come to your home. That way I can meet young Master Stevie in his own environment. That way initial tensions can be reduced and kept at the lowest possible level. What I mean is, it's good to catch the kid on his own turf."

"I'll come to the synagogue."

A pervasive sadness drifted into his voice. "So be it. Let's make a date."

We did.

nine

The interview with Emil Lieber was scheduled for the following Tuesday morning. Too long to endure. An empty time lapse that would suck me in and put me down. Turn me inside out. Make me crazy.

How not to think about the interview occupied most of my thinking. I devised schemes to keep my mind from Emil Lieber, from what he might ask me, from what he might say. I saw him as a corporate Svengali, able to manipulate and twist me until every morsel of self-condemnatory information had flowed across my lips.

Oh boy, did I want that job. As Jonathan Marras had said, it was perfect for me and I for it. Waiting was a killer. . . .

Until suddenly the waiting didn't matter. A flash of insight made me understand that the job was mine. It had to be. Here was an ideal mating, me and that job, meant to be. Emil Lieber and I would perform a complicated ballet in which the finale was already composed. A happy ending. I would be hired. My career would be launched anew. My life revitalized.

As my excitement increased so did my guilt. Personnel systems operator versus mother and wife. My loyalties were being torn apart and so was my concentration.

I didn't know what to do with myself. So I went to the playground with Stevie every morning that week and spent every afternoon concocting gourmet dinners that neither Stevie nor Walter really cared for.

I ironed Walter's shirts, sewed buttons back on and patched Stevie's corduroys. I also refrained from interrupting Walter while he was reading. Walter had gone through the latest issue of *National Geographic* and into volume nine of Will Durant.

Sybil took me shopping. She might disapprove of my intentions, but she bought me a new dress to wear for the interview with Lieber. She was certain I'd get the job.

"No daughter of mine is going to be turned down for anything."

She also agreed to take care of Stevie on Tuesday morning.

At last Tuesday came and ten minutes ahead of time I introduced myself to Emil Lieber's secretary. She waited until the precise moment of our appointment before taking me into his office. It was one of those huge rooms carefully designed not to look like an office. Two huge sofas and some green leather wing chairs. No file cabinets, no desk, and a telephone that resembled a shining phallus.

Emil Lieber looked like a Bavarian *Braumeister*. Round and ruddy with curly gray hair and a paternal smile, a deep warming voice. He led me to one of the green leather chairs.

"That is all right for you, Mrs. Pepper?"

I said it was fine.

"You never know about people. I'm an overgrown bear, so what is comfortable for me is not always for other people, women especially."

I said I was just fine.

"If you say so." He put himself into one of the sofas and contemplated me with scientific curiosity. "You have been very well recommended."

Beth Dooley and Jonathan Marras. I was batting one thousand.

He turned on a genial smile. "I will tell you about myself, to break the ice, yes. I am a vice-president with a long title which conceals a decided absence of substance."

"Oh, I'm sure not."

Again that smile. He looked the part of every girl's benevolent old dad, loaded with affection, tolerance and generosity. I started to smile back at him when I remembered that he was a VP at IFP and that he had to be a killer under the skin. I cut the smile short.

"I think you do not believe what I tell you. You are right to be skeptical, and that is a good sign. One for your side, as they say. I am an important man in an important position. Probably I shall become the next president of the firm, soon, I would think. I am a man to have on your side."

It sounded like a threat. I began getting cold again.

"Under my jurisdiction," he murmured softly. "You would be working directly under me."

Bad off-color jokes popped into my head. I suppressed them, every one. "Yes, sir."

"Your background is impeccable."

The job had to be mine. "Thank you."

"I'm impressed."

I almost curtsied.

"That's a very nice dress you're wearing."

What did he mean by that? "Thank you."

"I tell you what, I'll make a guess—you just bought it, brand-new?"

"My mother gave it to me for the occasion. Her gift."

"You are lucky. My parents died in Germany many years ago. Your mother must be a very nice woman."

"Yes," I said, surprised to discover I meant it.

"No man would do that."

"I beg your pardon." I sat up a little straighter.

"A man gets his suit cleaned, yes. A new tie, maybe. But a new suit for an interview, I don't think so. That is how women behave."

"I never thought about that."

"At certain levels of operation it is best to consider all factors of human behavior. Your husband, he likes the dress?"

"My husband?" The question startled me and for a long chilling moment I couldn't remember what he looked like or what he called himself. "Oh, you mean Walter," I said, relieved. "I think so. He didn't say. But I'm sure he did."

"Walter, that's his name. What does Walter do, if you don't mind my asking?"

"Mind? Why would I mind?" But I minded, a hell of a lot, I minded. What did Walter have to do with this job? "No," I ended, donning a neutral expression. "I don't mind."

"Just another morsel of meat in the stew of knowledge." He laughed to show me he didn't take himself seriously. Like hell he didn't. "Bits and pieces of information until a complete picture is formed. That's how we come to ultimate judgments here at IFP."

"What does Walter do?" I was stalling. He reads, I said to myself. "Walter's in advertising," I said aloud. Used to be, I tacked on in grim secrecy.

"Ah. And what does Walter think about the possibility of your going back to work, Mrs. Pepper?"

Good question. What *did* Walter think about it. Walter and I talked from time to time, but seldom communicated. "Walter is very supportive." Give 'em what they want to hear. There's a motto to live by.

"I'm glad to hear it."

I detected an atonal note of doubt in his Teutonic voice and that worried me. I gave him an encouraging smile. "Walter is very much on my side."

"I must tell you, were you my wife I wouldn't want you to work. Twenty-two years I've been married, Mrs. Lieber never had to leave the house, not once. Times have changed."

"I agree."

"I suppose you feel your rights have been compromised, Mrs. Pepper?"

"Oh, no. Not me. Just looking for a good job."

"Women talk about their rights a lot nowadays."

"I suppose so."

"My compliments to your mother, Mrs. Pepper. About the dress."

"I'll tell her you liked it."

"You dress like this all the time?"

I provided a precise answer. "It depends."

"We prefer our female employees not to wear pants in the office."

"I never wear pants." Another lie.

He folded his huge veined hands across his equally huge middle. "Life can be difficult for the ladies. The mornings, especially. Getting the kiddies off to school, getting hubby off to the job. The house cleaned, the shopping, the mending."

"My son isn't old enough to go to school yet."

He leaned forward, as if coming on a great discovery. "Who will take care of him, if you are at work?"

For a split second, I thought he had me. But I made a nice recovery. "Arrangements can be made." That had just the right touch of mystery to it, as if I knew something nobody else knew.

"Arrangements, of course." He drew his golden brow down into a series of fretful ridges. "When I last employed a woman at this level, certain problems resulted, I must tell you."

"Problems?"

He shifted around like a great, uneasy beast. "Take the wives of policemen. Policemen, the preservation of order in the society, all very necessary. But police-*women*, what about them? The wife of your average policeman doesn't appreciate her husband riding around in a car with a strange woman, even if she is also in uniform."

"I see," I said, not seeing at all.

"Such an arrangement is necessarily intimate, you see."

"Intimate," I echoed automatically.

"Too intimate. Too many shared experiences away from hearth and home. Too many temptations."

I imagined myself in a darkened prowl car next to some big handsome cop. Suddenly I am on my back and he is all over me, only his gun keeps getting in the way. What does it matter, cop or gun, as long as I get what's coming to me?

"The point is simple," Emil Lieber was saying. "Wives don't want their husbands spending a great deal of time with other attractive women. Insecurity exists in the life of every woman. Wives get jealous and jealousy can decimate a relationship, especially a marriage. Bound to be problems. Anticipate problems and you may eliminate them before they cause trouble. I must be sure about my people."

"You can be sure about me."

He looked me up and down as if peeking into the dark closets of my soul. "My table of organization calls for fifteen men. Should you join us, Mrs. Pepper, you would be the solitary female on staff. Fourteen men, one woman. Paths cross. Converging lines, you know. A certain amount of togetherness. Traveling together, evenings spent in the same city, the same hotel. You see what I'm getting at?"

Not really, but I wasn't going to say so. "Oh yes, I see."

"Frequently projects are joint."

"Joint projects."

"Exactly. Meetings. Lonely days, long nights on the road . . ."

"I know what you mean."

"You aren't bothered by the prospect?"

"No." What bothered me was Emil Lieber, everything he was saying. He had the tactics of a secret bully and I was becoming more and more uncomfortable in his presence.

"Speaking frankly. I believe in speaking frankly, Mrs. Pepper. Therefore I must say it, I don't know if we should hire a woman. For all the aforementioned reasons, I don't particularly care for the idea."

"I can handle it, believe me. I'm right for the job, for this work."

"I admit it, nobody could be better qualified. On paper."

"Then? . . ."

"Every applicant must be considered with equal care. I must think about it. I will think about it. You shall hear from me, from us, in no time at all." He had me on my feet and moving toward the door. "A letter, in a few days you'll receive a letter."

"If there's anything else I can tell you—?"

"I am impressed. Poise. Ambition. Experience. Very favorably impressed. Not to worry . . ."

"Not to worry," Xavier D.C. Kiernan said when I finished telling him about the interview with Emil Lieber.

"I've heard that before."

"Worrying does no good."

"What else have I got to do with my time?"

Kiernan never cracked a grin. He just wiggled around in the Eames chair, as if relieving an anal itch, keeping his eyes on me every second. The chair squeaked when it moved.

"A little Three-in-One oil couldn't hurt," I said.

"What? What's that about oil?"

"I want that job." I turned loose one of my medium-rare smiles, your normal begging-for-pity smiles. But from the inside my face felt like a sheet of crumpled paper. Be nice to the crazy lady, doctor. . . .

"Is there one good reason to believe you won't be hired?"

"Has a dog got fleas?"

Kiernan put on his bloodhound face. He didn't approve of my wise-guy persona. But I was shaky, freezing my bottom off, confronting a horrendous fate. Either Kiernan laughs or I cry.

"Could be I'm not qualified," I said.

"My impression has been you believed you were uniquely qualified for the position."

"You bet. I've got what it takes. A natural for the job. There is no reason for Lieber to turn me down."

"Then you're confident?"

"I wouldn't want to go that far."

"Doubts are natural to us all."

"Doubt, doubtful, doubting. Throw in skeptical, dubious, disbelieving."

"Then you're not as secure as you indicated earlier?"

"Secure! Me? 'It is hard for those who live near a bank. To doubt the security of their money.' "

"That's very good, you have a way with words, Libby."

"T. S. Eliot."

He surveyed me glumly. Kiernan credited invention, not memory. "You sincerely and honestly want to return to work, Libby?"

The bastard still didn't believe me. "Sincerely and honestly. Until it hurts."

"We should discuss the matter."

A heavy silence followed. At forty bucks for fifty minutes, I couldn't afford much silence. Even if it was on the cuff.

"Okay," I said at last.

"Okay?"

"Let's discuss the matter."

"Why, Libby?"

"Why?"

"Why do you want this job?"

"I already told you, in The Family."

"Tell me again."

"I have to say this, those characters in the group, are you positive they're on my side?"

"We'll all genuinely fond of our Libby. Tell me why."

"Productive activity is uplifting for a depressed psyche, you've said so yourself."

"Continue."

"Also there's the money. Wouldn't you like to get paid someday?"

"I expect to be paid someday. But money is not the primary question, I think. Let's discuss your emotional needs."

"It is the money! Either I get a job and a salary or the Three Little Peppers will have to hit the welfare line. Mention welfare and Walter gets constipation of the voice box. Talking about such unpleasant items as food, clothing and shelter offends my husband."

"How do you feel?"

"Walter's been out of work for almost a year. That makes me feel lousy."

"Very well. What if you took the job, how would that affect Walter?"

"He'd eat better, have money in his pocket. He could buy a whole bunch of new books."

"Tradition has the man as the breadwinner, Libby."

"I want my own thing."

"Ah-hah!" He almost pounced. He caught himself just in time, fell back into the Eames chair. "Certain principles have come into being with reason. These have withstood the battering of the centuries. . . ."

"Man does not live by principle alone."

"There are codes. Structures according to which individuals, families, societies exist and carry on. The Tablets, the Talmud, the Old Testament. You Jews have codified the ways of your people for four thousand years. A way to survive, to live, to confront your Maker. What code do you live by, Libby?"

"Morse?"

Behind his gold-rims, his gelid eyes glazed over. "It's your time, Libby, your psyche, your money."

"Do you take American Express?"

"Waste."

"Come on, Xavier, tell me the truth. When am I

going to get Lieber's letter? Will the news be good or bad?"

"I cannot foretell the future."

"I know a gypsy who tells you everything up to a year in advance, guaranteed. Only don't bring a lot of cash when you visit her. Her scam is—"

"Libby." It was a warning.

I gloomed up and slumped down. "It's been a week."

"That's not so long."

"It seems like a century."

"You feel pressure?"

"I'm pumped up to bust."

"What do you think can be done to relieve the pressure?"

Would you believe it, at these prices he asks *me.* "What do *you* think can be done to relieve the pressure?" Take that, Kiernan.

He handled it easily. "Each of us must create our own reality. Externals inevitably intrude and when that happens . . ." He gave me an eloquent shrug.

"I'll call them."

"I wouldn't do that."

"It's a good idea."

"They'll think you're anxious."

"I am anxious. About almost everything."

"Patience."

"Where do they sell it? I'll take a couple of pounds, your best patience."

"More jokes."

"Maybe they lost my address, can't get the letter to me?"

"I doubt that."

"Accidents happen. Big companies make mistakes. And the Postal Service is awful, rotten."

He put on one of those Freudian looks, a sort of Viennese smirk.

"They will contact you."

"That's your story."

He was on his feet, moving me out. The fifty-minute heave-ho, putting some other fouled-up floozy onto my couch. The man failed to recognize that mine was the Classic Case, right out of a text on abnormal behavior. He was getting an education, at my expense.

"You will survive," he murmured. "You will receive the letter soon. I prophesy it."

"Xavier, you'd be terrific in a tearoom."

By exercising extraordinary restraint, I was able to go until ten the next morning before phoning IFP. Three secretaries later, Jonathan Marras came on the line.

"Good morning, Mr. Marras. This is Libby Pepper."

"Who?"

That set me back and I struggled to locate some semblance of poise. "Libby Pepper. We spoke about the job in Mr. Lieber's division. You were very encouraging . . ."

"Oh yes, Mrs. Pepper. You thought I forgot you. I didn't forget you. How could I? You are the only female applicant."

"Mr. Lieber said I'd be hearing from him."

"Then you will, you surely will."

"You think so?"

"Oh, definitely."

"He said a letter."

"That's customary, a letter."

"I thought it might have gone astray."

"I doubt that. You'll get your letter, all right."

"That's what my husband says."

"He's right, your husband understands the workings of big business, I'm sure."

I wanted to say more, but what? "Well, thank you, Mr. Marras."

"You'll hear from us, Mrs. Pepper."

He was right. The letter arrived on the following Wednesday morning. I ripped it open, anticipation re-

ducing me to a quavering hulk. It was a first-rate letter, I thought, to the point, the way a business letter
should be written:

Dear Mrs. Pepper:

I regret no opening exists with International Food
Products at this time. Should a job become available
at some later date you will be notified.

Yours very truly,
Emil Lieber

I knew it, I knew it. I knew it all along.

part two

1972

ten

"No need to fret."

That was Walter's reaction to the letter from Emil Lieber. He was reading *Crying of Lot Forty-Nine* when I broke in, waving the letter wildly, fighting not to cry.

"It's just as well," he said.

The hell it is . . .

"No way things would've worked out. After all, we've got a home to maintain, a family life to preserve, a future to construct. With you working, what would become of us all?" He tacked on a smile to show he was only half-serious.

"I want the job," I wailed.

"I've been meaning to tell you." He hefted Pynchon, getting ready to plunge back into those densely written pages. "I've got something hot on the front burner. Good money, good prospects for advancement, good work. Sooner or later, you'd've had to make a choice, give up the job. You can recognize the logic of that."

My reaction to his logic was entirely hostile. The only game left to me was homicide. I longed to inflict a slow painful death on my ever-loving spouse. Not to mention Lieber, Marras, the entire executive staff of IFP. All done with much cruel mean skill to the accompaniment of much pain and verbal abuse. Torture suddenly seemed to be a most admirable human activity.

"The really big money," Walter said, "is in mail order."

What in God's name was he talking about? "I want the job," I mewed.

Walter, overcome with sympathy, groped my fanny. "Few of us get what we want out of this world."

Fuck you, I felt like saying, but didn't. I dislodged his hand with a disdainful bump and grind.

"Wallenstein and Smithton," he announced proudly.

"What are you talking about?"

Walter let go with a wet chuckle to let me know he *understood.* Not that he did, not for a second. He reached for my crotch, squeezing as if it were a rubber ball. I made a quick retreat, putting a cool distance between us. Over the years I'd noticed a powerful connection between Walter's rod and Walter's roll. Money and sex were inextricably linked for him, as if only a paid-for product could give satisfaction. How American can you get?

Maybe I ought to begin charging Walter. That would drive him berserk, his wife hustling tricks. At that moment turning hooker had a great appeal to me. Ten bucks a hand-job. Twenty for head. Thirty for a bang. And for half-a-hundred, the works.

Beautiful blue sky. You tell me your dreams, I'll tell you mine. Know how many lust-crazed men were pounding at my bedroom door, for pay or for free? None is how many. Zero. Zilch. Even loving Walter was only an occasional visitor.

"Wallenstein and Smithton, they're in direct mail advertising. They want me."

"You always loathed direct mail. You said it was the lowest form of the business, cheap, tawdry, personally offensive to you."

"I've reconsidered. I was wrong. Here is an opportunity to compose an ad and see the results where it counts—in dollars and cents."

"You always wanted to get into television commercials, you told me."

"My mind's made up."

"You've accepted the job?"

"They're going to call me."

Maybe they wouldn't call. Maybe they'd send him a letter—*We regret to inform you* . . . Let him find out how I was feeling. Mean, that's what I was. Mean and vengeful. A small person, right. Call me any name you want, I don't care. *I want my job* . . .

"Good luck," I muttered.

"Things will be better once I'm back on the job. We'll take a holiday, go on a trip. Where would you like to go?"

From angst to anguish. "You think of a place." In times like these, a girl needs her mother. I got on the phone to Sybil and gave it to her straight.

"They didn't hire me."

Sybil, the Queen of Sharps and Flats, gave it right back, fortissimo. "It's just as well."

They were a matched pair, Walter and Sybil.

"Why do you say that, Mother?"

"What about your son?"

"There are such places as nursery schools. . . ."

"Hah!"

"Daycare . . ."

"Yuch."

"Housekeepers."

"A child needs his own kin around him. Spend more time with your son. Read to him. Play with him. Take him to the Philharmonic."

Thoughts of Stevie monopolized my days, not to mention my conscience, which exerted a lunatic pressure on me to conform. Be good, it hollered in an English accent. Be bland and anonymous. Ignore the syncopated heartbeat of your alienation and conform.

"It's been nice talking to you, Mother."

"You're hanging up?"

"Thanks for calling."

"You called me."

Friday night was The Family Night. But there was no way I could face those jackals. In the misused name of love and compassion they would strip away my defenses and show me to myself for the once and future failure I was doomed to be.

I had to get out of the apartment and I did. Saying nothing to Walter, just going. I went to an X-rated movie. It was all about a man with an enormous prick that remained hard through a number of sexual episodes, few of which I'd even known were possible. At one point, the hero boasted of having forty-six orgasms in a single twenty-four-hour period. At once my mathematical talent came into play; that worked out to about twice an hour. What a liar.

Later, when I got home, I checked Walter's *Guinness* for the world's record. *Guinness* had no listing under "Fornication." On our wedding night we did it twice, though I couldn't swear that Walter got off each time. Walter was a silent screwer. A thrust or two, a roll, and a quick lurch into passivity. To judge by that blue flick, a great deal of possible action was not being served up to Libby Pepper.

I want my job.

I had transformed silent screaming into an art form. My head rang with the cry. Why hadn't I gotten the job? What had I done wrong?

I put myself into a hot tub and slipped down until water lapped at my lips and dribbled into my ears. Sweat trickled off the tip of my nose and I tried to catch the salt drops with my tongue. Mostly I missed and eventually gave it up.

My eyes closed and I felt myself going down into shadowed solitary. To be alone, stripped of sensation, emotion, all thought, that was the only safe territory. Beyond the shadows Darwin's predators were prowling and primed to kill.

But patterns of light and dark shifted to display the deficiencies in my character. There in the cracked mirror of my soul was the Star-Spangled Woman, unable to turn away from the tainted glory reflected in the glass. The ultimate narcissist.

Me, me, me, me . . .

It never occurred to me that an objective reality existed that shaped and directed my destiny. I could think of only one question: What had I done wrong? As if to keep some essential element of myself from dropping out, my hand went between my legs, holding on for dear life.

Those interviews—Dooley, Marras, Lieber. In what imperceptible and terrible way had I goofed? I reconstructed my time with Dooley. Called back everything Marras had asked me. My replies to Emil Lieber.

Undoubtedly my attitude had been bad. The smartass New Yorker jumped a millimeter under my skin, materializing without warning with a wisecrack, a dumb remark, a particularly unfunny joke. I felt like a stand-up comic not getting his laughs.

What the hell is wrong with me?

I could make a list. Come up with a million answers. Complete with citations, quotations, recommendations. The lady was a lemon.

I refused to dwell on the bad stuff. Instead I concentrated on my hand. It was busy and doing pretty well. Go, go, go.

By the time I made it to bed that night, Walter was sound asleep. I removed Pynchon from his chest, swallowed a Valium and shut the light. It couldn't have taken me more than two hours to fall asleep.

I dreamed. This time I was shut up in a room with a glass wall. Very thick, strong glass. On the other side of the glass people pointed at me, shouted derisively and made ugly faces and disgusting gestures.

I yelled at them to let me alone, to go away, and suddenly they were gone, and I was left to look through that empty glass wall. It was a lousy dream, mad, shabby, and at six in the morning when Stevie began to cry because his bed was wet, I almost didn't mind going to him.

eleven

On Monday, Walter went to work for Wallenstein & Smithton. That left me with the apartment, our son, and my thoughts. An intolerable triad. I sent Walter off with good wishes and a kiss on the mouth, saying how glad I was for him. What I was was miserable for myself. How petty can a girl get?

I want my job.

I felt like spending the day curled up in bed and feeling sorry for myself. But there was no time for that. At two o'clock I was meeting Rabbi.

The synagogue was in the middle of a block of fine old apartment buildings, each with a uniformed doorman wearing white gloves. On the corner, a drunk had passed out smelling of Gallo Hearty Burgundy. What New York needed was more cops and fewer doormen.

From the outside, the synagogue looked like a basketball court. From the inside, the synagogue looked like a basketball court.

Rabbi preened like a Big Ten coach when I pointed it out, trying to break the theological ice, so to speak, "An architectural stroke of ingenuity. Take a look at those pews."

They sat there, row after row of polished oak, hard

on the butt, hard on the lower back. "They look okay to me."

He did not take my meaning. "Be not deceived, dear lady. They *fold* up."

"No kidding!"

"Indeed. The outside stanchions collapse and tuck underneath. Each and every pew is hinged in two separate places—a third of the way along and two-thirds of the way along. That way we can very rapidly break down the seating and move it out into the appropriate storage places. Once this is done we bring in portable grandstands, portable baskets, portable public address system and voilà! A basketball court."

"Basketball . . ."

"No pale and flabby yeshiva Yids in this congregation, dear Mrs. Pepper. Basketball's the city game. Speed is required. Strength and quickness. Sternness of mind and body. My boys are rough and tough, aggressive in the ancient traditions, muscular Hebrews. Wild tribesmen they were then. My boys can do whatever they did."

"Out of Egypt . . ."

". . . into the wilderness."

"Up into the Promised Land."

"You grasp my meaning exactly, Mrs. Pepper."

"About the Bible class?"

"Saturday mornings. Beginners at nine, intermediate at ten, advanced at eleven." He smoothed his short spadelike gray beard, then pointed it at me accusingly. "Basketball," he intoned in a talmudic tenor. "Don't get the idea that I'm a roundball freak only. Not at all. I believe in a well-balanced program. Our football team is undefeated in three seasons in the New York-Westchester Ecumenical Athletic League. Our boys are rough, our boys are tough, our boys are determined."

"I'm sure they are, but—"

"No, buts, believe me. Also boxing. I do not expect every mother to appreciate boxing . . ."

"I very often would like to slug somebody."

He never cracked a smile. This was not one of your

laughing rabbis. This one could have made it across the wilderness barefoot in a lot less than forty years.

"The point is, Mrs. Pepper, to raise a new breed of Jewish youth. Healthy bodies, healthy minds. You see the direction we're going in?"

"War?"

"Ah," he said solemnly. "That's very good. 'War.' I must remember it. We also have handball. There's a sport that demands strength, coordination, excellent reflexes. Also tennis, squash, track and field, skiing in season . . ."

"And oysters, I presume?"

That got to him. "What?"

"A little joke, Rabbi."

"Ah." He plunged ahead. "We have a marching band, a pep squad. Spirit, that's very important. A sense of community. We cover the spectrum. Give us your boy and we'll return—who can say, a Hank Greenberg, a Sandy Koufax, a Maxie Baer."

"Stevie is only four years old."

"Plant the seeds early and all the rest will tumble into place."

"About the spirit, Rabbi—"

He would not be diverted. "There is also music. I myself am an opera freak. Beverly Sills is Jewish, you know. And Bernstein, of course."

I put on my most innocent expression. "He's Jewish, too?"

For a beat he wasn't sure of me. Then he waved an Old Testament finger in my face. "That's good, very funny."

"Could we talk about religion?"

"I will see to it. Your son will get a full dose. Oh, we'll fill him up with the stuff. By the time he's six, he'll be a full-fledged for-the-rest-of-his-life Jew. That's the way the pope's people do it, you know. Get 'em early and they never get away. The Commies use the same technique. Pragmatic Judaism, that's what we're after. Also art."

"Art?"

"Museum visits, that kind of thing. A small sampling of everything."

"Sort of a cultural antipasto?"

"You grasp my meaning, Mrs. Pepper."

"I would like the kid to know what it means to be Jewish."

"You bet. Our program turns out the complete boy, well-rounded, strong in body, alert in mind, fit for life in these United States of America, God bless . . ."

"Speaking of God . . ."

"Were we speaking of God, Mrs. Pepper?"

"Not so you could notice," I said on my way out.

Nothing went right. My life was up for grabs, and no takers. Nothing unusual about that, and I might have gone on drifting, stumbling, feeling sorry for myself, if not for the crying.

The crying began after lunch on the following Thursday. Outside it was raining, one of those chilling downpours that adds so much spice to city living. A slight pressure in my sinuses signaled the coming of one of those whopper headaches. My belly was puffed out a little more than usual and my mouth tasted sour. Naturally I blamed it all on my period.

But crying that way was a new and distressing ingredient. Especially when the tears kept coming and no matter how hard I tried I couldn't put an end to them. What really got me down was the realization that I *wanted* to cry, wanted to drown in self-deprecation and self-pity.

I went for the phone. Kiernan in a pinch. My cross and my salvation. Four digits dialed and I pulled up short. St. Xavier would surely prescribe a double dose of Valium, two Tylenols and some hot tea. Sybil could do as much, at a better hourly rate. I hung up the phone, took deep breaths in order to lessen the weeping, shaking and rattling, then called Cici.

"I must talk to someone."

There was only the slightest hesitation. "You'll have to come over here, my housekeeper called in sick."

"Is it all right if I bring Stevie?"

"Of course. The twins will love having someone new to play with."

Just like that. No Beautiful and Important People to interview. No handsome young men to entertain. No publishers lurking in the wings. Just come on over. I felt as I had felt when both of us were so very young, full of affection and friendship and hope for the future.

I herded Stevie down to Sixty-seventh Street and the Des Artistes, where Cici lived. It was one of those rococo old buildings that glamour and wealth cling to, made more desirable by the ghosts of famous people who lived and died there; and those who still live there. But none of that entered my mind then. I was concerned totally with my own present, not to mention a very hazy future.

Cici greeted me with a kiss on the cheek and promptly led Stevie off to some far chamber of the huge apartment to play with her boys. Returning, she settled me in a cozy book-lined room that she identified as her workroom, brought coffee and a drink, and put herself in a chair opposite, watching me obliquely. Naturally I began to cry again.

"Caught your husband in the hay with another chick, is that it?"

The idea caused me to gasp in relief and amusement. I stopped crying at once. "Nothing like that."

She frowned. "Then it must really be serious."

"Do you remember, Cici, how we used to talk years ago? What we were going to do, what we were going to become. Super-Mothers. Super-Wives."

I expected her to find that funny. She merely shook her head. "What fools we were."

"Were we?"

"Of course. Attaching all our dreams to the needs of other people. Mothers, wives. Why not just ourselves? Women."

"I suppose you're right."

"Of course I am."

"I believed it. When I became pregnant with Stevie

I was ecstatic. I quit work at once and swore I'd never go back until Stevie was old enough not to need me."

"When will that miracle come to pass?"

"My husband needs me, too." I sounded desperate to myself, my voice shrill and full of pleading as if I wanted her to agree with me.

"Super-Mother and Super-Wife, okay you made it." She sounded bitter, angry.

"Oh, no, not me. You, you seem to have it all in order, the different aspects of your life."

"Nothing's what it seems to be. I could tell you stories——" She broke off and a harsh laugh came out of her. "Super-Wife, that's a man's fantasy laid on us to their own advantage. Most of them swap one mamma for another, that's all."

"Is that why you went back to work after the twins were born?"

She shrugged. "Maybe I should have stayed home, I don't know."

I was confused. It had never occurred to me that Cici suffered doubts about anything. "Why didn't you?"

She shifted around, trying to get comfortable, obviously not making it. "I had lots of misgivings at the time."

"You did it anyway. You were able to do it all. Career, wife, mother." I waved my hand to take in the apartment. "All this, it all runs so smoothly for you."

"I told you, nothing's what it seems to be. I have a housekeeper, a cleaning service. There are standing orders at the butcher, the fruit store, the grocery. Twice-a-week deliveries are made automatically. We have a two-week menu, a different meal each night, then it goes back to square one again. Entertain? A catering service——food, drinks, servants, cleanup afterwards. You wake up the next morning, it's as if nobody was there, nothing happened, everything's the same."

The conversation seemed to have gotten out of hand, drifting away from my problem. "What made you go back to work?"

She measured me as if deciding whether or not to answer. "I simply could not tolerate the loss to my ego of not having my own work to do. My job. My career. I needed something that was purely mine. Does that make me sound cold, selfish?"

What she said gave rise to more questions about myself, about what I was trying to do.

"I didn't get the job," I said.

"The job?"

She'd forgotten all about it. A quick flush of resentment came and went. There was no reason for her to remain close to the twists and turns of my existence. I told her of my experiences at IFP. When I finished, I sat back and waited.

"In the letter, Lieber gave no specific reason for not hiring you?"

"Nothing."

"The bastard."

"He said there was no opening for me."

"But there were fifteen jobs, you said."

"All together, yes. There was one opening left."

"Maybe you weren't qualified . . ."

A hot tide of anger spread into my eyes. I blinked it back. "But I was, eminently qualified. Cici, I have had exactly the kind of experience they asked for. The right education, everything. If anything, I'm overqualified."

"Oh, the bastards."

"I'm confused. It's as if I've missed something basic."

"It was there from the start. Lieber, he let it out early, told you precisely where his head was at."

"I don't get it."

"Tell me again that business about his wife."

"Oh. That he wouldn't want his wife to work."

"Damn right he wouldn't. Better to have her home cooking and washing out the john. Cheaper help is not to be had. Do you see what I'm driving at, Libby?"

I shook my head no.

"Oh, Libby. It's the system. Most women have been

brainwashed by it. Male dominance is the game. That shitty business about your dress. 'Is this the way you usually dress?' You think he'd speak that way to a man? No way, believe me. And that other crack—'Who will take care of your child when you're at work?' Why not your husband? The idea would never enter Lieber's mind. Why shouldn't men get a good shot at the joys of parenthood for a while?"

I giggled. "What a mess that would be, Walter around the house."

"He can learn. They all can. *We* did. Cook, clean, pander to your men. Otherwise you're a failure, your femininity in question. What crap. Has Walter ever changed a diaper?"

"The smell made him sick."

"Yes, I know. My Robert, too. Poor sensitive fellows. Do they think we enjoy the stink of baby shit? And what about that other dandy remark, that stuff about cops?"

"Mr. Lieber believes that cops' wives don't want their husbands riding around with policewomen."

"Sure. As if every female cop has hot pants for those blue-suited fascists. Oh wow, Libby. You really put your foot into the full load. And without preparation. No wonder you're shook up."

"I guess I'm awfully dumb, Cici. I still don't understand."

"You don't know why you didn't get the job?"

"Not really."

"Because," Cici said, spacing out her words, "you are a woman."

"Oh," I said without thinking. "I can't believe that."

I had an acute pain in the memory. When I grew up—we lived on Riverside Drive, Sybil's social and economic compromise between Park Avenue and the Bronx—I loved to play the boys' games. Baseball, football, basketball, all of it. Also roller hockey, which I was not very good at, and punchball, at which I was a whiz. Boy, could I murder that pink spaldeen, sending low liners past the infielders.

Whenever I could elude Sybil's musical dictates, I'd charge down into Riverside Park, hunting for a game. The more I played the better I became. The hardest part was to be as hostile and aggressive, as mentally tough as the boys, as willing to do whatever was necessary in order to win.

Under certain conditions and provocations, fights broke out. No one could be pushed beyond a certain point. No one could be allowed to intimidate a player, to take away his best game.

So I taught myself to fight. Until I realized that the boys saw my battling as a weird and somehow treacherous act. An aberration. The boys seemed confused and often angered whenever I displayed my aggressiveness openly and sometimes refused to fight back when I struck them. It was as if they had surrendered some cultural power to me, at the same time removing me as an equal playmate. Until at last it sank in. As a girl I was expected to act like a girl. Feminine. Gentle. Curbing all those combative reactions.

In a thousand different subtle and overt ways I was made to understand that being female was a deficiency that made me strange and definitely inferior. In time I came to believe the boys were right. The passing years had changed nothing. They still wouldn't allow me to play in their games. They still were reminding me of my sexual shortcomings. Cici was right. The bastards didn't hire me because I was a woman.

I was outraged. Confused. And relieved that I would not have to go out into that deadly jungle day after day. But the pain kept returning, intensifying, making me want to cry out.

They can't do this to me!

I needed to talk about it. Inevitably I turned to Walter. He listened to the entire story without speaking. Finished, I sat back.

"That's it?" he said.

"Yes."

"And you believe they didn't hire you because you're a woman?"

"That's what Cici says."

"I never entirely trusted her."

"Cici claims there is an implicit bias against women in general."

"That's Cici for you."

We didn't seem to be making any progress so I ended the conversation and called Sybil, told her everything.

"Look for an alibi and you're certain to find one."

"I'm not looking for an alibi, just a sensible explanation."

"Be downstairs at ten tomorrow morning. I'll come by in a cab, we'll go shopping at Altman's."

I said I'd be there and hung up. That brought me around to Kiernan. From out of his Eames chair, he would curdle my spirit, stamp on my psyche, muddle my thinking. If Walter was the monkey on my back, Kiernan was the Great Ape.

I decided to give Cici another try. "Did you mean what you said?" I began.

"Absolutely. They cannot do that to you."

"But they did."

"They can't. Not legally."

"You mean there's a law about such things?"

"Yes."

"An honest-to-God written-down law?"

"State and federal. Just substitute the word 'black' for woman and see if what I'm saying doesn't make sense. Suppose they refused to hire someone because he was black or Jewish or Catholic . . ."

"They do."

"Not so much anymore. Because blacks and Jews and Catholics stood up to the bastards."

"Well, if you look at it that way——"

"Exactly. It's prejudice pure and simple."

I felt compelled to say something, not entirely clear about what I wanted to say. "The thing is, I made all the necessary arrangements. Housekeeper, nursery for

Stevie, daycare in the afternoon. I set up charge accounts with the local shopkeepers . . ."

"Libby, you have been screwed."

"I wanted to look right so I bought new clothes. I can't believe people still act that way."

"They do."

"So it seems."

"What are you going to do about it?"

The question put me off balance. I couldn't imagine any action I might take that could possibly alter the way things were. "What can I do?"

"File a complaint with the State Human Rights Commission."

"Oh."

"Or write a letter to the appropriate people in Washington."

"I see."

"If you still want the job, that is."

"Oh, I do, I do. The Human Rights Commission, that makes sense." And it did, being close to home with the prospect of a prompt response. I thanked Cici for her help and said I would act on her suggestions.

"You won't be sorry," she said.

I knew better than that.

twelve

My head tingled with all the goings-on, very little of it making sense. In pursuit of sanity, my imagination went fluttering off into flights of social and legal fancy. Head-movies courtesy of Libby Pepper Productions. Hollywood lives! In the dark creases of my brain.

Picture this—the Human Rights Commission. One of those handsome paneled offices in a gleaming white building with marble floors and immense windows, sparkling clean. A phalanx of great-looking men in Savile Row suits and Johnston & Murphy shoes await my appearance.

They come to their feet as I enter the sober chambers, lawyers every one, all dedicated to shielding poor little me from injustice and intolerance. They listen to my tale, unable to conceal their rising fury.

"Outrageous!"

"They did that to *you*?"

"Corporate swine."

The handsomest of the group, all charisma and strong leadership, calls for silence. He puts through a call to IFP.

"Emil Lieber!" he says into the instrument. "Mrs. Pepper is with us now. No, man, apologies will not suffice. Did you actually do to this lovely, charming and eminently-qualified-for-the-job woman what she reports you have done? You *did*? Unconscionable. How dare you do what you did! You can't do what you did. And never do it again. Women are people and don't you forget it. Mrs. Pepper is a credit to her sex, and you don't deserve her. She could revitalize IFP, make millions for you, man. All right, she'll be right over, if she doesn't bear a grudge. Give her the job, Lieber, or else."

He hung up and gave me his orthodontist's best smile. Then we all went under the board table and had a really first-rate orgy.

It was, I decided, time for me to put daydreams aside and act. I phoned the New York State Human Rights Commission. An uninterested voice said, "Where are you?"

"Home."

"No, lady," the voice said patiently. "Where did the alleged act of discrimination take place?"

"Alleged nothing," I shot back. "It really happened."

"Have it your way. Where?"

"International Food Products."

"Address?"

I supplied it and the voice grew more active, lined with a secret pleasure. "Okay, I got it now. So why are you calling here, lady?"

"You're the Human Rights Commission, aren't you?"

"Sure we are. Only you have got yourself connected to the wrong office."

"You're confusing me."

"The alleged act occurred north of Forty-second Street, which puts it under the jurisdiction of our up-town office."

"Uptown? . . ."

"Had it taken place south of Forty-second Street, well, that would have been a different matter. In that eventuality, we at this location would have exercised jurisdiction."

"What do I do now?"

"Go to One Hundred Twenty-fifth Street, naturally."

"Thank you."

"No sweat."

I discovered Stevie in the bathtub, the water about to overflow. I turned it off and opened the drain.

"More water!" he yelled.

"Mama has to dress you."

"I already dressed."

It was true. He was fully clothed, complete to his saddle shoes. It took some doing for me to get him out of those wet clothes, dried off, and into a clean outfit. I pulled off the entire operation with minor wounds to Stevie's ego and none at all to his flesh.

Once dressed, he headed for the television. "Wanna watch!"

"Mama has to go."

"Mama go, Stevie stay."

The going got a little rough after that but I finally made it into the street with him. On the corner, a man and his wife were bitterly cursing at each other while sharing a half-gallon jug of muscatel. The wife jabbed her finger into the man's eye. He recovered quickly and knocked her down.

Stevie cheered and wanted to watch the remainder of the contest.

"Beat it, kid," the man growled.

"Let's go," I said to Stevie.

"They're fighting, I wanna see."

"Rotten kid." The woman picked herself up, bleeding from the nose.

"A nation of spectators," her husband said.

"Participate or perish," the woman added.

"He's only a child," I protested.

"The child is father to the man," the man said sagely. He handed the jug over to his wife, who beamed lovingly.

I hurried over to the bus stop. At One Hundred Twenty-fifth Street, we transferred to another bus, heading east. I looked around and noticed for the first time that we were the only white people on the bus. Visions of muggers, rapists and crazy gangbangers danced through my head. I tried mightily to shrink out of sight. I must have succeeded for nobody noticed us all the way crosstown.

The Human Rights Commission was located in a store-front within eyeshot of the elevated railroad tracks of the Penn Central. I tried to imagine myself on a train leaving town, heading for some distant, sedate and secure suburb. I loathed this crummy existence I was leading.

"I wanna go to the playground," Stevie shouted. He tried to make his getaway but I was wise to his tricks and propelled him, flailing and crying, into the Commission office. Once inside, impressed by the majesty of the State, he quieted down.

I spotted a sign on a desk behind a low guard rail: INFORMATION. I made a beeline for that sign. Behind it sat a bony black woman stuffing envelopes.

"Excuse me," I began.

She kept stuffing, not looking up. "You do the talking, I'll do the listening."

"Is this where I file a complaint?"

"Right on, sister." A practiced head-jerk directed me to a stack of official forms. "Fill one in. Who did what to you."

"I've been discriminated against."

"Well, yes, you have. This is where you will get equity, justice and sweet relief from oppression, sister." She finally glanced up, staring at me for a long time. "You ain't black," she said at last.

"Never said I was."

She didn't crack a smile. "*You* have been discriminated against? That what you're saying to me?"

"Yes, that's it, I think."

She dropped a protective hand over the stack of forms. "Got to be absolutely sure."

I thought it over. "I'm sure."

She let out a great room-sized laugh. A gale of joy that exploded out of some deep dark corner of her soul. I didn't like the sound of it one bit.

"Hey, Sabitha!" she cried. A black woman halfway back in the room stood up. "Sabitha, we got us a case of discrimination here."

"That the one?" Sabitha crowed.

"Better believe, sister."

Sabitha began to laugh. And soon all the clerks at all the desks joined in. Then Stevie, light of my life, began to laugh. At *me*. I gave his ear a twist and he howled in agony and went to the floor. Slave-traders, I decided on the spot, had not been such bad guys after all.

"It's true," I managed to say.

Sabitha, a huge woman with a dozen chins, came forward. "Dig it, people. The honky lady has been discriminated against."

"I went for a job," I said.

A beautiful girl with a sensational figure pranced up to the guard rail for a good close look. She slapped her palms and wiggled her jutting fanny, performed a jerky dance routine. "Whooo! Whooo! The honky wants her rights 'tended to.' Well, all *right*." Smooth and funky, all parts in motion, she retreated to her desk. What I'd've given to be able to move that way.

The laughter grew louder, more oppressive, and I searched for a way out. But my legs failed to respond, all joints fused forever.

Fortunately the Lone Ranger came galloping up and all my troubles were over. Lanky and handsome in stovepipe jeans and scuffed boots and a sports coat from Brooks Brothers. No sheriff's star, no six-gun, but plenty of cool authority. My hero . . .

There he was. Lean and mean, the brightest, bluest eyes set deep behind smooth cheekbones, his skin softly weathered, his features artistically assembled. Young Gary Cooper must have looked almost this good.

"Hey there, Bubba," the woman at the desk said in a respectful voice.

"Hey, Frances," he answered. Easy drawl, rich tones

sliding up and down my libido. I stood up a little straighter. "Frances," he said. "Shame on you."

"Ah, Bubba." She went back to her work. The laughter had ceased. All was right with the Human Rights Commission.

He drew me aside, gazing down into my face, the most charming smile imaginable on his wide, Western mouth. "Gene Horn, ma'am. Folks call me Bubba. Seems to me like you might be in need of a helpin' hand."

"What? Oh. Yes. I came to file a complaint."

"That's surely what they do here. Frances, here, she accepts complaints and aims folks toward the proper course of action, ain't that a fact, Frances?"

"That's my function, counselor. From dawn till dusk."

"Frances is a truly good person, only some of the time she'd rather not let on. You listen to the lady's complaint, Frances."

Frances giggled. "You going to take on her situation, counselor?" She made it sound illegal and immoral, slightly uncouth.

The tall man patted her cheek. "Frances, you and me, we got to cut a hot trail, get it on gooooood, if you follow my meaning."

"Shoot, a cute country boy like you, you'd just wear me down first thing."

He turned the full force of his wide smile on me. My knees buckled and I began to quiver. "Frances will help you, ma'am."

"Thank you."

I watched him stride—I mean *stride*—over to where a middle-aged black man sat on a bench waiting.

"Keep your eye on Bubba," Frances said cheerfully. "He is highly regarded in these parts."

"I can see why."

Frances examined me with new interest. "That is one wicked cowboy."

"Not really a cowboy, is he?"

"A genuine turd kicker out of the Texas badlands. Also a honest-to-God lawyer. Good-looking sucker, isn't he? A mite pale for my taste, but . . ." She shrugged, grinned, waved a pen in my direction. "All right, I'm ready to hear your tale of woe . . ."

I told her what had happened at IFP and Frances wrote it all down. "Title Seven," she said.

"Ah," I said wisely. What, I wondered, was Title VII? I didn't dare ask. When Frances finished typing it all up, I signed an affidavit.

"That's it," she announced.

"What happens next?"

"Next you will receive a letter . . ."

That sounded alarmingly like Emil Lieber to me. One such letter was enough. I felt I should ask another question or two, underscore the seriousness of my intentions. But from the set of Frances' face, I assumed that nothing worth talking about remained to be said.

I was almost to the exit when Bubba Horn caught up with me. "Frances do right by you, ma'am?"

"I'm sure she did, Mr. Horn."

"Friends call me Bubba. But you have the advantage of me? . . ."

I told him my name. He repeated it and shook my hand. "Just as easy as comin' down a greased slide from here on out, Miz Pepper. The complaint goes into the hopper and steps with all deliberate speed up the line, then starts back down again."

"An investigation?"

"Nothin' like that. Some pokin' and pryin', that's all. Until one day a letter arrives."

"How long will all this take, Mr. Horn?"

"Bubba." He turned on that smile.

"Libby." I was too nervous to smile.

"A while. What has to be decided here is whether or not your case warrants a hearing."

"Do you think I should have a lawyer?"

"Not necessary. Surely you are acquainted with

somebody in the legal profession who can advise you on how to deal with this situation."

I shook my head.

He rummaged around in the pocket of his sports coat, came up with a card. "What we have here is my name and business phone. Now I am layin' no claim to bein' handy should you need help, but it'd surely be worth a phone call, you require some legal assistance."

"I appreciate that."

"Stay in touch, Libby Pepper. Could be old Bubba can do you some good. Sure nice to meet you, ma'am." He started to walk away, turned back. "You plannin' to get off a letter to the Federal Equal Employment Opportunity Commission?"

"Who?"

"Can't harm you any and those people down in Washington are the only ones that have enough enforcement muscle to make it worthwhile."

"I'll write them."

"You do that, hear. Only thing is you got a limited period of time for filin'."

Before I could thank him, he was on his way back to the man on the bench. He looked lots better to me than Gary Cooper. Better even than Robert Redford.

That evening I wrote a letter to the Equal Employment Opportunity Commission in Washington, venting my spleen on Emil Lieber and that corporate monster, IFP. I rewrote it twice, corrected misspellings, improved the grammar and polished the syntax. Then I typed a clean copy.

I mailed the letter the next morning and felt a lot better for having done so. As if I had accomplished something really outstanding and brave. As if I were truly fighting back. But of course I knew better.

thirteen

Write it off. Nothing was going to come of it. The complaint, the letter to the EEOC, those were mild and relatively ineffective ways of striking back. Okay. It was done. My feeble counterattack, having been made, was over. A flea bite on the back of an elephant would be noticed more. They—Lieber, Marras, IFP—were the winners. Somehow my life had slipped into failure and defeat, and it was almost impossible to remember when I did good things, controlled my existence, and won more than I lost. How had I turned away from all that? What had I done to myself? What had I allowed to be done to me? A terrible rage boiled up under my skin, but against who or what I didn't know.

To me, Cici was the flip side of all my failures. The embodiment of all that I had longed to become, and didn't. For the first time I understood that I had been in competition with Cici to become Super-Woman. I still was. But it was no contest.

The following Saturday night Cici had a party and invited us. Naturally Walter didn't want to go.

"I won't know anybody," he said.

"We'll meet new people."

"Go without me. I'll babysit."

I insisted that I would not go without him, but

the more we discussed it the more the idea appealed to me. In the end I gave in and said I would go alone.

I wore the black evening skirt and blouse Sybil had bought for me at Saks. Very carefully I applied make-up, not too much and that done as sneakily as possible. I liked looking like the Dragon Lady, but I didn't want anybody to think that I was doing it deliberately. One last glance in the mirror convinced me that I might pass muster among Cici's fancy friends.

Cici's apartment was a duplex, huge, meandering, passages leading to unexpected rooms and other passages. By the time I arrived, there were people clustered together in pairs, trios, groups, simultaneously talking, talking or laughing, laughing, in counterpoint to the gladiatorial clink of ice in tall glasses, charged by the slow sweet drift of pot smoke. On a balcony looking down on the living room, a rock band was pounding away. The decibel count was outrageous.

Everyone was beautiful. Stylishly pluperfect, clever, witty, and clearly very sophisticated. As if they'd just stepped out of Bloomie's display windows. I felt like Cinderella, after midnight.

There were familiar faces everywhere. People whose names I knew, or felt I should know. Actors and singers and even a couple of newspaper columnists I recognized. And an army of beautiful women in see-through blouses and exceptionally fine nipples. I wondered, where could I get such a set of nipples? The men were all lean, handsome, leaning into the wind like Italian racing car drivers.

A waiter put a drink in one of my hands and a canapé in the other. I nibbled and sipped and looked for Cici. After a while I gave it up and stood still and tried to decide what to do with myself.

A voice at my ear intruded. "Darling, how excellent to see you again!" A lushly constructed woman in orange and yellow moved in on me, stroking, kissing, talking swiftly. "How long since the last time? Months, I imagine. Not a *year*. Oh, it can't be that long. Last summer, I'm certain, at Jay's party at the Pines. My

God, you were hilarious. That story you told, the one about the crippled plumber, simply hilarious. Tell it again this evening, darling, you must. Lewis loved it. Repeats it constantly, but not as well as you tell it. You will come to dinner. Next Wednesday a week at nine. Hillary will be there and John-John and Sidney. The economist, you remember. He was crazy about you, dear. My heavens, don't you look sensational. Sexy as ever, you naughty creature. At nine, then, Anita?"

"I'm Libby Pepper."

"Oh, that's funny, Anita. Did you make it up yourself. Pepper as in 'salt and.' Just too droll, my dear. You're incognito, yes. Well, good, wait till I tell Lewis. He'll love it. Now where is that motherfucker?"

She plowed into the crowd and disappeared.

"Incredible woman, isn't she?" a voice said behind me. I turned to see a man with a face like an English muffin. He wore thick glasses and an ironic grin. "Lucy Dragge, she's everywhere. Talks like it's going out of style."

"There's something I should tell her."

"Nobody tells Lucy anything. What could you possibly tell her?"

"That I won't be at her dinner on Wednesday."

"Ah-hah!" It was a gasp more than a laugh and his cheeks went pink and his eyes teared. "That's good. Listen, I'm Harry Ellenbogen." He offered his hand. It was immense and surprisingly strong.

"You must be a piano player," I said, trying to free myself from his grasp.

He held on. "Don't struggle, it's useless. What do you mean 'piano player'? Is that a crack?"

"Okay, let go of the hand. The flesh is disintegrating."

He laughed some more and let go. "You're funny."

"Especially when I don't mean to be!" For a moment he seemed bewildered, almost hurt, as if I'd damaged him in some way I failed to comprehend. I set out to make amends. "Okay, you're not a piano player. What then?"

He leaned forward, his weak eyes soft and without penetration behind the thick glasses. "A professional meddler." He waited for me to react. "Ah, well, a social psychologist."

He struck me as a man running a bluff and convinced his bluff was going to be called. One of those men who never quite make it to where they want to go. A marginal man.

"What does a social psychologist do?"

He inched up on me like some great shuffling beast, anxious to rub flesh. I backed off.

"I won't hurt you," he protested. "I ask questions," he went on. "For a living, I mean. Make lists, get it all down on paper."

"What down on paper?"

"Whatever I find out. Why is it people in New York never have conversations?"

"What do they have?"

"Trouble," he answered quickly. "Ah-hah!"

"Not funny, Ellenbogen."

He sobered at once, tried to move in on me again. "What I mean is you have to identify yourself. Job, rank, professional status. What do you do?"

"Nothing, really."

"That's wonderful. It's very hard to do nothing. Even to be a derelict requires a certain amount of effort, planning, getting through the day."

"I'm a wife."

He seemed disappointed. "And a mother?"

"Yes."

"You keep a house, right?"

"After a fashion."

"You must shop, food and all."

"Yes."

"So you cook, clean, shop, raise a kid, be nice to your husband. Boy, have you got a rotten job."

"I think you're right. I went looking for a real job."

"And?"

I told him about IFP and he asked good questions, listened to my answers.

"That it?" he said when I finished.

"Yes."

"Title Seven."

"It keeps coming up."

"You don't know about Title Seven?"

"Tell me about it."

"This is grand," he said, rubbing his huge hands together. "Absolutely grand."

"It's not so good, I didn't get the job."

"Let me tell you, what they did to you, it's worth real money. Coin of the realm. Five thousand, at a guess."

"Say again." I began to feel nervous.

"Inflationary dollars, of course, but dollars nevertheless. The peso is in trouble and the franc is open to question. Get it in dollars."

"Five thousand dollars?"

"I have written a book on the subject."

"What are you talking about?"

"Discrimination. Bias. Prejudice. You think people can go around dumping on people just like that? Well, they cannot do it. There is a law."

"I know that. I filed a complaint—"

"Hah. Read my book, you'll learn what you should do. It's the definitive text. I use it in all my classes. I teach, too, you know. It's called, *You Can Sue*. Get a copy, it's very good. You must sue."

"Oh, I couldn't."

"Sure you could." He gave me his card. "Get in touch. Private consultations at reasonable fees. Better than these sharpie lawyers who'll rob you blind. Don't let the dirty rats get to you. They cheated you, they damaged you, they insulted you. Sue, sue, sue."

"But," I said, "it was such a little insult."

fourteen

I bought Harry Ellenbogen's book. Eight hundred pages of small type, dense legal terminology that kept me going to the dictionary. It took me two days to finish the introduction and the first chapter. Perhaps it was the definitive text to Ellenbogen but to me it was a bust. Twelve-fifty down the drain. I put it aside and a few days later noticed Walter reading it. He seemed to be enjoying it, too.

Everybody had suggestions. Walter said to forget it. Ellenbogen wanted me to sue. Cici told me to file a complaint. Bubba Horn was willing to give some off-the-cuff legal advice. But none of them was involved, not the way I was, with fears and feelings and palpitations of the heart whenever I thought about *the* job.

One day the letter arrived. On official stationery. The State Human Rights Commission, with a facsimile signature at the bottom. The type blurred before my eyes and I had to squint in order to decipher it. It said that my complaint had been received, noted and a hearing scheduled for the following Wednesday at ten A.M. Also, if I couldn't make it I was to call a day in advance and inform them accordingly. My knees knocked, my heart pounded, and my stomach shifted around crazily.

A *hearing*.

Either I was coming down with something brutal and fatal or I was scared out of my wits. No matter which, I needed help bad and fast. Naturally I called my husband at work.

"Who is this?" he began.

"It's Libby."

"Libby!"

"Your wife."

"You're not supposed to call me here unless it's an emergency."

"This is an emergency."

"What's wrong with Steven?"

"Stevie? Nothing, it's me."

"You had an accident?"

"You could say that. You know that complaint I filed?" When he made no response, I hurried on. "My job."

"Oh."

"They want me to come to a hearing."

"A hearing."

"The Human Rights Commission."

"What's the emergency?"

"They want me to appear, to testify."

"I can't talk about it now."

"I'm petrified, Walter. I'm turning into jelly. I'm peeing in my pants."

"Don't be vulgar. You made the complaint, you must have expected this."

"No, no. I mean, I didn't think they'd actually *do* anything about it."

"Every action," my darling Walter said in clear, forthright tones, "brings about a reaction."

Divorce Walter. Yes, that's what he deserved. On second thought, divorce would be too good for him. Any single man in New York is fair game for those millions of horny women you see looking so beautiful on the East Side. Those barracudas would latch on to Walter in a minute, drag him off to bed where he'd have nothing but fun and games. Not on your life. No, no; divorce was out.

I tried Cici. Surely she could advise me properly on how to conduct myself at the hearing. Cici would calm my jingle-jangled nerves. But she was out of town, researching the oil fields of Oklahoma for an article entitled "Women in Oil."

Who next? What about Ellenbogen? Not only was his book unreadable but the man was charged with lecherous intent. I remembered how his eyes had gleamed behind those Coke-bottle glasses of his as he looked me over. Ellenbogen would have liked nothing so much as to get me alone in his office, helpless, vulnerable, so he could diddle around. No way, my man.

Sybil? Forget it. My mother would take me shopping for a new pair of shoes, something frivolous and fancy, when I needed fur-lined boots to keep out the cold.

Then I remembered Bubba Horn. Of course. The Cowboy Lawyer. Friend of the depressed and the poor, the oppressed and the weak. Old Bubba would help. After all, on the Richter scale of neediness, I rang up no more than a six-point-five.

He answered his own phone, which I took to be an indication of his genuine humanity. "Well, Libby, sure is nice to hear your voice again. Things movin' all right for you?"

I told him I had a problem and he said why didn't we have lunch. We went to one of those small but very elegant and expensive French restaurants in the East Fifties. In threadbare plaid slacks and an old turtleneck, I felt very much out of place. In his faded jeans, boots and sports coat, Bubba looked as if he belonged anywhere.

He ordered a cold fish appetizer in a lemony sauce, rack of lamb, potatoes and zucchini sautéed in butter, coffee and a chocolate mousse. Plus a Chablis that went for around ten bucks a bottle.

"You're some kind of cowboy," I said.

"Just a farm boy. My daddy has a little piece of land up in the Panhandle. Nothin' very fancy. Town's named White Buffalo, and there ain't much high livin' goin' thereabouts. Miserable country. Wind comes whis-

tlin' down out of Canada in the winter and the sun
bakes you crisp come summer. I have got to say it, it just
warms this country boy's heart to sit across from such a
purty lady for some civilized talk."

"What I really need is some legal advice."

"Ask me anythin' you want, Miz Libby."

I handed him the letter from the Human Rights
Commission. "They're having a hearing."

"There you are, life is just waddlin' down the old
cow path."

His drawl was getting thicker with each mouthful.

"Shouldn't I have a lawyer?"

He gave a sweet, country smile, shy, diffident, appealing. "What you don't need most of all is a lawyer.
What we have here is just a piddlin' little hearin'."

"I am somewhat apprehensive."

"Nothin' to it."

"Filled with trepidation."

"Lean back and hang in."

"I'm scared stiff, Bubba."

"Not one single thing for you to worry about. Brainy
as you are you'll rope and tie those uptown critters all
by your lonesome self."

"I am? I will?"

He planted his elbows on the table, chin in hand, and
examined me with those hard, bright blue eyes. I
squirmed. "Yes, ma'am, I am convinced of it."

"You are?"

"I have seen such as that before."

"What's that, Bubba?"

"It's right out front with you."

I grew uneasy.

"You," he said. "You are one of those highly intelligent women who aim to keep it tucked away like it
was a crime against nature, Yale and God."

"I went to City College, myself."

"There you are. Let it all hang out, Libby, be yourself. I have discovered how it is with some of you New
York intellectuals. You're afraid that intelligence in a

woman equals shrewdness and shrewdness equals unat-
tractiveness and makes for unfeminine qualities. Well,
I am here to tell you not to believe that for a minute.
Intelligence pops right out of those pretty big brown
eyes of yours and there is no way to hide it."

Oh, boy, could he talk. Either he was the greatest
talker in town or a bullshit artist supreme. Which might
amount to the same thing. No matter, I sure did enjoy
listening to him.

"About the hearing," I said in a small voice.

"You go in there scared, they'll sniff it out and
swarm all over you."

"They?"

"Well, sure. The company is bound to be well represented."

"By a lawyer?"

"It's the way big outfits work."

"Maybe I should have a lawyer, too."

"There will be a kind of arbiter. Sort of a judge. Im-
partial, of course. He'll listen to both sides of the
argument and—"

"Decide?"

"Consider the facts and render a judgment. Eventually."

"Eventually?"

"Man has to consider what he's heard."

"What if he renders against me?"

"That's what his function is, to decide whether or
not you were justified in making the complaint."

"That doesn't sound so bad."

"Just say to yourself that you're goin' to enjoy every minute."

I was still not convinced. "No lawyer?"

"Lawyers cost money and don't necessarily shore
up every weak beam in the barn. How do you like
the wine?"

"It's excellent."

"I reckon you've come here before."

"Never. Walter and I, we don't go out very much."

"Imagine that. A man's got a smart-lookin' wife, makes good sense to travel her around, make her feel good."

"Is that what you do with your wife?" My God, I was half-flirting with the man.

Bubba put his tongue in his cheek. "Tell you the truth, Miz Libby. Just haven't been able to work out the time for marriage, and such as that. All this legal backin' and fillin'. I mean to tell you, it just saps a man's time and energy. Not fair to rope and brand a woman thataway . . ." He tapped the side of his perfect nose.

He roused all my latent skepticism, not to mention curiosity and dormant libidinous attitudes. "Are you for real, Bubba? That name? . . ."

"Folks put that on me when I was little. Seems I kept saying it to everybody . . ."

"And that cowboy drawl of yours, those boots . . ."

"It's you Yankees talk strange. Back in White Buffalo . . ."

"That's another thing—there really is a White Buffalo?"

"Gettin' to be a metropolis, almost. Four hundred and thirty-two livin' souls, black and white, Mex and Chinese. Best eatin' establishment up to and includin' El Paso is the Chinese restaurant. Make the tastiest tacos in West Texas. We got us a Sears catalogue store, back counter of Herv Martin's store. Mostly he sells tractors and farm tools and such. And a honest-to-Jesus indoor cinema playin' a movie show every night, 'ceptin' the sabbath. Odd you not knowin' all about White Buffalo."

"Your father has a farm in White Buffalo?"

"Just outside of town. Itty-bitty place. Once a year I go down to give Daddy a helpin' hand."

I could see it clearly. Bubba's poor old father, bent by too many years of stoop labor on unyielding land, unable to hire help, needing his son's assistance at harvest time in order to make it through the winter. Bubba had good instincts, a sound family background, solid roots in the Texas soil; no wonder he had dedicated his life to helping those less fortunate. I almost reached out and touched him.

"Helping me this way," I said. "It's very kind of you."

"This prejudice business, I am positively opposed to it. Bias toward women, it is an insidious disease festerin' across the land, liable to break out anywhere.

"You take old Tom McKinney, one of my best friends. Went to school with ole Tom in Austin. Smart fella, Tom, been around, traveled, reads, knows how things work. Well, Tom, he operates a chain of fast food eateries. Calls 'em Stuffins and Muffins, so help me. Now here is this worldly wise man, smart as a whip, and he is about as chauvinistic as you can get. He's got gals workin' his places in just about every spot he can put 'em. Why, you say? 'Cause ole Tom has it figured that he can pay them less and work them harder. Says so himself, he does. Listen to what I am tellin' you, I have got a great deal of friendly feelin's toward Tom in spite of his backward business policies. Man knows he is wrong, you see, knows what he's about, and does it anyway. Says business is business. Well, if a person like ole Tom can do thataway then I say a company like IFP has likely as not done a grievous wrong to lots of women, especially you, Libby."

"Let's hope the arbiter agrees."

Bubba leaned my way, those gunfighter's eyes riveted on mine. "I am about to hand over some very excellent advice, free of charge. When you go to that hearin' you go innocent and none too smart. Same as if you just come out of the piney woods and got not the slightest idea of where it's comin' from."

"Play dumb, you mean?"

"Precisely." Before I could object, he went on. "Keep your nose to the wind and sniff out their intentions. But give them nothin' they can hang you with. What you got to make them believe is that you are there to put yourself into their manly hands. Roll over on your back and wave your feet in the air like some kind of a helpless pup, you hear me. Let 'em scratch your belly. Let 'em tug on your ears. Let 'em chuck you under the chin. You stay as loose and as cool as my ole granny, and that poor ole lady's been dead more'n fourteen years now." He grinned, quick, white, engaging. "Those big-company people, they'll roll right over you, you give 'em half a chance."

"So I don't give them the chance."

"Keep a low profile. Do not provoke them into drawin' down on you, if you know what I mean. Helpless, innocent, weak, stultifyin'ly ignorant."

"I don't know if I can carry it off. I'm scared. I'll be scared then. And I'm not really dumb, or innocent, or helpless. At least I don't want to be."

"Do like I say and you'll be stronger than all of 'em together. You got my word on it."

"I'll do my best." I wanted to please him.

"Be sure to look the part. Be sure to put up a colorless target, nothin' those folks will want to shoot at."

"Nothing too provocative, you mean?"

"A teensy bit of makeup ought to do her. And one of those dicky-poo blouses, something sweet and virginal, so's they don't pay too much mind to your ever-lovin' body."

I blushed. "I'm a married lady."

"No tricky touches, like wearin' no brassiere."

Was this a natural part of the lawyer-client relationship, a discussion of my boobs? Then it occurred to me that he was talking about bras, I was thinking about boobs. What kind of a pervert was I?

"Now, Libby-gal, this is all of a piece, our entire battle plan. You go in there, a solitary, helpless citizen put upon by an oppressive corporate giant. I tell you, it's a beautiful composition, a work of art."

"You're the artist."

"Nothin' to it."

"And it's going to work?"

"Guaranteed."

"I hope you're right."

He stroked my hand and gave me that great white

smile. I got my hand back as soon as decency permitted. Ole Bubba was deadly, a threat to life and limb, not to mention other more delicate parts of me.

On the way out of the restaurant, I fell a stride or two behind and noticed that he had one of the world's great asses. Tight, round and strong.

Whoop-e-ti-yi-yi-yo!

fifteen

Bubba and I parted at the corner, shaking hands and smiling secretly, as if we had something special going on. If we did, I'd missed it. But then my perceptions had always been slow. Or was it my ability to process my perceptions? How nice if something real and worthy had come into being between Bubba Horn and me. A deep and lasting bond, stronger than love, richer than friendship, more exciting than lust. I wanted desperately to be a woman who could persuade a man to do anything.

As I wandered around inside my head, I kept searching for a phone. In New York, that search cools the blood rapidly. In the first booth I came to the instrument had been ripped off the wall. A block later another booth, the phone in place. It took my dime and gave back no dial tone. Finally, in a drug store in Rockefeller Center, I located a telephone that worked. I called Sybil and got no answer.

I decided to go home. At a bus stop on Eighth Avenue the full vigor and cultural energy of the city descended upon me complete with living color, stereophonic sound and an awful stink. A bearded man tried to sell me some hashish. A hooker offered to do to me what had never been done by man, woman or beast. A seven-foot-tall black man in a yellow jacket and green boots guaranteed me a net income of five hundred dollars a week—"And fuck the IRS," he added—if I'd put myself under his professional guidance. I spotted an empty cab and dived in, nearly hysterical.

The driver made it up to Sixty-ninth Street in about twenty seconds, giving me palpitations, ulcer pains, and the sweats. He grinned back at me and said he'd forget the fare in exchange for a little head. I flung a couple of bills his way and fled, overtipping as usual.

Back into the apartment, and breathing hard, I locked, bolted, and chained the door, and braced a strong chair under the doorknob. I still felt unsafe. New York, as they say, is a constant adventure. A source of unbridled creative force. The cultural center of the universe. Some say it's the best possible place in the world to bring up a child. There was no way I was going to be able to live through it.

I made a ham loaf for dinner, with a caramel sauce. The meat was overcooked and the sauce congealed. Nobody even noticed.

I did the dishes, bathed Stevie and gave him a half-hour of playtime. Then I read *The Cat in the Hat* to him. Then I sang him six or eight songs, including "Happy Days Are Here Again." Then he said that he might go to sleep if I would stay with him while he listened to a Winnie-the-Pooh record. I lay down beside Stevie on the bed and immediately went to sleep. He woke me in order to turn the record over.

It was past nine-thirty before I was able to tiptoe into the kitchen and make some instant coffee. I splashed cold water on my face, and tried Sybil's number again. Still no answer.

I carried my coffee into the living room. Walter was reading *Light in August.*

"Sybil isn't home," I said.

He didn't look up. "She must be out."

"Having a good time," I said without enthusiasm.

"With Mr. Michaels, probably."

Listening to some string quartet, I supposed. Or having supper at the Russian Tea Room. My mother's distaste for the West Side of Manhattan was almost total, excluding only the Russian Tea Room and Carnegie Hall. Both possessed a certain cultural cachet, an East Side flavor.

"They remind me of London," she had once declared in a bout of nostalgia.

"How?" I had dared ask.

She replied disdainfully, "Don't be silly."

"I've been calling all day," I said to Walter.

"Sybil's an active woman."

"I know. But—"

He marked his place with his forefinger, raised his eyes to mine, full of literary forbearance. "She might have gone away for a few days."

"My mother!" The idea startled me. "Go away without telling me? We call each other every day."

"Three or four times a day." Walter smiled to indicate he was being pleasant. Walter was pleasant, considerate and often concerned. Whenever possible, that is. But no matter how hard he tried Walter seemed to exist at some distance from the rest of us. "Anyway, you keep complaining about how much Sybil bothers you . . ."

"She's a difficult woman to take."

"Why not enjoy her absence. It doesn't happen often."

He was right, which in no way prevented me from worrying. "Maybe something happened."

"To Sybil? What could possibly happen to Sybil?"

"She might have been mugged."

"No mugger in his right mind would dare lay a hand on your mother."

I agreed with that. Sybil gave off a rather intimidating aura, a presence of self that kept other people from coming too close.

"I'm worried," I said, after a while.

"Well, I'm not. Not a bit."

Of course he wasn't. His parents were alive and warm in Florida, safe among the shuffleboard addicts.

"You're right," I said. "I'm being silly."

He began to read again.

"I can't help worrying," I said.

He put the book in his lap. "That's your nature, to worry. Do you want me to go over there, check out the apartment?"

That really scared me. If Walter was so certain nothing was wrong, why was he suggesting such a dramatic and uncharacteristic act? "That's very nice of you, Walter." It was, I insisted to myself. Sweet, almost. All right, Walter, no divorce. At least for a while. But stay in line. I stood up. "I'll phone again in a few minutes."

Walter gave me a little squeeze. "Suppose I call the manager of Sybil's building. Ask him to look in on the apartment . . ."

"That really shakes me up," I said.

"In that case, I won't call."

"You think there is something the matter?"

"No. Just a precaution. To allay your fears."

"Oh, my God!"

"Forget it, Libby. I won't call."

"How else will we know? Call."

"You're sure?"

"No. I'm not sure, not of anything. No, don't call. It's silly. I'm overwrought is all. My nerves are on edge. I'll take half a Valium."

"Take a whole one."

"Only if you call."

"You think I should?"

"Call. The manager. The manager of her building. He's to go right up to Sybil's apartment and see if she is there. That's all. Is that so much to ask? A small favor like that. Sybil takes care of him lavishly every Christmas, gives him too much. I want my mother . . ."

Walter made the call. "The manager's not there," he reported.

"What? What do you mean he's not there?"

"He went to a basketball game."

Rabbi Basketball was winning the war. "At a time like this!"

"His wife is there. She's sending the elevator operator up to the apartment with a passkey."

"Oh, my God!"

Walter sat back down and began to read. I checked up on Stevie; he was still breathing. I filled the tub and undressed. The phone rang and I got to it before Walter could mark his place. It was the wife of the manager of Sybil's building.

"It's Mrs. Markson, Mrs. Pepper," she said. "George went up there, rang the bell, knocked. When no one answered, he went inside. Mrs. Markson was lying on the floor, Mrs. Pepper. Unconscious. I think she's had an attack of some kind . . ."

Stroke!

What an awful word. What a cruel and devastating thing to happen to my mother. Sybil, so charged with vitality and zest, so purely conceived and designed to live at a high pitch, and go on.

We stood in a neat little triangle outside the Intensive Care Unit in Mount Sinai Hospital, Walter, me, and Herbert Barger, M.D. Barger was strictly according to the AMA book. He came complete with Park Avenue office, two receptionists, three nurses, a white Corniche Rolls, a military mustache and a stethoscope jutting out of an immaculately tailored pocket.

"Ah, no," I groaned.

Barger cocked his neat round head in what passed for professional commiseration.

"How serious is it, Doctor?" Walter delivered his lines with sober intensity, one man to another.

Barger practically sighed in relief, did a half-turn in Walter's direction. Clearly, hysterical daughters were not among his favorite people. A reasonable husband was right up his medical alley. He cleared his throat as if to address a collection of his colleagues.

"Let me explain." The man was on his own turf, try and stop him. "What we have here is a stroke, I want to emphasize, not a heart attack."

"You already said that," I said.

"So I did, Mrs. Pepper." His lips shifted around, and he showed his teeth, as if he were saying "cheese," for the camera. He oozed patience and understanding. He leaned, he hovered, he put on a long face. He did everything at once, except rub my belly. "So as to eliminate any confusion. What we have here is a cerebrovascular accident. The human brain must have a constant flow of blood in order to provide the oxygen it requires, not to mention other nourishment. Should the flow be interrupted, either by blocking of large or small arteries or veins or by bleeding from a blood vessel into brain tissue, the reaction in that part of the body controlled by the portion of the brain affected is immediate.

"Now." He broke sweat, all warmed up and rolling, enjoying himself. "The blocking may be intracranial, within the skull, or it may be extracranial, outside the skull. An obstruction of the carotid artery in the neck would be a good example of the latter. Am I going too fast for you?"

"Will there be a quiz on Friday?" The words shot out of me accompanied by what I hoped was a disarming smile.

Walter tried to cover up for me. "Very clear," he said. "Very interesting."

Our house would soon be blessed by a medical encyclopedia, I could tell.

Barger picked up where he'd left off with no loss of verve. "Usually a thrombus, a clot that remains in place where it originally formed, causes the blockage. But in the case of an embolism, the clot travels through the bloodstream and blocks off a blood vessel elsewhere. I'm not being too technical, I hope . . ."

"Oh, not at all," Walter assured him. "I might ask you to recommend some books . . ."

I knew it!

"Many excellent works on the subject." Barger grew cheerful. "Be pleased to make up a reading list for you . . ."

"Appreciate it."

"My pleasure."

"Please go on," I said, trying not to scream.

Barger recognized my unstable condition. "Of course, dear lady. A stroke comes on suddenly. There is no warning, most of the time. It can attain its peak within minutes or even seconds of its inception. Sometimes it may take as much as a few hours to run its course, the attack, that is. One thing we know, the processes leading up to the onset have certainly been going on for an extended duration.

"Depending on various factors, a number of occurrences may follow a stroke. The victim may lapse into coma. Or remain conscious. He may collapse to the ground. Blindness may set in in both eyes. Or in one eye. Or in half of one eye, that condition being known as hemianopsia. Dizziness may ensue, a reduction of feeling in various portions of the body, stiffness in the neck, difficulty in swallowing, loss of the sense of smell. You can see, the possibilities are endless."

"I never knew any of this," Walter admitted with a substantial amount of pride.

"Few people outside the profession do, Mr. Pepper. But isn't that as it should be? Everyone to his own trade, as they say."

"Who?" I said aloud.

"What?"

"Who says that?"

Walter jumped in. "Your point is well made, Doctor."

Barger checked me out obliquely, as if only his peripheral vision was operative. "I believe in Mrs. Markson's case the blockage may very well be in the arteries of the neck rather than inside the head itself."

"Is that good?" Walter said.

"Relatively. In a major stroke . . ."

"Major!" The voice was shrill, distant, and faintly familiar; it was mine. "My mother is going to die."

"Now, Libby," Walter said.

"Now, Mrs. Pepper," Barger said.

"Tell me the truth."

"In your mother's case, speech is somewhat impaired . . ."

"You mean my mother can't talk?" Sybil had always existed at the top of her lungs. She had chattered, declaimed, argued, pontificated, gossiped, criticized, babbled nonstop for all these years. A Sybil without speech was no Sybil at all. Deprived of that pleasure, she would swell up and burst into a million frustrated syllables. Things were worse than I had imagined.

"There is also . . ." Barger said, voice hushed to convey new seriousness. Did he think what had gone before was a comic routine? "There is also what we call hemiplegia."

Walter said, "Ah," as if he understood. I said, "What the hell is that?"

"There is a decided flaccidity on one side of Mrs. Markson's body—the right side."

"What? What's that mean?"

"Mrs. Markson is partially paralyzed."

My throat closed up and I gasped for air. "My mother's going to die."

"Much too early to talk about dying," Barger answered.

Too late, I told myself. Too late for so many things. All the talks Sybil and I had never had. The confidences never exchanged, the hopes never revealed, the mistakes never admitted and cried over, or laughed about. What kind of young girl had she been growing up in Poland? She never mentioned it. What kind of life had she had before she married? Did she know many young men? Did she have many boy friends, sweethearts, lovers? She never told me. What had she dreamed about, longed to do, yearned to be? How was it in the early days of her marriage to Sam Markson when they must have talked and planned for the day when he would be a famous concert violinist and she would conduct a musical salon known worldwide? Once, I remembered at that moment, Sybil had men-

tioned how she and Sam had saved in order to buy him
a Stradivarius. But they never accumulated money
enough and Sam always had to make do with a lesser
instrument. It was the story of my parents' lives, and
mine.

"When," Walter said to Barger, bringing me back
to the horrible present, "will we know more?"

Barger had all the words laid out in a neat rank, all
shiny and sterile. "The first twenty-four hours are the
most crucial and dangerous. Even the first two or three
days. But if—let us say after three weeks, we may see
some degree of improvement."

"Three weeks before we know if my mother is going
to live?"

Barger drew down his Sandhurst mustache in sober
contemplation. "I was referring specifically to the ex-
tent of the paralysis, Mrs. Pepper. Your mother's life
is ultimately in God's hands."

Something was out of whack with my world. The
rabbis were athletic directors and the doctors were
hooked on God. Barger delivered his best bedside
smile, full of phony encouragement. He couldn't fool
me. Nobody made house calls anymore.

They said I could see my mother. For a few minutes only, as if I could tolerate much more.

One look and you knew that it was all wrong. A
scruffy little room with drab walls and a single, tiny
window, the shade drawn. If she had the choice, the
Sybil Markson I knew would have been up and gone
out of that depressing cubicle. A place for a corpse
not a patient.

In one of those hospital beds with guard rails drawn
up, Sybil seemed insignificant and helpless, not at all
like my mother. A tube ran into her nose. A needle
had been shoved into the back of her hand. Her skin
was gray, her eyes were closed. I kissed her cheek
and spoke softly.

"Mother . . ."

For a long interval, nothing. Then her right eye rolled up to reveal a yellow orb glowing with hostility. The right side of her mouth moved and I leaned closer.

"Call me Sybil . . ."

sixteen

Nothing helped. There was no mental trick I could work to keep from remembering how Sybil looked in that hospital bed. The layers of accumulated style had been peeled back and the artistically designed sophistication shattered. Replaced by an aged body that functioned only by half. A face out of kilter, frozen into a grotesque mask distantly reminiscent of its former self. The English accent had been muted by the clot that traumatized her brain.

"Look what happened to me," she had complained. Her head hurt, she said, she couldn't move her arm, her leg, couldn't see out of one eye. She wanted to know how she looked.

"She's got to live!" I screamed when Walter got me back to our apartment.

He hesitated. "It might be a blessing if she didn't."

Killing was too good for him. I longed to wipe him out, turn him into an unperson who had never existed, not in fact nor in memory. "What are you saying?"

"Even if she survives, she may be paralyzed."

Sybil paralyzed. Limping through the rest of her days in pain and despair. Not fair, not fair. "She couldn't stand that."

"That's what I mean. Let's have a drink."

"No."

Walter poured some Scotch into two glasses, gave me one.

"No."

"Drink it."

I wanted to kick and scream, to roll around on the floor, to cause trouble for Walter, for Barger, for the whole damned world.

"To be perfectly honest," Walter said, "you surprise me."

"What does that mean?"

"You never seemed particularly fond of your mother."

I had the urge to strike out, give pain. I opened my mouth to speak, to retaliate, but no words came forth. All the antagonism I'd developed toward Sybil. Her cultivated nagging, her constant push, push, pushing. As if only she knew the right way to do things, the right way to live. As if only she had the answers for her ugly duckling second-born, unwanted, accidental daughter. She'd never given full approval to anything I'd done. Or to what I was.

What if she died?

Guilt oozed out to my nerve endings like spoiled milk. I ran to my son's bedroom, afraid the sins of this blasphemous mother would be visited upon my only child. Stevie slept the sleep of the good and the pure, or at least the very young. I admired the perfect form of that angelic face. See that beautiful profile; worth a million in cool cash on the open market. Where had it come from? Sam Markson had owned a beak humped and twisted like a street vendor's pretzel.

Sybil, on the other hand, had undergone one of the great nose jobs of the century, thanks to an English surgeon of delicate skill and artistic hand. Somehow I had inherited Sybil's new nose, passing it along to Stevie. So much for heredity.

Back in the living room, Walter was nursing his drink and reading his book. He indicated my glass.

"It will help you relax, go to sleep."

"I don't want to sleep."

"You can't stay up all night."

"My mother is dying."

"You heard the doctor, it's too soon to speak about dying."

"When is the right time?"

Walter changed his tactics. "Barger's doing his best."

"He's a mechanical man. He treats diseases, not people."

"A doctor can't get involved with every patient. They'd go crazy."

"Why not? I'm going crazy." I started out of the room. "I have to call Candy."

"There's a three-hour difference in time."

"Sybil's her mother, too."

"I'll call."

"No. She's my sister."

He nodded his agreement and went back to his book and his drink.

I waited for the operator to make the connection, trying to remember what my sister looked like. Or sounded like. Trying mightily to summon up some familiar vision out of the past. Nothing came. Sisters had become strangers.

Three thousand miles away, a voice came on saying, "Yes?" Never a hello or a how are you. Just that faintly superior "Yes?" as if the caller had interrupted her during a particularly sensitive moment.

"Candy." I could hardly get her name out.

"You'll have to speak up." All that authority, lined with criticism of lesser, less competent beings. Namely me. Putting into clear focus the limits of my insecurity. Who in hell did she think was calling, some sexual weirdo after some long distance action courtesy of Ma Bell?

"It's Libby."

"Libby?" She sounded more puzzled than pleased. "Why are you calling me, Libby?"

"Is it a crime? . . ." I began, and began to cry. "Oh, Candy . . ."

"What's wrong? Is it that creep you married? Well, it's about time. Divorce is a woman's most precious weapon. Don't let the bastards do it to you twice, I know. When did it happen?"

She sounded so much like Sybil, it frightened me. "Candy, it's Mother."

A long silence ensued and I began to believe she'd hung up on me. "She's dead," Candy said. Her voice was guarded, as if all her emotions had been herded into a safe place behind verbal barricades.

"Mother had a stroke."

"Not Sybil. I don't believe it."

"We were at the hospital."

"That's not like Sybil, to allow life to punish her in any way."

Why *punish,* I thought irritably. Did Sybil honestly deserve punishment? Did any of us?

"Poor, poor Sybil," Candy tacked on.

That, too, sounded strange. Nobody ever pitied my mother. Even her disappointment in Sam Markson had been diverted to her advantage. Second fiddle or no, Markson had delivered Sybil into that magic mellifluous world of music and musicians, composers, conductors, sellers of sheet music. I made a mental note to bring Sybil a gift, a rare and wonderful recording.

"What do the doctors say?" Candy asked.

"Doctors," I snarled into the phone.

"I know what you mean. I was once married to a doctor, if I remember correctly. I'll come right away, Libby." There was a minimum amount of enthusiasm in her voice.

"You don't have to."

Why let her off the hook? Sure, come. Take up some of the burden, big sister. Shed some tears, suffer some pain.

"No, I think I should. After all, it's been a very long time since we saw each other."

Our mother was dying and Candy saw a chance to

mend sisterly fences. Any excuse for a party. I noticed that I was no longer crying. "Yes," I said. "A very long-time."

"I'll catch a flight out tonight."

"I'll meet your plane."

"Don't bother. I'll stay at the Plaza. Check with me there in the morning. After nine, if you don't mind. I need to catch up on my sleep. It will be good to see you again, Libby."

"Yes," I said. "It will be good to see you again, Candy." It surprised me to discover that I really meant it.

"Are you all right, Libby?"

"How can I be all right," I flipped back, "when I'm still alive?"

seventeen

In the morning, in the kitchen, drinking bitter coffee and listening to Stevie shout from his bed that his immediate surroundings were flooded, I inspected the avocado plant. The pit, to be more accurate. For it was little more than that still. A pale uncertain root poked tentatively into the water, the start of a new life. The symbolism was not lost to me. I phoned the hospital.

"There has been no change," a mechanical voice said.

"Are you a person or a recording?"

"I am a person." There was a click and the line went dead. Person my Aunt Fanny.

I decided to talk to Barger, voice to voice. Another pipe dream. An answering service was what I got. "If you will give me your number and name Doctor will contact you presently."

Give you nothing! I slammed the phone down, then called the Plaza. Candy had not yet checked in. I had the phone in my lap, finger poised to dial again. Who could I call? Almost anyone would do. Out there a whole world existed ready to turn away from me in my time of stress.

I decided to find someone, someplace, to look after Stevie for the day. I needed relief from motherhood.

Two hours and eleven calls later, I located a daycare center on Eleventh Avenue willing to lend a hand to a panicky mother. I got some dry clothes on Stevie and rushed him over there before they could change their mind.

Back at the apartment, I tried Barger's office again. A nurse answered and said Doctor wasn't in but Doctor would phone when Doctor came in. Up yours, Doctor.

Next the hospital. "There has been no change."

The Plaza. Mrs. Candace Loughlin—my sister's current married name—was in suite 814. I was hyperventilating by the time they hooked us up. Candy sounded energetic, enthused, envisioning what she called A Fun Visit to the Big Apple. Her words, I knew better. She'd be lucky to get out of town alive.

"Come on down," she commanded. "We'll have breakfast in the room."

That sounded hazardous, closed into a small space alone with a sister I barely knew anymore. I came up with a terrific alternative: Chock Full o' Nuts on Madison Avenue. We compromised and met in the Palm Court.

Candy was a larger version of Sybil. An elegant woman with frosted hair and superb cheekbones, eyes that tilted up at the corners. She had managed to take on that glossy Southern California look, perpetually suntanned and glowing with good health. You knew she ate sunflower seeds, organically grown vegetables and a minimum of red meat. One look opened a catalogue of ancient insecurities. She was the kind of woman who, on a nude beach, would appear modest and unassailable.

We embraced, kissed, and said things like How Long It Has Been and Why Don't You Write More Often and so on and so on. Candy ordered eggs Benedict and coffee for us both and announced that there was No Place Like New York.

"Bet on it," I said.

The irony was lost on her. "You're lucky to live

here. Active socially. Always on the go. Meeting famous, interesting people. There's an electric energy to this city, a creative thrust. This is the center of things. Art, music, the theater."

"We don't go to the theater anymore. Too expensive."

That amused her. "Only a native New Yorker could say that without sounding slightly pompous. I imagine none of your friends has ever visited the Statue of Liberty."

"I haven't."

"You see."

I didn't, but I wasn't about to argue the point. "What I'd like to do is go to Marineland."

"Marineland! But, darling, that's for tourists."

"Precisely."

Enough chit-chat. Candy decided to get down to basics. "I suppose we should talk about Sybil."

"Not necessarily."

"I find it hard to believe, Sybil ill, I mean. It's not like her."

"She didn't do it on purpose."

"There you go, Libby. You always were the clown of the family."

Ugh.

"There's something positively immutable about Sybil, as if she dwelt outside the normal situations that affect most of us. Safe behind an invisible screen. Oh, you don't know what I'm talking about, do you?"

I remembered the dream and the glass wall that cut me off from the rest of the world. The dream had occurred twice more. "Just keep it coming," I said with a smile that hardly represented how I felt. "After a while I'll get your message."

Candy patted my hand. "Poor dear. You're upset, aren't you?"

"Me? No. You want to hear about Sybil?"

"Oh, yes, please. Everything."

So I told her. Everything. When I finished, she called for some hot coffee and said Poor Sybil.

"We can visit her this morning."

She shuddered. "No reason to rush. Is she all wired up? I don't do very well in hospitals, you see. But you, Libby, you're in such firm control. I envy you your confidence and strength." She had obviously confused me with Nurse Edith Cavell or somebody. "Later, we'll visit Sybil later."

She went at her eggs Benedict with concentrated fervor. There we were, two people linked by blood and upbringing and considerable common experience, yet with very little to say to each other. I felt a strong urge to make an emotional connection with Big Sister, to renew old affections, interests, shared experiences. I took a deep breath and began to tell her about the job at IFP.

That engaged her interest at once. She listened attentively, asked good questions, even made a few notes.

"You are a nervy one," she said, when I finished.

As smart as she was, she didn't know me at all. "I'm scared silly."

"Not many people would have the guts to fight a major corporation."

"Just one small step. A routine complaint. Nothing will come of it, I'm sure. The hearing will just be a waste of time."

"Is it soon?"

"A few days. Maybe I can get a postponement. With all that's going on——"

"Don't do that. Get it over with, force the issue, that's my policy. Give 'em hell."

I didn't know what to say.

"You'll do just fine. You always were the brainy one in the family."

I did well in school, but that doesn't mean much. A good memory, pay attention, and you can't miss. "You're the one who accomplished something with her life."

"I've been married more times, if that's what you mean. Working on number four right now."

"I thought it was three."

"Sometimes I get them confused, call this one by number two's name. Also, they tend to say the same things, the same ideas expressed in almost identical language, as if they were all cut out of the same pattern. I never planned on being so much married . . . I might as well have stayed with the first one."

"But you didn't. When things go wrong for you, you take steps. You change your life . . ."

"My husband, that's all."

"You don't let life kick you around. That takes courage, decisiveness."

She eyed me quizzically. "Trouble in the nest, sister?"

"Nothing like that," I said too quickly. "It's just that —I wish Walter were more . . ."

"The bedroom?"

For the first time, I became aware that Candy and I had never before discussed sex. Never touched on the subject. Nor love. Nor guilt. Nor disappointment nor happiness. Nothing intimate, serious or important to either of us.

"We used to share a bedroom," I said.

"The same bed."

"We slept together, but we never had any conversation."

"We talked a lot."

"We talked, but we never said anything. I guess the difference in our ages . . ."

"Maybe that's it. When I got married the first time you were—how old?"

"Twelve. I envied you a lot. Getting a husband, getting out on your own, getting a room of your own."

She laughed softly. "You got our room."

"I slept there but it was always your room."

"I see what you mean."

"I dreamed of changing places with you, traveling to some exotic land full of adventure, strange sounds, smells, people. Where was it?"

"Fort Bragg, North Carolina. The silly ass was a paratrooper."

"He was very handsome in his uniform, I remember that."

"He was a fool. A thirty-year man."

"Moe, his name was Moe."

"You can remember that? He kept breaking his leg, always the right leg. Every time he jumped."

"What happened to Moe?"

"Last time I heard he was behind a desk in the Pentagon. The fool broke his leg too many times to do anything else."

"That bedroom was an empty place with you gone."

"We did have some good times."

I stared at her. "After you left, it was as if it had never happened. No high points, no low points. No vivid memories."

"That's the way life is."

"I hope not."

"You always were the idealist in the family. Anyway, it's better that way. Better not to feel the squeeze after you've screwed up time after time. All those deals that fall through. All the love affairs that go nowhere. The marriages that are empty, sterile, so very dull. Believe me, living isn't easy for some of us."

"You were always on the go, Candy. On your way to Europe, South America, all those glamorous places."

"You get tired of it."

"When I saw pictures of you in the newspapers with that racing driver . . ."

"Roberto. Another fool. Drove like a madman, on or off the track. Ended up with a steel plate in his skull and his brains scrambled."

"I envied you all that excitement."

She grimaced. "Did I ever tell you about number three, Leopold, the doctor? He insisted that he was descended from a Hungarian king, or was it Slovakian? In any case, Leopold split his time between men and women. Once in a while he worked me into his schedule, long enough to tell me about all the other sexual goodies he was tasting. Leopold enjoyed going into detail and he had a lot of details to go into."

"Why did you marry him?"

She laughed, a hacking sound without mirth. "I have this tremendous drive for power, my dear. I'm always trying to turn life around."

"You didn't succeed with Leopold?"

"Hardly. When last heard of Leopold was living in Milan with an Italian industrialist."

"Small loss."

"Oh, I wouldn't say that. Leopold was a fascinating man and never dull. No, never dull. And now I'm married to Abner."

"And you have two children, a successful business. You and Abner are a very good team."

"Abner is—well, Abner *is*. Like no one else I've been married to, that's for certain."

"I read that article about you in the *Times* business section. It said you were one of the most successful women in America. You must be very happy."

She didn't answer for a long time and when she finally did speak it was to change the subject. "We shared one chest of drawers in that room . . ."

"One of the drawers was missing."

"Yes. And one closet."

"And that terrible Murphy bed with the awful springs that kept poking you in the back."

She began to laugh. "I think it was that bed that sent me off with Moe. I needed a good night's sleep."

I was laughing too. "I hated that bed."

"We did share some moments together, Libby. We did."

"We lived together. We were sisters."

She looked me right in the eye, that clear California surfing look, exploratory and hard. Whatever she sought she failed to find for she turned away.

"I had to take care of you, Libby. I was only seventeen, just a girl, too. Sybil, Sybil had her music, her friends, a life without room for two scruffy daughters."

"What about Sam?"

"Sam. He was around. Just around, practicing on his fiddle, never getting any better. I was your baby-sitter, Libby. I fed you and bathed you and read stories to you. At night I'd sing you to sleep. When you were older, I took you for walks."

"You used to tell me about the boys you knew, the places they took you, the movies you saw. I've been a movie fan ever since."

"Do you still take walks?"

"In this city? Not anymore. There were walks we were going to take, but never did."

"Were there?"

"We were going to walk across the George Washington Bridge to New Jersey. You were going to tell me how the stock market works. You knew all about it and I wanted to know what you knew. But you went away before we could take that walk."

"And you never found out how the stock market works?"

"I don't know anyone who knows how to make money."

"Maybe we'll take that walk one day."

I knew better than that. "Maybe," I said.

Later we went up to Mount Sinai. The nurses said Sybil was resting comfortably and doing as well as could be expected. Candy went in first. When she came out, her face was set and her eyes were dry and shining.

Afterward we went to a bar on Madison Avenue and spent the rest of the day drinking. When I got home, I fell across the bed and went to sleep, didn't wake up until the next morning. Walter had covered me with a warm blanket and he had slept on the living room couch. Good old Walter.

eighteen

The following day, Candy went back to California.

"If you really need me, I'll stay," she said.

"I'm sure I can handle things."

"Oh, I'm sure you can. You're so good at this sort of thing, Libby."

What sort of thing was she talking about? This was my first encounter with my mother having a stroke. My experience was severely limited, I felt like saying. I resented her departure, resented being left alone to deal with the daily realities of Sybil's illness. But I was unable to ask her to remain. Unable to voice any criticism of my sister. Unable to do anything but smile and wish her a good journey.

"There are so many loose ends out there," Candy explained.

"Your business." I wanted to make it easier for her. Why?

"And I do have a family to worry about. You understand?"

I understood almost nothing. Not Candy's problems nor my own. There was only the ever-present *now* and a succession of difficulties to be dealt with, if not overcome.

Candy laughed briefly. "For a C.P.A., Abner can be an awful klutz with numbers."

"You go back."

"If anything happens . . ."

"I'll phone you."

"Yes. Call collect. The business pays for it, anyway."

"Collect, yes. I'll remember."

"It's only a few hours away. I can always catch a flight. Sybil understands. I explained that I wouldn't be able to stay very long."

"Sybil can be very understanding."

"I'm so glad we had this chance to talk, Libby. After all this time, you have no idea how much it means to me."

She was right. I had no idea at all.

Two mornings later I went up to One Hundred Twenty-fifth Street for the State Human Rights Commission hearing.

Standing on the street in front of the Commission office, I wanted to run away. But I lacked the courage to do so. After all, they were expecting me in there. All those important men, they'd planned their morning to accommodate me and the least I could do was show up, go through the motions. So I took a deep breath and made myself go inside.

At the rear of the store, beyond the guard rail and past the ranks of desks and clerks at work, was a wide space dominated by an old oak conference table. The kind of table they used to have in school libraries. A dapper little black man in horn-rimmed glasses hurried to greet me, hand outstretched.

"Mrs. Pepper, I am Leon Stephenson, Mrs. Pepper. Regional director of this division of the New York State Human Rights Commission. I will serve as your hearing examiner during the hearing."

"Arbiter" Bubba had called him. "Hearing examiner" was much more imposing, loaded with authority. He was awfully short to be a regional director, but I was impressed nevertheless. Intimidated, if you want the truth.

"I'm very pleased to meet you." If I had been a Catholic, I would have kissed his ring.

"The others will be along momentarily. You can put your coat on that rack."

I obeyed and returned to the table. Stephenson motioned me into a chair at one end of the table. "Smoke, if you wish. There's an ashtray . . ."

"Thank you, but—"

"Also a legal pad and some pencils, should you have to write down anything."

I took my seat and looked over at Leon Stephenson, who looked at me. I smiled and he smiled. He fingered a brown folder on the table as if it might blow up without warning. "Your file," he explained.

That upset me. It had never entered my mind that there was actually a file on me. "I'm not important enough to have a file," I said mildly.

"Oh, yes, you are."

It sounded like a threat. Yes, definitely a threat. I sneaked a look at him. Light reflected off his glasses so I couldn't see his eyes.

"Everybody has a file," he said. "How else are we to keep track of things?"

"Right on," I said, trying to be one of the gang, so to speak.

He turned away, as if I'd made some embarrassing social gaffe. He looked at his watch. "They're late."

"Oh, that's all right."

"You're sure you don't mind?"

"Oh, I don't mind."

"People don't have much of a sense of time these days."

"It's all right, I don't mind."

"Nothing to be worried about. Just a friendly little hearing."

"I'm not worried. A little nervous, maybe. But not actually worried."

"Oh, don't be nervous."

"I already am."

"This is simply an opportunity for me to obtain a fair story from both sides. A conference, a little get-together in order to resolve a small misunderstanding. I listen to your story and to the other side's story and consider all the facts. That's all there is to it. Later I render a judgment. Not a trial, or anything like that. No need for you to be nervous. How about some water, Mrs. Pepper? Would you like some water? Coffee? Tea? A Coke, maybe?"

"Nothing, thank you. I'm fine."

"Yes, I can see that. Just fine. While we're waiting, you could fill in this little questionnaire. Sort of a fact sheet, designed to tell me something about yourself. Background, age, birth statistics, marital status, et cetera, et cetera."

"I'm married."

"Of course, *Mrs*. Pepper." He delivered a quick thin smile.

I smiled back and looked over the questionnaire. "All these questions?" I said.

"Oh, yes, all of them. Of course if you are unable to answer any of them leave the spaces blank."

"It's all right?"

"It's all right. Just an information sheet is all."

I had just completed the questionnaire when the delegation from IFP arrived. Emil Lieber, Jonathan Marras, and one other man. He worried me.

Emil Lieber took my hand in both of his and said how glad he was to see me again, as if we were old friends. "You're looking very well, Mrs. Pepper."

Jonathan Marras said, "Hello, Libby." He, too, thought I was looking very well. I wasn't so sure.

"Do you know John Hannah?" Lieber said. John Hannah was the third man. "Mr. Hannah is a vice-president of Galapagos, Limited, the parent company. Based in England, you know, with worldwide holdings—" Sybil, I remarked to myself, would have been on *their* side. "IFP is small potatoes when you consider the wealth, power and economic might of Galapagos." Lieber acted as if he knew something I didn't know; I didn't doubt it for a second. "Mr. Hannah is chief counsel for Galapagos . . ."

Now I knew what Lieber knew. "A lawyer!" Bubba Horn, giver of legal advice to the downtrodden, the scared and the lonely, had assured me I wouldn't need a lawyer. I forced myself to look at John Hannah.

He had a face like a falcon, eyes like bright blue marbles and a tilt that made me believe he was getting ready to pounce. He was tall, lean, sinewy, and though he was in his middle years, he had the ambitious look of a newly minted Princeton graduate on the make, which I'm sure he'd once been. He lifted his upper lip in what was meant to be a smile and revealed sharp fangs at the ready. He was, obviously, a highly trained, very expensive, practicing murderer.

I squeezed myself together, but not in time. A couple of drops seeped out of me. I had wet my pants.

"Shouldn't I have a lawyer?" I murmured.

"Not to worry," Leon Stephenson said. "I will see that your interests are protected."

"Let's get on with it," Hannah said.

I shuddered.

Lieber opened his Crouch & Fitzgerald attaché case and passed out sample boxes of sugared breakfast cereal to Stephenson and me. "Great stuff for the kiddies. Here we have a breakfast bar, chock full of vitamins and other good things. Tastes like a Milky Way. Try one, Leon."

"Later, Emil."

I was getting nervouser and nervouser. They all took seats at the far end of the long table, as if I had something catching. I was isolated, apprehensive, the same way you feel in a dentist's chair when he comes down at you with his drill.

Leon Stephenson nodded my way. "Please begin, Mrs. Pepper."

"Begin?"

"Yes. Give us your version of the events that have caused us all to assemble here today."

Once more the story. Just as it happened. Just as I remembered it. And it seemed to me that I was using the same language, repeating myself, convinced that the recitation was without impact, without drama or interest. As far as I could tell, no one at the table seemed overly concerned with what I was saying and so it came as a surprise to me when Emil Lieber broke into my narrative.

"That comment about your dress," he pointed out tartly. "It was a compliment to your taste. I was making a passing remark, hardly a criticism. In no way to be construed as criticism."

I slipped back to a previously prepared defensive position. "You asked if I dressed that way all the time."

"I don't remember saying that."

"Why would you ask such a question, Lieber?" Leon Stephenson said.

John Hannah answered in a scabrous falcon's rasp. "Seems like a most reasonable question. The job being discussed would bring the employee into direct contact with the company's clients. Inevitably the company is concerned with how the worker looks, her attitudes as expressed in dress."

"Exactly," Lieber said smugly.

I looked around. They were watching me, as if to keep me from escaping. "But Mr. Lieber, you said, 'If you were my wife I wouldn't want you to work.' You said that."

"You misunderstood me, Libby."

"Hardly an expression of company prejudice," Hannah tacked on.

Lieber gave a short laugh. "One man's opinion, Libby. Mrs. Lieber has been a mother and a wife for twenty-two years, never a complaint. That's all I was saying to you. You didn't understand."

"You wanted to know how I would take care of my son if I went to work."

"I was concerned for the welfare of your child, that's all. Concerned for your husband, your family. That's all."

I shot a glance at Leon Stephenson for guidance. He was fiddling with some papers on the table in front of him. "Let's keep it moving," he muttered.

"Mr. Lieber told me that he'd had problems earlier when he hired a woman . . ."

Lieber gave me a placating smile, spread his fleshy hands. "That was at another firm, Libby, another job."

Hannah leaned my way, his lips extraordinarily thin. When he spoke, they hardly moved. "Do not blame IFP for the hiring policies of other corporate entities."

"A lot of traveling with men," Lieber said. "I was trying to protect you, Libby."

Protect me? Was that what it had been about? Had I misread everything, allowed my paranoia to interfere with and block off reality? I shuddered and clenched my thighs tightly.

"Protect," Hannah said. "Emil was looking out for your self-interest."

"You misunderstood everything," Jonathan Marras said.

Had I? I wasn't sure, not now. I struggled to clear my mind, arrange my thoughts. "Mr. Lieber said to me, 'I don't know if we should hire a woman. I don't like the idea of it myself.'" I sat back with a certain amount of satisfaction, breathing a little rapidly. That was the clincher. Stamp my case won. Lieber could not deny having said it, not when he actually said it. Bubba Horn had been right all along. I had no need of a lawyer. No one could have presented my case better. Any right-thinking person could see that I had been deprived of the job because of my sex. Gender, that is. Because I was a woman.

Lieber shook his head heavily. "All along I had only your best interests in mind, Libby."

"The point," John Hannah said, "is that Libby simply wasn't—and isn't—qualified for the work. The job has—had—certain strict and rather lofty requirements. Libby, I have studied your application, the record of your interview with Mr. Lieber, and no other conclusion is possible. You just don't measure up."

I made plans to slaughter John Hannah. A swift, efficient death. The other side of my brain urged me to throw myself upon his mercy, beg him—the company—to reconsider. To hire me in some lesser capacity. *Be nice to me, please.* I began to wonder if perhaps I was less than normal, less than sane. Surely I was not a person who knew what mattered to her. Everything I thought, everything I did, the world that I perceived; all of it seemed just a little bit off center.

Leon Stephenson's cultivated tones brought me back to the present. "I wonder, gentlemen, eventually did you hire a man or a woman to fill the opening?"

What a terrific question! I should have thought of it. Waves of love and good feelings went out from me to Leon Stephenson. That's what I needed—some protection, some comfort.

"A man," Lieber said.

There. Proof positive of what I was saying. It was all done, victory mine at last.

John Hannah said, "A highly qualified man. An accountant by training and experience. Are you an accountant, Libby?"

"No, but—"

Hannah made a gesture of dismissal. "The best people, the most qualified, happened to be men. Pure coincidence, nothing more, Leon."

I scribbled a note to myself, a reminder to ask some devastating question or other.

Hannah jabbed the air with a sharp bony finger. "You're making notes."

Immediately the pencil fell out of my hand. "Just a reminder . . ."

"What are you doing, Mrs. Pepper?" Stephenson asked.

"You said it was all right for me—"

"Yes, yes."

"No, no. No notes," Lieber cried.

Hannah snapped out the words. "Stop it. At once."

"I thought—"

"If you had been thinking, thinking clearly, none of this would be necessary."

I collected a small amount of courage. "I can make notes if I want to."

Hannah showed his fangs. "There is no reason for a transcript to be made of these proceedings."

"Just some notes, for questions." My resolve was sliding away.

"Unless," he insisted coldly. "Unless each party thereto is supplied with a clean and corrected copy, attested to as to accuracy. Is that your intention, Libby?"

I pushed the yellow pad to one side. Hannah nodded agreeably and leaned back.

"Do you have something to say at this point?" Stephenson said to me.

I felt like weeping. "They never told me they wanted an accountant."

"Nonsense," Hannah said.

"It was not in the *Times* ad."

"You can't get everything into a small ad."

"No one said anything."

"Perhaps you let it slip by."

"I generally have a good mind for details."

"Generally."

"Yes."

"But not always."

"We're all human."

"Which does not qualify us all for every position. A lack of accountancy experience is a major weakness in an applicant. In your case, it meant you were unemployable."

Stephenson shifted around in his seat. "Emil, did you really say you didn't know if a woman should be hired?"

"So many people, so many interviews."

Hannah added, "A man doesn't remember everything he says. Perhaps, if it was said—*if*—then it might have been said in jest."

"It was no joke," I dared remark.

Hannah glared at me and I shrank back in my seat.

Stephenson consulted the papers on the table. "Ah," he said, with the joy of discovery. "Mrs. Pepper, you were born in Europe."

All mental operations came to an abrupt halt. "Yes," I whispered.

"Where?"

"A small town in Poland, near the German border. It's part of East Germany now."

"And, Emil, you are not native-born either?"

Hannah objected but Stephenson indicated he wanted an answer.

"I was born in Munich," Lieber said.

"That's Germany, too."

"Last time I heard."

Everybody laughed. But not me.

"It seems to me that we are coming to the core of the problem. Mrs. Pepper is Jewish, Lieber is German."

Lieber was on his feet, his face pale. "No, no. I came to this country when I was a boy, six years old, or less. I am a citizen for a long time. One hundred percent American."

"Jews and Germans," Stephenson cooed, not to be deflected from his chosen course.

"It's because I'm a woman," I insisted. "I was only five when I arrived in this country."

"I am specially sympathetic to the Jewish people," Lieber said. "I give money to Israel regularly. Israeli bonds. United Jewish Appeal. I planted a tree outside of Haifa on a hillside, a beautiful tree."

"I'm not even religious," I said.

"Please," Stephenson said, cutting us off. "I will conduct the hearing. Let the chips fall where they will. We black people, we know all about discrimination."

Abruptly, and without my really knowing it, my

fears dropped away. I was on my feet. "It's because I'm a woman!" My voice wailed and waffled.

All sound drifted away. Typewriters ceased clicking. Laughter faded. Conversations ended in mid-sentence. Somebody coughed.

Unforgiving eyes were fixed on me. There was a right and a wrong way to behave in front of the Human Rights Commission. Obviously I had erred. Flushed with shame, I sank back into my chair.

Leon Stephenson shook himself like an angry lion. "Mrs. Pepper, don't you see what you people are doing? Don't you know you people are causing a great deal of trouble for us? The law—Title Seven wasn't designed for people like you. Title Seven was designed for people like me. People like you have spoiled it for people like me. The steam has gone out of the civil rights movement. Nobody cares about black people's rights anymore. You women. You white, middle-class women. You liberal, well-to-do, pseudointellectual phony sophisticates. You people are spoilers, did you know that? Yes, spoilers. All that energy being taken away from poor black folks. All that money. Giving out with that jive about women's rights and women's liberation. Can't you see the damage you're doing?"

They were stomping and cheering, clapping their hands. All the clerks, interviewers, secretaries; all the way out to the front guard rail and beyond. Leon Stephenson rose and bowed left and right, raised his hand for silence, and resumed his place.

At least I think that's what happened. I couldn't be sure of anything because the edges of the world went out of focus, nothing solid anymore, and I clung to the arms of my chair lest I slip off the edge of reality. I blinked and John Hannah shimmered into view, the separate images flowing finally into one. He was tilted my way like an avenging angel.

"What gives you the right to make such a complaint?"

I thought I'd made that clear.

"IFP is a sovereign institution given over to the production of goods required by a complex and growing society. Implicit in its existence and continued growth is concern for the welfare of its stockholders, officers, workers and, not incidentally, the consumers, all of whom are sorely beset in these hard times of rampant inflation and unemployment. Where does it say IFP has to hire *you*?"

"Yes," Jonathan Marras echoed. "Where does it say that?"

Before I could respond, Hannah went on in scathing tones. "Your mode of dress." Oh, if only Sybil were here to answer that scurrilous charge.

"Your blatant form of behavior . . ." What? What's that? What did he mean by that?

"Primary, secondary, tertiary obligations on your part would have placed the company in an unfavorable position and these are but a few of the factors mitigating against your employment. Company policy —any company has the right, the obligation, to generate policies in its own best interests—policy is unbending in certain matters of dependability, competence, morality. Your credentials left much to be desired. The job was not coming to you . . ."

My heart was flipping around again and it was almost impossible to draw sufficient air into my lungs. Attacks were coming from all quarters and I filled up with resentment and rage and pain. But I choked back the desire to strike out, remembering Bubba Horn's admonition to remain demure, ladylike, proper and precious. Had he said all that? Throw myself on the mercy of the court. Wasn't that what he advised me to do? Nothing was very clear to me. I reined in my aggressive tendencies and spoke in a sweet little voice that could give offense to no one.

"I thought I was very well qualified for the job. Overqualified, even. And I was dressed all right. Attractively but sedately . . ."

"Provocatively . . ."

"Oh, no, that's all wrong. Anyway, I thought this

conference was to set out all the facts in an orderly fashion so that you, Mr. Stephenson, can arrive at a fair and objective determination."

"I know my job, Mrs. Pepper," Stephenson said stiffly.

Another mistake, I told myself.

"It was," Hannah said smoothly, "simply a question of getting the best man for the job."

"Man!" I repeated. "You see!"

"Figure of speech," Lieber shouted.

"That's all it is," Marras tossed in.

"Pettiness in a pretty woman is not attractive," Hannah said. He clicked his fangs ominously.

Leon Stephenson cleared his throat, gave it his best *Porgy and Bess* baritone. "We all know what Mr. Hannah intended, don't we?"

I did; I wasn't sure about the rest of them.

"As a matter of fact," Lieber offered, "the person we did hire came on the payroll about a week before we notified Mrs. Pepper."

Stephenson frowned. "Why the time lapse?"

"Nothing conspiratorial, Leon," Hannah answered. "Normal office procedures. Perhaps a slight administrative breakdown."

"They do occur," Stephenson said sympathetically.

They, I informed myself righteously, had kept me dangling until they were able to find someone, anyone who appeared reasonable for the job. As long as it was a man.

"May I ask a question?" I raised my hand. I had to pee a ton . . .

"No!" Hannah ripped out. "This is not a trial body. Cross-examination is out of order. The company is not obliged to respond to further hectoring and badgering. There is no precedent . . ."

"Oh, let her ask a question," Stephenson said. He seemed bored.

I addressed myself to Emil Lieber. "How many female executives work at IFP?"

"Don't answer," Hannah snarled. "That's a sneaky question."

"I don't have the information at hand," Lieber said contentedly.

Marras whispered in his ear and received a dirty look in reply.

"He knows, Marras knows."

"Makes no difference," Hannah said.

Lieber addressed the tabletop. "I don't have to tell you anything."

"Attaboy, Emil," Marras said happily. "Stonewall it."

"Ah-hah!" I cried. "They're holding out."

"Nobody's holding out anything."

"You are, you are."

Stephenson said, "Give us an answer, Emil."

"I won't."

"He doesn't have to," said Hannah.

"Tell the truth," I insisted.

Hannah glared some more. "Don't tell her a thing."

"They're concealing evidence," I protested.

"This is not a trial," Hannah responded.

"What are you hiding?" I said to Lieber.

"Nothing. All right, I'll tell you. No women, no women executives. If that be discrimination . . ."

"Coincidence," Hannah said.

"These things happen," Marras said.

"None?" Stephenson said. "Not even one?" He sounded disappointed. "Ah, well, it seems to me we have arrived at a point of diminishing returns. What more can either side say? I have listened to both arguments, gathered a great deal of information, sufficient for me to arrive at an equitable determination. Both sides will be notified when I reach my decision."

What a shiftless performance. I'd muffed it, when I might have won. They had dealt with me as if I were a child, a little girl, without regard for my ambitions or my intelligence, had bullied me whenever it suited them to do so. Bubba Horn had advised me badly and what was worse, I had gone along. I felt pretty bad.

John Hannah wandered down to my end of the table, smiling and friendly, suddenly a very appealing and attractive falcon. It was very clear to me that he was certain he had brought a great victory to his team. He took my hand in his, full of Ivy League grace and charm.

"You're really a very nice girl, Libby. I know you'll never do anything so foolish again."

part three

1972

nineteen

Bubba Horn took me to Daly's Dandelion for lunch. On Third Avenue opposite Bloomingdale's, naturally. And just as naturally, everybody who goes there looks fantastic. Like the models in a slick magazine advertisement for a foreign sports car. You know the look: tight French jeans, glazed leather jackets from Italy, expensive dark glasses from Hollywood. Men and women, from the rear you could hardly tell them apart. A quick butt survey revealed that the best three out of five belonged to women. Could that be the root of my problems?

Bubba arrived eighteen minutes and twelve seconds late, not that I was counting. He folded himself into a chair and called for a dry Rob Roy on the rocks.

"Is that what they drink in White Buffalo?"

He gave me his famous white grin. "Mainly it's Pearl's, beer, that is. You sure lookin' good, Libby. What's happenin' on your side of town?"

"Anybody ever tell you you never pronounce your 'g's?"

He took my hand and counted the fingers. Satisfied, he tickled my palm in a way that put dirty ideas into my head. "I do a thing like that folks'll run me outta White Buffalo. Town charter says so."

I took back my hand and he never noticed. "What do people do in White Buffalo?"

"Go on squirrel safaris, ride circles around the Burger King, keep count of the tumbleweed blowin' through the place, such as that. Oh, it's lots of fun."

"Sounds like it."

A waiter brought the Rob Roy and Bubba knocked half of it back without blinking an eye. He was a man of many parts. "When you telephoned, you said you had a problem."

"I could make a list."

"I'm listenin'."

"There's life in general and life in particular."

"In that case, why not just say how the hearin' went."

I made a face.

"That bad?"

"I knew they'd never let me have the job."

"Has ole Leon handed down his determination?"

"Not yet, but I know what it's going to be."

"I reckon nobody's about to accuse you of bein' an optimist. Now you just hang on, it ain't over yet."

"That's easy for you to say. It's not your fight." Bubba had been polished to a smooth perfection, with an added flash of brilliance. He had subtlety, grace and a clear insight into what living was all about. How different he was from any other man I knew. In fact, I'd never known anyone remotely like him. He was strange, exotic, unlikely. Unique. Or at least that's how I felt at that moment. "A lot of what's happened is your fault," I said, careful not to be unkind. "Most of it, I think."

He pursed his perfect lips. "How come you say that to ole Bubba?"

"Nobody else is within range."

"Fair enough, but I ain't the one tryin' to shoot you down."

I'd called him for help. No reason to give him a hard time. "They practically admitted what they did.

The guy they hired isn't half as qualified as I am. They really are prejudiced against women. They did discriminate against me."

"No doubt in my mind."

"That Mr. Stephenson, he's hooked on the fact that I'm Jewish and since Lieber is German, he tried to turn it into a case of anti-Semitism."

"That's Leon for you. He likes his prejudices clear-cut, traditional. Anything new puts his teeth on edge."

"They yelled at me. A lot. They made me very nervous."

"Sumbitch."

"Yes." I checked him out of the corner of my eye. "It might have helped if I'd had a lawyer."

"Can't be sure of that."

"I feel like the victim in a rape. After a while you start to think maybe you did let him do it . . ."

"I wouldn't pay too much mind to what went on this time. You can never tell about ole Leon, he might just come down on your side."

"Not a chance." I watched him drain the rest of his drink in one smooth swallow. He wasn't even breathing hard. "This boy wasn't even on the premises in question."

"You were the one told me to dress and act demure, modest. Sedate, that was one of your words."

"I did say that."

"Well, it's not me. I mean, sure I was frightened and unsure of myself. But there's a lot of fighter in me. When I was young I had lots of fights, with boys, too. I have never been demure."

He looked me up and down like a judge at a stock show. "I certainly am pleased to hear you say that."

"Don't flirt with me, Bubba."

"A little ole farm boy don't flirt. He just goes at it, if you follow my meanin'." He switched on a grin.

"Oh, I follow, all right." He had an arsenal of grins, and I had no idea what any of them signified. He used them for punctuation, change of pace, emphasis, to lighten his words and to give them extra meaning.

With that smile, the man had a repertoire of untouched entendres. "I know all about you farm boys." Oh, my God, I was flirting with him. Shame, shame, an old married lady, a respectable mother. I felt as skittish as if this were a first date, or an illicit assignation. The idea tickled my fancy and scared hell out of me at the same time. Another split in me—the suffering victim on the one hand, the lusty hedonist on the other.

"I reckon you mean the way a country boy goes at it with the beasts in the field and all that." Honey dripped from every word.

"I don't believe it. You never did it with an animal, did you? Did you?"

The grin came sneaking along, slow, insinuating, worrying me half to death.

"Not just any animal."

"Which ones?" I said like the fool I was.

He let me have it right between the eyes. "Only the ones that I truly loved," he drawled.

I struggled to keep a straight face. "Isn't it time we discussed my case?"

"You name it, lady."

"The case. What if Stephenson hands down a negative judgment?"

"Then you file an appeal, to the state capital."

"Will you help me write it?"

His eyes were bright and shining blue. "Anytime you want, you just come runnin' to ole Bubba. He'll do right by you, hear . . ."

Oh, boy, did I hear.

twenty

It was not easy. Since Sybil had had the stroke, I'd been visiting her twice a day. I would hold her hand and talk, say whatever came into my head. Not let myself think or feel too much. I told her about Stevie, exaggerating his words or deeds in order to divert her, making Stevie seem cleverer than he was, more inventive, more amusing. She never laughed. I told her, too, about Walter's new job. If she cared, she gave no sign. I told her she was looking better and that soon she'd be up and around again. She believed neither statement, nor did I. But she never disputed anything I said. Never criticized nor made suggestions nor mocked me. That was not like my mother.

I brought her a recording of Toscanini conducting Berlioz's *Romeo and Juliet*. I told her that Millstein was going to be at the Philharmonic. I told her about the hearing, that I did not anticipate a favorable decision. Half her mouth moved and I bent closer and heard, ". . . inside and out, there is only desolation . . ."

So much desolation. I was empty, depleted of resources, victimized by fatigue of the spirit and the flesh.

"I've had enough," I told Walter that evening. "I'm going to call Stephenson, tell him to forget the whole business. I don't want the damned job."

Walter stared at me. "Of course you do."

"It's not worth it."

"You can't give up."

Walter sometimes surprised me. I never expected this reaction from him. "I'm tired," I said.

"You must fight those people." He reached for his book: *Everything You Always Wanted to Know About Sex.* Was there hope for us yet?

"Why? Why should I fight them? I can't win. I won't win."

"The condition of your mind eludes me, Libby."

"I don't understand you, either, Walter. Why do you want me to keep fighting?"

"You can't let them push you around."

I left Walter with the book and took a hot bath. Sweat broke on my brow and lubricated the jammed gears of my mind. It had been a very long time since Walter had displayed so much enthusiasm for anything. Important changes seemed to be taking place. What were they?

I rooted around in the clogged corridors of my mind, cleaning out some of the emotional sludge, trying to think straight, to put the pieces together. After a while a coherent picture began to form. Those who dumped on Walter's wife automatically dumped on Walter. I was, after all, his personal slavey. Held in thrall, yes. But also to be protected from alien hostile forces. Since this was a war Walter could not make himself, it fell on me to make it for him. For us.

Only one problem with that: I was a lifetime loser. That was clearly confirmed two days later in a letter from the New York State Human Rights Commission which declared that "no cause has been found" for a complaint against International Food Products. Leon Stephenson had signed it with a flourish.

Creep . . .

"I'm all right," I said, staring up at the meandering crack in the ceiling.

"Whatever you say, Libby."

I sat up and looked directly at Xavier D.C. Kiernan. He inspected me glassily through the gold-rims and pursed his prissy parochial mouth. He shifted around in Mr. Eames' rosewood and leather creation, squeaking softly.

"It doesn't really matter," I said.

He lifted his brows in question.

"That I didn't get the job."

Down came the brows.

"I knew they'd find against me."

"You knew it?"

"Yes."

He waited.

I waited. He won; I told him. "It's because I'm a woman."

"Are you telling me that the New York State Human Rights Commission is biased against women? Half the population."

"There's a war on. I'm just finding out. Between men and women."

He ignored that. "Let's be sensible."

I wanted to pound on his pale seminarian's face. "I was qualified," I said, trying to keep my voice under control. Xavier looked with disfavor upon people who made a scene. "I am qualified. Nobody could have been more qualified."

"Let's examine all the possible causes . . ."

"Of what?"

". . . for your not being hired."

"I told you—"

"Did you present yourself in a favorable light? How were you dressed? Did you in fact have the correct credentials? After all, there are many intangibles involved in hiring someone."

"You're on their side."

"I'm only trying to help."

"Help!" I cried and glanced up at the ceiling. The crack was growing wider by the second, and soon all of it would come tumbling down, beams, roof and all. "I think I'm going crazy."

"The word is inexact. What we attempt to do here is provide depth and breadth to the various disciplines—psychology, sociology, anthropology, genetics. To synthesize all the knowledge of twentieth-century mankind into one solid . . ."

"I feel so tentative, transitional. Neither here nor there."

He looked wise. "Of course."

"I have limited access to my own feelings."

"Exactly. So here we seek a meaningful, intelligent, revealing dialogue."

"I don't know. Men and women, I'm beginning to think we're traveling along alternate roadways to madness. No wonder I get depressed, hysterical, confused."

"I would hesitate to characterize you as a hysteric, Libby. On the emotional side, yes. Not as objective as one might prefer, no. Somewhat dislocated in a social sense, perhaps. But hysterical—I'll have to think about that."

"The trouble is, I've decided, no real value is given to women."

"We are discussing Libby Pepper, not women in total."

"Especially me."

"Do you value yourself?"

"You must be kidding. I feel humiliated . . ."

"Humiliated, that's worth exploring."

"Furious."

"Furious. What are you angry about, Libby?"

"Ashamed."

He blinked as if not expecting that one. "Let's go back to furious. At whom are you angry, Libby?"

"You."

"Me? I'm here to help."

"Hah. Walter."

"What has Walter done?"

"Nothing, that's why I'm angry with him."

"I see. Anybody else?"

"Myself."

"Now we're getting somewhere."

"Also Sybil."

"You're angry with your mother because she's ill? You feel she's betrayed you? Deserted you? There we have it. You blame yourself."

"Am I my mother's keeper?"

"You do feel guilty?"

"I didn't do it, your honor."

"Of course not. But we must blame someone, isn't that the way you feel? Who would you like to blame?"

I gave it a little thought. "God."

Xavier actually raised a finger along with his brows. "God?"

"Yes, God. Births, marriages, other natural disasters, they're His province. Let Him feel guilty."

"Since when did you become a believer, Libby?"

"Since Rabbi."

"Rabbi?"

"They never use names, you know, or articles. Just Rabbi. As in Rabbi wishes you to know. Or Rabbi will see you in a moment. Also doctors."

"Doctors?"

"As in Doctor says. And Doctor has examined Patient."

"I see."

The hell he did. Xavier saw almost nothing at all. I gave him a grin I had borrowed from Bubba Horn. "Rabbi is Head Coach for the entire Upper East Side. You didn't know that, did you?"

"Hmmm."

"Not including Spanish Harlem, of course."

He checked his watch.

No way he was getting rid of me that easily. "You're right," I said. "We've wasted enough time. Let's get down to some serious headshrinking. There's the question of affairs—"

"Affairs? What affairs?"

"Sexual affairs."

He went from pale to pink and back again, as if someone had changed the lighting on the set.

"Lately," St. Xavier droned, "you have been greatly obsessed with sex, I believe." No major commitment there. Xavier was a cautious man.

"You know what Céline said—'There is nothing, Monsieur Baryton, between the penis and mathematics, nothing at all.' Isn't that great?"

He frowned. "What does it mean?"

"Beats me; ask Céline."

He swiveled from left to right. "To get back to affairs? . . ."

"You're interested, are you? Okay. I am beginning to get the idea that there's a man in my life."

"Your husband."

"No, not Walter. Another man."

"I see."

We were back to that.

"This man, you're having sex with him?"

"Not so fast. He hasn't laid a glove on me yet."

"It would be best if you kept it that way."

"You take a dim view of extracurricular fornication, don't you, Xavier?"

"Approval and disapproval is not what we are about here."

"You mean you're not hanging around the confessional anymore?"

"Does it please you to have fun at my expense?"

"What I want to know is whether or not you think it would necessarily harm a person's marriage if she did it with somebody who was not her husband?"

"I am not Solomon, Libby. I don't make predictions."

"I remember."

"You intend to sleep with this man?"

"Sleeping is out. Either it's some plain and fancy screwing around or forget it."

"This is not a laughing matter."

"You bet it's not."

"Are you asking for my permission? Is that it?"

"I don't know what I'm doing."

"You're entertaining the idea, however."

"Let's say I find the idea extremely entertaining."

"How does that make you feel?"

"Not too bad."

"Guilty?"

"Guilty, but not bad."

"Consider the sixth commandment, Libby."

"I have considered it. And the Puritan Ethic, the injunctions of the Bishop of Rome, also the Law of Diminishing Returns. There's just one small problem."

"And that is?"

"Bubba hasn't even tried to cop a feel."

Xavier never cracked a smile. He cleaned his glasses, slid them back on his thin nose. "Perhaps . . ."

I hung on his words.

"Perhaps you should have an affair."

I was startled, stunned, shocked. I said so.

"There are some women who believe an affair with a man not their spouse gives life a little spark, renews excitement, provides . . ."

"A little fun?"

"Do you think such a relationship would help your marriage?"

"Relationship! I was talking about playing around is all. Get involved and you get hurt. See what you've done, you've given me something else to worry about."

"The experience might prove to be disappointing. It might not live up to your expectations. The grass is not always greener on the other side of the hill."

"On the other hand, it could be a terrific boost to my self-esteem."

"That's always possible," he said, standing. "Time's up. We'll continue next time."

A beardless Indian in a white jacket came out of my mother's room. "Mrs. Pepper?" His inflection was pure Gunga Din, vintage 1930-ish. Strip him down to jockey shorts and give him a pig bladder full of water and he'd even look like Sam Jaffe. Cary Grant,

Victor McLaglen, Douglas Fairbanks, Jr., all playing at Kipling. What a terrible movie it was; I loved every minute of it.

"What's wrong with my mother?" I cried.

He handed out the usual Now, Now, along with a Shall We Sit Down Somewhere And Talk, steering me by the elbow to a small waiting room.

"She's dead!"

"Not a-tall, not a-tall."

"Let go of my elbow. Who are you anyway?"

I was sure he said, "Dr. Siddhartha." He flashed his scrubbed-down teeth at me.

"I want to see my mother."

"In a moment, dear lady."

"Now, now."

"Mrs. Markson appears to have lapsed into a coma." Take that, dear lady.

"Appears to? Aren't you sure?"

"We are sure."

"My mother's dying."

"Mustn't leap to conclusions."

"Why aren't you helping my mother?"

He never blinked an eye, came right back with the official AMA line. "The best medical care in the world . . ."

"You've got her all wired up. Tubes running in and out of her, all those infernal machines. And she's still getting away from you."

"You don't understand."

"Of course not, you idiot!" I yelled at the top of my lungs. Siddhartha blanched. "Butchers!" He slithered along the wall, trying to escape. I trapped him in a corner.

Some of the visitors sneaked looks from behind old copies of *Modern Medicine* or *Playboy* in the mistaken belief that this was the six o'clock news. The noise brought three nurses running.

"What's going on?" one of them said, reaching for my pulse.

Siddhartha pointed my way. "She's a little upset."

"Why, it's Mrs. Pepper," another nurse said. "Mustn't shout, Mrs. Pepper."

Another doctor materialized. Seeing the weight of numbers was on his side, he advanced displaying a quizzical smile and a stethoscope. He was Oriental. No wonder your son and mine can't get into an American medical school. JFK was right, life isn't fair.

"Everything all right here?"

A nurse smiled. "We're in control now, Dr. Chan."

"Charlie Chan?" I said. My life was turning into a festival of 1930 movies.

"Very funny," he said, not cracking a smile. "Irving Chan, out of Wichita. You have a problem, Mrs. Pepper?"

They all knew me. And were ganging up to divert my attention while Sybil slipped away unnoticed.

"Problem? Why should I have a problem? Just that you are permitting my mother to die unmolested."

"What does she mean?" Chan said.

"Do something about it!"

"She has the best of care."

"No more propaganda! That rotten doctors' union."

Chan protested. "Doctors aren't unionized . . ."

Siddhartha said, "Of course the Teamsters have approached us."

"That's where the muscle is," Chan explained.

"Where's Barger?" I cried.

"*Doctor* Barger," Chan said. His eyes turned to glass at the mention of the name.

"Why don't we let him in on the secret?" I said.

"Doctor Barger has been notified," one of the nurses said.

And here he comes now! Like magic, the authoritative click-click-click of metal-plated heels grew louder. Down the corridor in a tight triangle, Dr. Barger trailed by two grim-faced assistants. Interns, residents, nurses, all flattened against the wall lest they make physical contact with the Great Man and so draw his ire.

"What's going on?" Barger snarled.

Chan pointed at me. "She's making a fuss."

"Snitch!" I hissed. He shrank back.

"Mrs. Pepper," Barger said soberly, "I am deeply distressed."

"Why? Is your mother sick?"

"As a matter of fact, she's quite well."

"My mother's dying."

"That's a rather unscientific assumption on your part. Of course, sooner or later each of us does die."

His face looked hard to me, chipped, polished marble. The face of a man who had never dared to feel too much. His mouth opened and closed and I forced myself to pay attention.

"Patients often remain comatose for extended periods and come out of it with no medical explanation. Not that I am able to promise anything."

"Pull the plug, let her go now. My mother doesn't want to be a vegetable."

"Plug? My dear woman, there is no plug. Your mother is being given no extraordinary attention. We are not at that stage."

"What are you trying to tell me?"

"Only that Mrs. Markson is in a coma. She is a long way from death. You may, if you wish, speak to her."

The old palpitations came back, the difficulty in breathing. I began to tremble with an incoherent rage. "Is that your idea of a joke?"

"The last thing to go is the patient's hearing. Should you choose to speak to your mother, she will hear you."

I couldn't afford to take any chances. I went into Sybil's room and put my face close to her. A thick, cloying scent rose up from her. She was breathing quietly, as if peacefully asleep. All the tubes, the wires, the pins and needles were gone. I forced myself to speak aloud to her.

"It's Libby, Mother. Everything will be all right. Doctor Barger told me so. Soon you'll feel better. Soon you'll be out of here. I love you, Mother . . ."

Everybody knows it's not right to lie to your mother.

twenty-one

I phoned Bubba Horn. He said, "How do. How can I help you?"

"You said to get in touch if the Commission turned me down. They turned me down."

"I'll be dogged, that Leon. He sure is not a man to depend on. Well, I reckon you are just goin' to file an appeal, that's all there is to that. And I am goin' to make it a can't-miss proposition. Tell you what, this is one of my busy days. Why don't you skip on over to my office, no, that won't do. What do you say to my apartment about six o'clock?"

What I said was Six O'clock Would Be Just Fine. What I meant was I was scared on a number of different counts. I called Walter at Wallenstein & Smithton and told him I had to meet my lawyer. He said terrific and he'd take Stevie out to dinner. Maybe a corned beef sandwich at Fine & Schapiro's.

The afternoon loomed up long and difficult. Complete with guilt and anticipation, not to mention a large dose of uncertainty about a lot of things. Therefore—I went to the movies. First, *Klute,* with Jane Fonda. Jane played a hooker in this one with the proverbial good heart under a hard shell. I figured she was a lot like me. Or how I would like to be, maybe. Actually it was a very depressing flick, moving along slow and straining to make an Important Statement about Life.

When I got out it was still early and I looked around for something else to do. *Panic in Needle Park*. One laugh after another about junkies. Who needs it?

It was almost four o'clock and still two hours to kill. I went to see *I Never Sang for My Father*. With a title like that, I had a right to expect music and dancing and a stand-up comic or two. Instead I got a guy who discovers how much he loves his father only after the old man is dead. You can imagine what that did for my morale.

By the time I arrived at Bubba's apartment on the twenty-first floor of a high rise on East End Avenue, I was in need of liquid refreshment. Bubba wasted no time putting a glass in my hand.

I inspected the surroundings. An obvious lair for unsuspecting females. Texas-style. Masculine signals everywhere. A coiled lariat on one wall, plus a set of rusty spurs. A bison's head glared down from the far side of the room. A rack held three shotguns, two Winchesters, and a .22 target pistol, all behind glass. On the floor, zebra skins, a brown bear rug without head, and a tiger skin. A guitar rested against the arm of the couch.

"You play?" I said like a fool.

"Can a cat have kittens?" Down went the glass, up came the guitar. Bubba began plucking at the strings, voice lifted in a mournful twang that managed not to seem out of place in these lush surroundings:

> She kissed me, she hugged me, she called
> me her dandy,
> Trinity is muddy and the Brazos quicksandy,
> She kissed me, she hugged me, she called
> me her own,
> But down by the Brazos, she left me alone.

He put the guitar aside and retrieved his drink, gave me one of his shyest grins.

"Very nice," I said.

"Weaned on music like that. Honest-to-God cow-boy ditties."

I appraised him from a distance. "I don't get it, Bubba. A New York lawyer, slick and smart. You live up in the sky in sybaritic splendor. You dine in expensive restaurants and order great French wine. Then you go into this poor farm boy act of yours . . ."

"Fact is fact. Part of me always will belong back in White Buffalo on Daddy's piece of land."

"I'd like to meet your father."

"Jimmy Guy? He is some kind've a dude. He can't figure out what his ever-lovin' child is doin' up here among the heathens and the foreigners, rubbin' skin with colored folks and such as that. You up to another tumbler of drinkin' whisky?"

He went away, hips sassy and slow. A man who knew a lot more than he let on. He worried hell out of me.

He came back with the drink and sat close to me. Closer than was desirable. No, closer than was good for me. "I am goin' to put together one of the world's great appeals. It will put those hard-hearts up in Albany into shock. It will snatch them back to reality. It will teach them humility and humanity. Goin' to do all this just for you." He touched his glass to my glass and smiled a small but insinuating smile. Definitely insinuating.

I shifted away, but not too far, struck by my human frailty and the duality of my nature. "I appreciate what you're doing for me, Bubba."

He leaned my way and the delicate scent of expensive cologne drifted into my nostrils. No hint of the barnyard on Bubba.

"Mean to tell you, Libby. There ain't a single thing comes free in this world."

"Don't talk dirty." I made a valiant effort to suck the words back in. What could I have been thinking, to say a thing like that? It hung on the air between us.

His right eyelid rolled down, in no hurry to get where it was going. "Is that what I'm doin'?"

"That's a bad tic, Bubba. You ought to see somebody about it."

"I was layin' my best wink on you."

I stood up. "This is crazy. I must have been crazy to come up to this . . . place."

He stood up. Tall, lean, smelling good, looking good. Not fair, not fair. I backed away. "Keep your distance, Bubba. None of your Texas tricks, you hear me!"

"Yes, ma'am." He seemed to be getting taller and considerably wider. Either my eyes were playing tricks or he was closing in on me. There was nothing wrong with my eyes. Except for the nervous blinking.

"Just you remember, Bubba. I am a mother, a married lady, true to my husband always, up to now. Don't get the idea that I'm weak and helpless just because you have me trapped in your lair."

He spread his hands. "The door's not even locked, Libby."

Oh boy, was he tricky. "Anyway," I said, "Sybil is in the hospital." I began to weep.

He put his arms around me and stroked my hair until I felt better. "Who is Sybil?"

"My mother. She had a stroke, she's in a coma, she's dying."

"You don't want to leap to conclusions."

Siddhartha had said about the same thing. "You should've been a doctor."

"Jimmy Guy always said that. Wanted me to study veterinary medicine, to tell the truth. Felt it was economically sound, havin' a vet on the ole place."

"Oh, God!" I disengaged and moved a few feet away.

He followed in a more or less casual manner. "Prayer's always in order when a loved one is feelin' poorly."

My legs were beginning to tingle from the knee down, at the same time vibrating from the knee up. It might have been the drinks, but I suspected that Bubba had a decidedly intoxicating effect on me. Watch him every second, I warned myself.

"I don't believe in miracles."

"Got to have faith."

"You some kind of a religious nut, Bubba?"

"You Hebrews, Libby, you are the people of the Book. In my heart, I know you are a believer."

"Let me out of here," I said without conviction.

"Don't tell me you're an agnostic?"

I emptied my glass and he relieved me of its heavy burden. I sat down on the couch. "I have to go," I said.

He sat down next to me. "There's still the appeal."

I stood up. He drew me back down. Up close, those hard bright blue eyes were paler than I remembered. More and more he looked like something out of one of my best fantasies. This fantasy would be a real winner, I thought. Perhaps I ought to rush right home and get into bed, give it full freedom to flower. Then Bubba went and ruined everything. He kissed me. No little peck on the mouth. This was a real lip-moving, sucking and spitting wet kiss. His tongue was long, thick and hot, touched all bases without haste.

"Find any new cavities?" I said, when he finished.

"Lady," he said, making it sound like John Wayne about to go for his six-gun, "I am kissing you."

"Is that what it was?"

"That's not funny, Libby. This is no time for levity."

"You're making me very nervous, Bubba."

"I fancy you a whole lot, Libby."

"You Texans are all liars, champions every one."

"That hurts, it surely does."

"You could look it up."

"I mean every word, cross my heart, so help me."

He kissed me again. And there was his tongue, again, sliding between my teeth, working its way around the inside of my cheeks. I tried to figure out exactly what was going on inside me. There were a lot of powerful feelings in conflict.

Scared—yes.

Turned on—absolutely.

Confused—I made an attempt to examine the value-

cost ratio of what was involved here. If I let him go on
this way, what would I gain? If I let him go on this
way, what would I lose? If I didn't let him—and so
on and so on.

Since my brain refused to function in an efficient
fashion, I decided to ignore any moral or ethical considerations that might enter into the decision-making
process. After all, those questions had been asked
many times over the centuries by many men and wom-
en. I was hardly likely to come up with any fresh in-
sights.

Instead I directed my attention to a rational examination of my companion. For a long, panicky moment
I was unable to remember his name. Then it came:
Bubba. What a ridiculous name, a child's name, or a
child's pronunciation of the word "brother." In any
case, another example of arrested rural development.

I considered Bubba's kiss. He did it quite well, I
decided. Tender-strong, so to speak. Not forcing anything, allowing time for emotions to come into play. I
gave his tongue a little suck or two. Nothing serious,
just a playful expression to test it out. Nice.

Encouraged, he shifted around into a more strategic
position, rubbing my rib cage in what I took to be a
warning of better things to come. I let myself respond,
keeping my head empty for a while. Very cleverly he
located my breast and knew at once what to do with it.

I melted into the action, a lot of thick, gooey feelings
now, giving back some moves. A little pushing and
rubbing, your ordinary friction. Gradually I realized
that he had his hand under my blouse, was at work on
my bare breast. I made an effort to clear my head and
by the time I did he had surrounded my nipple with
his lips.

"Better cut that out, Bubba."

In answer, he went faster.

It was difficult not to respond. Difficult to stem the
terrible curiosity I felt about what was happening,
what might still happen. I could not deny that I *liked*
what he was doing—and somehow one of his hands

had worked its way onto my fanny, kneading, poking, generally doing a good job. I reminded myself of my obligations, of my position in the normal social order, of who I was. At that moment I found it difficult to remember *my* name.

I made up my mind. I would put a stop to this silly child's game and leave. But that was hardly a viable alternative. After all, I had come to Bubba for legal advice and I still very much needed that advice.

About that time the curiosity gave way to a certain delicious weakness, a warm tension that ran along the inside of my thighs, and tiny explosions went on in my belly as if an awakening was taking place. I said, "I'm a married woman."

He was undressing me and doing it quite well.

"I was married once. Cute little gal from Kansas. Came on fast, finished off slow. Tell you about her sometime."

"Don't bother."

He was over me then and then I was over him. I was never sure who was doing what to whom for my head closed off my mind and opened itself to my senses. No more was I watching, only reacting in strong gasping thrusts, the tightness clutching every nerve. I was trembling, unable to breathe. All senses were brought down to a fine edge, and my heart pounded in my ears, pulses throbbing across my middle, my breasts hard and demanding. Behind my closed lids, everything was blood-red. I smelled his manly sweat, and felt with an intensity that could easily become pain, half-wanting to pull away but driven by some secret force to become harder and rougher until I reached a point from which it was impossible to turn back. The pressure built up to the screaming level, but what came out of me was a muffled moan, and I was abruptly alone in all of this, apart, separated. Tension induced rigidity, and pressure swelled and broke over me in terrible waves of fright and pleasure. Then, a quick warning shot, another. Pulsations ran along my torso, focused and

grew stronger and built until they burst, and on in tiny
explosions, reminders. The rigidity was replaced by
flowing exhaustion, a soft, warm liquid in which I
floated safely.

I became aware of Bubba again, lying next to me,
his eyes closed, breathing easily. I felt grateful and
loving and so I touched him. His eyes still closed, he
sang softly:

> The girls of Little River, they're plump
>   and they're pretty,
> The Sabine and the Sulphur have many a beauty.
> On the banks of the Neches, there's girls by
>   the score,
> But down by the Brazos, I'll wander no more.

twenty-two

I felt good.

Vibrating with good health. Girlish. Excited and hopeful. And what was even better; no shame. Not even a dollop of guilt. I had come through unscathed. A little sweaty, sticky, and ripely scented, but psychologically untouched. Xavier would be devastated.

The subject of infidelity was not strange to me. From time to time I had conjured up in my imagination hot, thumping wrestling matches with any number of men. Men of my own creation mostly. A few real men who, in my wishful thoughts, were made considerably better than they were. But the fantasy men were best, perfect in every way, willing and able to perform to my commands.

"Way to go, Stud."

Self-recriminations always trailed close behind my fantasies. What kind of a woman would entertain such thoughts? What kind of a wife? What kind of a mother?

But the real thing was different. No negative sentiments. Only the sweet aftertaste of Bubba's long wet kisses.

Walter was a semidry kisser. And not much of that. One or two quickies and it was bing-bang time. With

Walter, you had the feeling he always had something better to get on to.

In the early stages of our marriage, I had tried to enlist Walter in a round or two of erotic conversation. He was, he made very clear, against Dirty Talk. To Walter screwing was a sanctified activity, performed by well-married people. In the dark. Quickly. And quietly.

"Walter," I used to say, "even nice people talk to each other in bed."

He gave my behind a friendly pat in reply. Piece on earth . . .

So it was. Talking we did not do. Kissing was kept to an absolute minimum. Any other oral pastime was considered a definite no-no.

Walter did not believe the human mouth was intended to participate much in lovemaking. Occasionally in a fit of frustration I tried to get Walter to put his face between my legs. Such efforts were always bluntly rebuffed.

"You ought to be ashamed of yourself."

"I won't tell anybody."

"I never did such a thing in my life."

"Try it once."

"No, no."

"If you don't like it, you don't have to do it ever again."

"I won't like it."

"You might develop a tolerance. You don't have to go into ecstasy over it. As long as you do it."

"No."

I bargained. "I'll do it to you."

"Don't be disgusting."

"I'd probably enjoy it."

"I'm beginning to think you're not normal."

That reminded me of Xavier D.C. Kiernan, who characterized my oral urges as "unresolved sucking desires, infantile genital play." Undoubtedly correct, I told him at the time. But it didn't change anything. I still wanted to give it a try.

Once, catching Walter off guard, I made it all the way down to the root of our trouble, tongue working fast, before he caught on. He yanked me up by the hair.

"That hurts," I complained.

"Don't dare do that again."

"I think you dislodged my scalp."

"You're acting like an animal."

So there I was. An unfaithful wife. And apparently no worse for the experience. All that humping and bumping and rolling around, all that wonderful slipping and slurping in smelly human excretions.

"Like a couple of hogs in slop." Bubba had a way with words.

I was looking forward to doing it all again. Bubba promised we would. He swore to make himself available to me whenever it didn't interfere with his being a People's Lawyer. That's what he said he was and I was very impressed by it. He also vowed to supply some rare, valuable and foolproof legal instructions which would aid me in pursuit of my job.

"You won't forget?"

"Forget? No way I'm about to let a juicy little pussy like you out of my mind."

You can't hardly find a lawyer like that these days.

Life went on. Carrying me from high to low, with a good portion of it lived in between. Hours spent in Bubba's apartment on his couch, his bed, on the tiger skin on the floor. We did it standing up in the kitchen, the door of the fridge cold against my ass. We did it sitting on the john in the bathroom. We did it back to front and watched ourselves in the long mirror on his closet door in the bedroom. I perceived dark and mysterious aspects of myself never before noticed, qualities of flesh and character only lately discovered.

And I shopped and cooked and cleaned the apartment on West Sixty-ninth Street. I read to Stevie and spent long periods playing with him, and these were surprisingly good times for both of us. I was careful not to disturb Walter when he was reading.

And every day I visited Sybil.

A diminished woman. Shrinking all the time. Putting the vibrant person she had once been farther and farther away. Her skin drew taut and her cheeks caved in, bones jutting fiercely. Once so lively and threatening, overflowing with life; now pathetic, a grotesque memory of my mother.

Each time I came I would kiss that withered face. I would put my mouth against her ear and offer encouragements, downright lies that she would not have believed could she hear them. Nothing I said comforted either one of us.

The nurses insisted Sybil could still hear. Of course they were full of shit, but I dared not stop talking lest they were right. One nurse told me about a long-comatose patient who one day opened his eyes and was alert, healthy, unchanged from before his coma. All without satisfactory medical explanation. They told me stories of people who had been pronounced dead and returned to life with wondrous tales of visits to the Other Side and of messianic figures cloaked in Blinding Light.

Where There's Life There's Hope, they insisted. Also Don't Give Up the Ship, God Is on Our Side and A Ballgame Is Never Over until the Last Man Is Out.

Sybil was a living corpse. Once, when I spoke to her, her breathing turned rapid and harsh. Frightened, I called for help. The head nurse took Sybil's pulse and pronounced her all right.

"They do that sometimes," she said with what was intended as a supportive smile. "Keep talking to your mother, dear, she appreciates it."

That evening I phoned Candy. "Mother's failing. She can't last much longer."

Candy exhaled. "I suppose I should come east."

Come, I almost screamed. Come and hold my hand. Come, Big Sister, so I can cry on your shoulder. Come and be part of this family again. Come, let us talk . . .

I was immediately ashamed of myself. How petty I

was. After all, Candy had a husband, children, the business. "There's no reason for you to come now."

"I guess you're right."

Sybil turned gaunt and gray. Her upper lip pulled back, exposing her teeth in a harsh, accusatory set. A hostile mask, an agonized twist of regret and resentment, and anger. She was furious at what had happened to her and held us all responsible. Barger, Candy, Walter, poor Sam Markson. But mostly she was angry at me. I didn't blame her.

One night I dreamed and saw Sybil's face. Not that sprightly pseudo-English face but the shriveled old crone of that hospital bed. The face in the dream filled up with bloat and blocked out everything else. I gasped and coughed, and woke in terror, hearing a vengeful cackle that might have been Sybil's voice. She sounded as if she were enjoying herself. I wanted her to leave me alone, go away, die. I began to tremble in the bed next to Walter, and turned cold. Would Stevie one day wish that I would hurry up and die and let him get on with the business of living his own life?

My visits to the hospital grew shorter. Less frequent. No one seemed to notice. Doctors, nurses, attendants, they were all less involved, less concerned about Sybil. Everyone had written her off, we were all waiting for her to die. I allowed myself to think about Sybil less and less and more and more about Bubba Horn.

In his bed there was only his flesh and mine. Pleasure given and pleasure obtained. Energy expended and reclaimed. The smell of human beings in heat was good, reminded me of freshly baked bread. I wanted more of him, couldn't get enough, and I told him so.

"You sure do simmer." He jiggled one of my breasts. "Look at that little fella stand to attention." He gave it another tweak. He was, it appeared, enamored of my left breast only.

"I," he announced, looking me right in the eye, "have used your lower regions to my great and everlastin' satisfaction."

"Is this the end of the line, Bubba?"

"What a revoltin' thought! All I'm suggestin' is a little variation on the theme."

My pulse quickened, as they say. My throat dried up. I licked my lips.

"Bubba, you are a West Texas pervert."

"A dyin' breed." His hand came to rest on the back of my head, fingers steady and alarmingly strong. "Any objections?"

"Suppose I say no?" He moved me forward, down, on a collision course with his crotch. Mustn't blink, I warned myself. I didn't want to miss a thing.

"Shoot," he murmured. "Why would you do a thing like that?"

"You're pretty sure of yourself."

I was inches away and the pressure on the back of my head increased.

"Take it," he commanded.

I liked what I saw, what I smelled, the way his cock enlarged into a beautiful pink banana. I couldn't remember ever getting this close to one before. I tried to look everywhere at once, anxious not to miss a trick.

The penis is connected in front of and to the sides of the pubic arch. In the flaccid condition it assumes a cylindrical shape. In the erect condition it assumes a triangular shape, one side of which forms the dorsum. It is made up of three cylindrical masses of cavernous tissue bound together by fibrous tissue and covered with skin. Two of the masses are lateral, the third is median. The latter contains the greater part of the urethra.

"Give head, lover."

I sniffed here and there with results that left me gay and light-headed. I embarked on an extended visual examination, dropping a soft kiss along the way, delivering an affectionate tongue stroke on impulse. Here I was at last in eye and mouth contact with a male organ. The real article. Long, gently curving back toward his belly, fat and growing redder by the moment. It seemed to twitch and jerk under my gaze, inviting additional ministrations. I kissed the hot soft tip and in my excitement it almost got away from me.

Walter drifted up into my consciousness. Walter, dedicated to doing everything in the dark and to a limited amount of blind groping. How long had it been since last I had looked upon the male organ? I couldn't remember, nor did it matter now. I gloried in the present, in the marvelous invention this part of a man was . . .

"Go on, go on."

Kissing and licking, flattening my lips against him. He seemed to swell and grow larger, the hardness of him causing me to feel faint, dizzy, crazy. My mouth traveled along the length of him in both directions, huffing and puffing like one of the Harmonica Rascals, bringing forth a rather eerie but satisfying razzmatazz.

Cerebral or spinal stimuli increase the supply of blood to the blood sinuses. The increase in the size of the sinuses results in compression of the deep veins because of the elasticity of Buck's fascia. Erection comes about as a result of mechanical engorgement of the blood sinuses.

"You like it." He was demanding reassurance, not asking a question.

"Not bad," I teased.

He didn't think it was funny. "That tool has been highly praised by some of this town's most beautiful women."

"I'll bet."

He sat up. "Tell me your honest opinion. Don't spare me, Libby. I value what you have to say."

"Best I've come across lately."

"Lately! When have you seen better?"

"It's been some time."

"How much time? Days? Weeks? Months?"

He gave me too much credit. "I left my diary at home. Can't we get back to the business at hand to mouth? You seem to have lost interest."

"A temporary diversion." He told me what to do to make him operative again. In no time at all, he was in first-class working order. He gave a name to what I was doing, to what it looked like, gave me a name. I was familiar with the terminology.

He said, gasping and rasping, "Take every bit of it."

I pulled back for relief. "If I do we'll be irrevocably joined for life."

"Don't stop."

"Don't shove."

"Don't talk."

"Don't hurt."

"All the way down."

I obliged, determined not to miss anything. I explored his balls, the delicate golden hairs, the gleam of perspiration in his crotch. He was, I noticed with some dismay, surprisingly tight-assed.

"Do it all over."

"Give me a minute."

"Oh, oh, there, there."

"Did I miss a place?"

"Oooh."

"Ahhh."

"Wow."

The scrotum consists of two layers, the integument and the dartos tunic. On its surface the scrotum is divided into lateral portions by a ridge which proceeds ventralward to the under surface of the penis and dorsalward along the middle line of the perineum to the anus . . .

"Oh, boy!" Bubba said, in what I took to be a compliment. "Nobody ever . . . not even one time . . . oooheee! That is so goooood!" He was howling and squirming, making it difficult for me to stay aboard.

"Oh, ah, oooh. Now!"

"Now?"

"Yes, ma'am, now. *Right* now."

Damned if he wasn't telling the truth. There ensued a considerable amount of heaving about and noises like a man in the throes of a coronary.

There is one ejaculatory duct on either side of the middle line. Two centimeters in length, it is formed by

*the union of the duct from the vesiculae seminales with
the ductus deferens, commencing at the base of the
prostate and running ventralward and caudalward
between the middle and lateral lobes, and along the
sides of the prostatic utricle.*

Some time passed before Bubba summoned up
strength and desire enough to speak. "You have a very
rare gift, little lady."

"You mean, I come up to your standards?"

"Beats a kick in the ass."

"What a sweet thing to say."

"Only way to go."

That's Bubba. He encouraged me in all my ambitions.

Bubba's letter of appeal to the Human Rights Appeals Board in Albany was salted with legal qualifiers
and modifiers. It was oblique, obscure, and set off no
bells in me. I worked it over. I added and subtracted,
changed words, paragraphs, sentences. I pushed com-
mas and put in a half-dozen exclamation points. I
made it exceedingly clear that IFP had discriminated
against me and that Emil Lieber had admitted his
bias. I also made it known that I looked upon Leon
Stephenson as a pretty dumb character.

"Uh-uh," Bubba said, when I let him read it over.

"What's wrong with it?"

"Not a gosh-darned thing. You got a way with the
language, sister, to the point, powerful, drawing blood
down the line."

"So?"

"So it is just a mite too strong for my taste." He began to strum his guitar, sing "Streets of Laredo,"
slightly off-key, I noticed.

"Not a single curse word in there."

"You sure come down heavy on ole Leon."

"He was no help at all."

"Well, now. Seems likely you and Leon are goin'
to face each other down one more time. Scratch his
back and chances are he'll scratch yours."

"I want what's coming to me."

"Course you do. So do we all." He put the guitar aside and located my breast. Same one as always. He gave it a couple of squeezes. "Let's fornicate, or somethin', my lady."

"I want to get this letter right, Bubba," I said, fighting for time, my resistance waning. I felt like a character in a Tennessee Williams one-act play. "They're coming at me from all sides, Bubba. I want my job."

"The fox never enters the henhouse by the front door." He kept trying to uncross my legs.

"You think I'm going to lose the case?"

"That's for the Appeals Board to decide."

"That's a swell answer, Bubba." I let him get my legs apart, which ended the conversation at once. For a long time our mouths were too busy, or too full, to do much serious talking.

I had to admit it, I was feeling good. My confidence was growing and I was convinced that I was getting better at all this all the time. At the very least, I was enjoying it more. Concentration seemed to be the secret, giving yourself over to the moment, to the pleasure of whatever was happening. There were times when I couldn't tell where Bubba's body left off and mine began. And that, let me tell you, was damned nice . . .

Bubba thought I was someone special. Something special, anyway. He said as much.

"Your husband's a lucky man."

"He is?"

"Got you handy day and night, he has. It's always there, all he's got to do is reach out and grab hisself a handful."

That was me, a handful. Only Walter wasn't grabbing much at all. These encounters with Bubba had provoked my imagination, increased my sexual appetite, done wonders for my skin tone. I yearned for more and more, over and under, in and out. Unhappily for me, Walter stuck to his routine; once a week, whether he needed it or not.

Don't think I didn't try to change the situation. I

brought pressure to bear. A new, brief nightgown which hid nothing when I displayed myself to him in a soft light. I might as well have been bundled up in a furry parka. I blew in his ear. I licked his neck.

"What's the matter with you?" he wanted to know.

"Let's play around a little."

"Not right now," was his favorite answer.

Was it possible that Walter was carrying on in some lewd and lascivious manner with someone else? What a stunning idea! Was he getting all he needed elsewhere? Did that account for his ongoing coolness?

"Do you have a lover, Walter?"

From the look on his face, it was evident he thought I'd flipped out. "What kind of a question is that?" He shook his head. "Certainly not."

"Why not?"

He looked up from his book. "Marriage imposes obligations on each of us."

"What if I had an affair?"

"Don't be ridiculous."

"What if I went down on another man?"

"Libby! You are not that kind of a woman."

"You won't let me do it to you."

"I believe that kissing should be restricted to the mouth."

"For sanitary reasons?"

"There is no need to prolong this conversation."

"I'm sure there are women you'd like to sleep with, Walter." I pressed my case.

"Only you, Libby."

Bullshit, I said to myself. Aloud, I said, "You think no other men want me? Is that it?"

"Many men do, I'm sure. You're a very attractive woman in many ways, Libby. But I'm sure of you."

"Don't be too sure."

He gave me a smug smile. "I know your character."

In which case he knew more than I did for I was convinced that I had a very small amount of character. There was that about Walter, he respected me in a lofty, old-fashioned way. And he loved me, I was

sure of that. All those notions about what a wife
should be, what a woman should be, what a marriage
should consist of. Walter was, in his remote and removed way, a dear man. Considerate and protective,
a family man.

No. No divorce. At least not yet.

twenty-three

Stevie had been attending the West Side Children's School for almost a week, nursery through grade six, plus extended day. And the change in him bordered the miraculous. He came home each day filled with secret delight, clearly having had a good time but careful not to impart too much information about his activities to either me or Walter. Nursery school was Stevie's private world and it looked like he meant to keep it to himself.

I told Walter how pleased I was with Stevie's progress. But Walter had his doubts. Walter avoided change whenever possible. Something in his deep past had fixed him on a steady, virtually unalterable course. As if to deviate might send him over the terrible edge of this planet. He avoided new experience lest it be catching and deadly. My husband was not what you would call flexible.

Stevie in school, Walter at Wallenstein & Smithton, Sybil in Mount Sinai. That left me with lots of free time. Whenever possible I put myself into Bubba's bed, but his legal practice frequently interfered. I spent many an afternoon at the movies. Or shopping. I had lunch with Cici occasionally and once she invited me to go to a literary party with her. I accepted reluctantly since I never felt at ease in large groups of people, never did very well at parties. Had I known how this particular party would affect my life, I might not have gone.

The People's Press was the host, the party to honor its newest author, Luellyn Sue Sherbert. She had written a graphic book about her adventures on a prison farm in South Carolina. You might remember Luellyn Sue. She's the young black woman who separated her lover from his cock with a rusty fishing knife when she caught him with another girl.

The party was held in a bookstore on Upper Broadway. Millions of books, old and new, on shelves, in bins, stacked in dusty corners. Walter would have been in his glory.

Soon after we arrived, I lost contact with Cici, found myself backed into the stacks, staring at a row of Marx, Fanon and Eldridge Cleaver. A tugging at my skirt drew my attention and I looked down to see a stout little man gazing up at me, a snaggle-toothed grin on his fat face.

"Hi, there," he said. "You almost got me that time. Those are pretty good-sized feet you've got, anybody ever tell you?"

"They're not so big."

"Ah, it's okay. I seen worse. What you got is really fantastic legs." He began stroking my calf.

"Cut that out."

"Don't worry, nobody can see."

"You're looking up my dress."

"And I like what I see, baby."

"Don't do that."

"Solid legs, I like 'em solid."

"You're a dirty dwarf."

"That's a rotten thing to say. Okay, so I'm on the diminutive side, but I'm normally proportioned. That makes me a midget."

"You're fat."

"That wasn't so nice either."

"Take your hand out of there."

He spoke intimately, "Suppose I just duck under

your skirt, eat your muff like crazy. Nobody'll ever know the difference."

"Get away from me, you perverted pipsqueak." I headed out of that book-lined cul de sac.

He yelled after me. "You won't find anybody better. Things being what they are, I get lots of practice."

I went looking for Cici to tell her I was leaving. I found her talking to a woman about my own age with shining dull-brass hair.

"Meet Mae Ives," Cici said.

Under that improbable head of hair, Mae Ives had the face of an imp with bright eyes and a pleasant, smiling mouth. She shook my hand briskly and said, "Hi."

"I've been telling Mae about your case," Cici said.

"I guess I've blown it," I said.

Mae Ives frowned. "That's defeatist. There's always another way with these things. I'd like to hear the complete story."

"You'd find it boring, I'm sure."

"I'm a good listener."

"Mae could help," Cici said.

"Oh," I said, trying to end the conversation.

"Let me tell you," Mae Ives said. "Any time a sister rises up to confront the pigs in their own territory, that is . . . beautiful."

"Mind if I tell Libby, Mae?" Cici said.

"Tell her."

"Mae here ghosted Luellyn Sue's book, you know."

"No, I didn't know."

"She did, start to finish."

"Well," I said, in what I meant to be a complimentary tone. "That's swell."

"You should be impressed," Cici said. "Mae is one hell of a writer."

"I am impressed."

"Don't be." Mae Ives laughed. "I dig the way you are. Not turned on by all the phony bullcrap going down about writers and other so-called creative types. Let's talk, Libby."

"All right."

"Give you a call."

"That would be nice."

And two days later she did call, and invited me to have dinner with her. I explained that I had a husband and a child who required a certain amount of attention. I kept all news about the Texas Plowboy to myself.

"Your husband can take care of himself for an evening," she said firmly. "Do him good to find out what it's like to care for his child."

I decided she was right and told Walter I was going out with a friend. He took it like a man. "Steven and I will have a very rewarding evening by ourselves." Looking at Stevie, he said, "I'll read you stories."

Stevie wailed, "I want to watch TV."

Mae took me to a restaurant on the East Side run by a fat lady. She said it was a hangout for literary types and even Jackie Onassis sometimes came there. From the look of the place, and the taste of the food, and the prices charged, I couldn't figure out why anybody would go there.

While working over a chewy piece of veal, I told Mae about my attempt to get a job with IFP. She listened attentively until I was finished. Then said, "Title Seven."

Everyone kept talking about Title VII, nobody explained what it was, what it did, what it meant to me. Before I could ask, Mae Ives was talking again.

"My impression of you, Libby, is that you're some kind of an upfront lady."

What did she mean by that? I chose to let it slide. "Nothing will come of my complaint."

"Have faith."

"In what?"

"In sisterhood. Women are strong, women are good, women will eventually triumph."

That sounded all right to me and I said so.

Mae Ives patted my wrist. "Freedom road is wide open to all the sisters, just come on board."

"Sounds like the West Side Highway."

"That's good, very good. This male-dominated society has always defined freedom for women in sexual terms agreeable to men. You follow my logic?"

"I never thought about it that way." I liked what Bubba and I were doing. It made me feel good and I wanted to keep it going. "My husband is not as sexy as he might be."

"There you are. The inadequate male utilizing marriage as a safe harbor while he traps you into cooking, cleaning, washing, ironing, bearing children . . ."

"Just one child."

"You get the picture."

"I wanted to have a child."

"Don't be diverted from the issues."

"I guess there's something in what you say."

"I've been there, I know."

"You're married?"

"Been. Twice. Twice victimized. Bear the scars and pain still. Casualties in the war between the sexes, that's what we are, you and me. Our right, our duty, is to do something about it. Take up the cudgel. Go into action. The choice belongs to us. Up to now what did we have?"

"What?"

"Suburban matron or lonely weirdo."

"I live on West Sixty-ninth Street." She didn't seem to hear me.

"Screw that noise. They had us by the short hairs. Unpopularity was the most subtle, sneaky, debilitating weapon in their dirty arsenal. To be unpopular—wow! What could be worse?"

I couldn't think of anything.

"Unpopularity wiped out plenty of the sisters. Destroyed the poor dears. Trying to live up to distorted, corrupt, disgusting male standards." She leaned forward, voice pitched low, intimate, caressing. "No matter what anybody tells you, you don't want to get your hair straightened . . ."

My hand went up to my head instinctively.

Mae Ives manufactured a victorious grin. "There, you see."

"Walter's not so bad," I felt compelled to say.

"Who is Walter?"

"My husband."

She made a face. "Men offer what? Masks is what. Pretend lives. Even the damned masks are fantasies, male fantasies for us to act out. They don't allow women to be their gutty selves. Nobody wins that game. If you are going to get it on with fantasy why shouldn't it be your own head trip?"

I agreed with that and said so.

"Bet your sweet ass," she muttered. She stared into my eyes. "We can help."

"We?"

"We militant feminists."

"Help who?"

"Help you."

"Me! How?"

"Your fight is our fight. We are with you all the way. We are living in a fragile historical moment. You must know that."

"I guess I do. Actually I hadn't thought about it much."

"You should. A lot. Who represents you? Legally, that is?"

"Oh, nobody."

"You don't have a lawyer?"

No way I was going to tell anybody about Bubba Horn. Anyway, he wasn't actually my lawyer.

"You're beautiful," she said.

"Ah, no I'm not."

"I think you are. You walked smack into the jungle by yourself. Sister, you are courageous, yes. But terribly naïve. The savages will eat you alive."

I had been wondering if Bubba did that to women. I hoped so. At least once in a while.

"Oh, it's only a job," I said.

"*Your* job."

"I admit it, I do have that feeling."

"They took it away from you."

"I guess you could say that."

"Of course they did, the bastards. So you fight back."

"I didn't do much."

"Libby, there is much more involved here than merely your private interests. Women's rights are at stake. Every time one of us allows one of them to shit on her it's as if they're all shitting on all of us."

"I'm not sure I understand that."

"No more men's turds."

"That would make a great advertising slogan."

She frowned. "This is important and very interesting. It holds out a great deal for us both. Let's not end it yet. We'll go back to my apartment and talk in comfort. There are ways in which I can help you, I'm certain of it."

I said all right, but I couldn't stay too late. Husband and child, you know. If she heard, she gave no sign.

Mae Ives lived in a glass and polished chrome building on Second Avenue, sleek and neat. Her apartment was starkly furnished, a minimum of possessions, a miminum of decorations. All black and white with just a hint of pink in a cushion and a wall hanging. Everything struck me as being terribly expensive. She placed a snifter of brandy in my hand and a Janis Joplin tape on the stereo.

" 'Cheap Thrills,' " she said. "You want to smoke some dope?"

"I don't think so. But thanks anyway."

She shrugged. "Janis is incredible, pure heart, pure woman. She was bi, you know."

I didn't know. In fact, I'd never thought about it, one way or another.

"Janis got it on with everybody, anybody. A real lady. What I'd like you to do is attend a C.R. session."

"C.R.?"

"Consciousness raising. Tell your story to the sisters, the true tale of how this fucked-up society has imposed itself on your existence, forced you to perform in ways not in your own best interest. Limiting your freedom."

"I could never do that, speak to a group."

"Sure you could. Just sisters. Like you and me. You'd be surrounded by love, wired into our activities. Many of the sisters take Personal Protection. Karate, judo, like that. Any motherfucker tries to put his sexual hangups on me I'll fracture his collarbones. Poor baby, you are not tough, are you? Sweet is what you are. Soft and pliable. I like that. But it's not the only way."

She touched my cheek with her knuckles. "What a very exotic face you have."

"I'm Polish," I said.

"Poetic. Sensual. You remind me of Brontë, Charlotte, that is."

I felt as if I'd betrayed Sybil, not saying I was descended from Tartars. As if I'd consigned my mother to a premature grave. I shivered.

"Poor baby, you're cold." Mae Ives put her arms around me. "Let Mae-Mae warm you."

She had arms like steel bands.

She kissed me on the mouth.

I tried to stand up. She kept me in place. "Please let go of me, please."

"You don't like me." She scowled, voice low and rough. "Why don't you like me?"

I unlaced her arms. "Oh, I do like you. I really like you."

She came at me again and I stood up. My feet crossed and I fell to the floor. She came after me but I scrambled away.

"Where are you going?"

"Home."

"What's wrong with me?"

"Not you. It's me. I'm sorry, I'm just not that way."

"Of course you are. We all are. You, me, Janis . . ."

I backed toward the door.

She crawled toward me. "Men are not necessary. There's nothing a man can do for you I can't do better. I would love to do cunnilingus on you . . ."

I reached for the doorknob.

"I'm really very good at it."

The knob wouldn't turn in my sweating hand.

"I know some dandy tricks . . ."

The door came open and out I went.

"One time," she cried after me. "You've got nothing to lose!"

twenty-four

"Poor Mae," Cici lamented over the telephone.

"Why not poor Libby?" I wanted to know. "She scared me pretty good."

"Mae is a sexual compulsive."

"Whatever that means. You might have warned me she was a dyke."

"Oh, it's only a phase with her. Until she got into the radical feminist movement, Mae went from man to man, like a little bunny rabbit. When she changed her politics, she changed her sex partners. She makes a pass at everybody."

"And I thought it was my overwhelming appeal. You could have let me get a little ego satisfaction out of it."

Cici was amused. "Personally I like Mae. She does good work for our side."

The conversation was making very little progress so I told Cici I'd talk to her soon and hung up, much to my surprise. It seemed to me that other people were always terminating my phone calls. Feeling surprisingly good, I headed uptown to Mount Sinai.

One look at Sybil and all the good feelings evaporated. Her breathing was coarse and uncommonly loud. Her cheeks were flushed and the skin was drawn tighter than before, dry, translucent, ready to disintegrate. With her upper lip curled back, she turned a defiant snarl to us all. I shivered and hurried back to the nurses' station.

"My mother doesn't look good."

The nurse examined her chart. "Mrs. Markson's running a fever," she announced casually.

"They put the tube back in her nose."

"Doctor thinks it best that she have oxygen."

"I could hear her breathing."

"Yes, you can hear her breathing."

"It's not good?" I said, looking into the nurse's face. Her features were arranged in an empty, institutional display. A wall off which you were permitted to bounce your fears and any faint residual hopes.

"It's not good?" I said again.

"I would say—Doctor should be along soon. He'll explain."

I drew my own conclusions, none of them encouraging. I went back to Sybil's room. I put my lips against that withered cheek, then hurried away, fighting to keep my emotions in check, not to think about anything.

I went to a movie. *Cries and Whispers,* courtesy of Ingmar Bergman. A real laugher, full of pain and human anguish. Just what I needed. That was the last Bergman picture I would ever see. At three bucks a throw, I can get depressed anywhere. There was always my own life to look at, for example.

I walked over to Lexington Avenue and climbed aboard the first bus that came along. By the time I reached Forty-second Street, I had it all figured out. The idea had been simmering in some shadowed corner of my brain for some time and now it had stepped out into the light where I could examine it thoroughly. It was, I decided, a terrific idea. Well, not bad. And potentially productive. I was tired of hanging around waiting for life to happen to me. I was going to kick fate in the butt, get things moving.

I presented myself to Beth Dooley at the Executive

Placement Service and to my surprise she seemed genuinely glad to see me.

"Sorry it didn't work out at IFP."

"They don't want women in key jobs."

She drew a veil over her eyes. "I can't comment on that." She arranged a bright smile on her face. "I didn't expect you to still be available, with your credentials."

"I haven't been looking. I guess I wasn't really ready to go back to work."

"And now you are?"

"I think I am."

"You're not sure?"

"I'm sure."

"You're bright, Libby. Personable, with a good education and extensive experience . . ."

Hey! That was me she was talking about. Keep it up, the old punchball player needed all the bracing she could get.

"There's an opening here at the agency."

That made me stop and think.

"We have been searching for another interviewer. I'd break you in myself, if you're interested."

"I'm not sure I can handle it."

"I'm sure. Salary plus commission, after a breaking-in period. The money is good, Libby."

"Do you want an answer right away?"

"Take a couple of days. Think it over."

I said I would and abruptly discovered I was back in the street. Somehow I made it back uptown to my apartment. No memory of how I'd done it remained. Bus? Cab? On foot? No answer came. Suddenly I was aware that I was slumped on the floor of the foyer alongside the blue and white Chinese umbrella stand, sobbing wildly. After a while I found myself in the bathroom. I turned on the tap in the tub and thrust my head under the cold fall of water. It felt horrible but I maintained that stance for as long as I could.

Dripping, I raised myself up and popped a pair of Valium, then stripped down and rubbed myself with a towel until I was dry. I put on a flannel nightgown, a pair of Walter's woolen ski stockings and got into bed. I either dozed off or went blank again. When I came back to myself, I was only cold around the edges. I reached for the phone and called Candy.

"What is it?" she started out, a hint of annoyance in her voice. As if I'd interrupted something important.

"Sybil is practically dead."

"Practically?"

"Not entirely dead. Not entirely alive. It's just that her heart won't quit beating. Why won't she let go?"

"Sybil never let anybody off the hook."

"She's making terrible noises."

Over the long wire, I imagined I could hear Candy assembling the various aspects of her character in order to deal with her crazy sister. "What you're saying is she's worse."

"No way of getting worse. Being dead would be an improvement."

"Libby!" Big Sister was shocked. What did she know about my life? Or about Sybil's dying? "Get hold of yourself, Libby."

"Any particular part?" I giggled, and gasped for air.

"Libby!" More of a warning this time. As if Big Sister was afraid. Of what? Of Sybil's imminent demise? I doubted she cared one way or the other. More likely she was worried, lest I lose control and Sweet Candy would have to step in, take over.

"Libby," she said once more. This time with a learned firmness in her voice. The voice of Corporate Authority. Big Sister was, after all, Big Businesswoman. "What does the doctor say?"

"Doctor says socialized medicine is bad for doctors."

"Save the jokes."

"Dying, that's the biggest joke of all."

"All right." Threat, threat coming. "I'll phone Dr. Barger myself, long distance."

"Dial direct, you save money."

"Have you no respect?"

"Not for Barger. I don't like him at all."

"All right, you don't like him. But he has a very good reputation. He costs a great deal."

The ultimate recommendation, his fees are high. "He reminds me of Adolphe Menjou."

"Who? What are you talking about?"

"Adolphe Menjou. He was in the original version of *The Front Page*. A little man, very dapper, spoke very fast, with a waxed mustache. Politically he was somewhere to the right of Genghis Khan."

"Libby . . ." A note of desperation crept in there, as if she was trying to tranquilize me, keep me legally sane and on the Right Track. "Tell me about Mother."

"No more string quartets for Sybil. No more secondrate musicians. All that's left is tears and a heavy hand on the organ. She wore juniors, did you know that? Never put on an ounce. She . . . looks . . . awful . . ."

"Dammit, this comes at such a bad time."

Death has a way of interfering with life. How bloody inconvenient.

"One of the shopping centers," Candy explained in a rational, businesslike manner. "The note's come due and—would you believe it?—damn Abner, he was supposed to be on top of everything. We don't have the money. 'Let it flow,' Abner kept saying."

"It must be nice to owe somebody a lot of money."

She snapped back. "What's that supposed to mean?"

"Well, you have to be pretty well established to run up a large debt."

"I don't understand you, Libby."

"You're not the only one."

"This could mean the end of my entire business."

"Just one little shopping center?"

"Everything's linked. Financial threads woven with more threads. A complicated tapestry of debts and cash flow and private agreements."

"Bribes?"

She ignored the question. "The suppliers, the unions, the landlords. Licenses, the fire department, the water

department, you have no idea. Oh, goddamn Abner—
'let it flow.' My whole life is flowing away."

I almost felt sorry for her. But not quite. I was the
one who needed help.

"Well," I said flatly. "I only called to let you know
how Sybil was doing. I figured you'd want to know."

Candy breathed out. "If what you say is true . . ."

If.

"Then there's nothing I can do. Sybil won't be aware
of me if I'm there or if I'm here."

Always sensible, that's my sister.

"Talk to Barger, Libby. Find out how much time
Sybil has left. If it's serious, I'll get on a plane, right
away."

Serious . . .

"I'll do that," I said.

"You'll call me back? Collect."

"Sure."

"I'm only a few hours away."

"Talk to you." I hung up. I lay back on the bed and
fell asleep almost at once. When I woke Walter was
standing at the edge of the bed. One look and I began to
cry. He held me until I quieted.

"Is it over?" he said.

"Soon."

"We'd better go to the hospital."

"You'll go with me, Walter?"

"Of course."

"Oh, I'd appreciate that. I truly would."

"I'm your husband." He managed to invest the words
with a quiet force. I began to suspect there was much
more to Walter than I had ever realized.

The nurse on duty gave us the Party Line: "There's
been no change. Doctor will talk to you, I'm sure."

So I went into that gray cell and looked down at
Sybil. That giving and selfish woman who had made me
cry and made me laugh. Sybil Markson, who had in-
vented herself. That exception to all of life's rules. That
exceptional person. My mother. Sybil.

Die, Sybil, die. And let us all rest in peace.

The next morning Barger called. "I'm sorry, Mrs. Pepper. Your mother died twenty-three minutes ago."

I was willing to bet he could have ticked off the seconds as well. I thanked him for calling and he said if there was anything he could do and I said thank you, anyway, and goodbye, and goodbye. So very polite, so very civilized, so very full of crap.

"Not to worry," Walter said. "I'll take care of everything."

Good. Because I was capable of taking care of exactly nothing.

I placed a call to Candy around noon. "Damn," she said. "This screws up everything."

Sybil couldn't get anything right.

"I'll be on the next plane."

"Swell," I said, and I hung up.

I called Cici. She said she wanted to be at the funeral but she had to go to Sacramento to interview Jerry Brown, whoever the hell he was.

I called Bubba Horn. He said he guessed we wouldn't be able to see each other for a while. "Your momma and such as that."

"Not seeing each other won't bring her back."

We made a date to meet at ten the next morning. At his place.

Beth Dooley called to ask if I'd reached a decision about the agency job.

"I want it."

"Can you start on Monday?"

"Yes."

So it went. Lose a mother, find a job. Things could be worse.

That night Walter held me until I fell asleep. In the morning, he was still holding me. Poor Walter, he hadn't been able to read himself to sleep.

Bubba and I came together on his couch. We locked mouths and I fastened on to his tongue for fear of falling off.

After a while he went to work on my breasts. *The* breast. He seemed to have taken permanent possession of it, the left breast. I swallowed a mouthful of his drool and broke contact.

"You always work the same side of the street."

"What's that?"

"The same breast."

He laughed. "A man gets into bad habits."

"It's not bad, just a little boring."

We resumed kissing and he slid his hand between my legs. That went on for a reasonably long time.

"You're missing the place, Bubba."

"Beg pardon, ma'am?"

"Don't get your feelings hurt, Bubba. *The* place, you're rubbing all around it. Shift a shade over to the right, and slightly lower down."

"There?"

"About a half-inch lower."

"There?"

"You're getting impatient, Bubba."

"Nobody ever complained before."

"I'm not complaining, just trying to help. Both of us. There, that's perfect."

We kissed and he rubbed and I squirmed. Then I stopped.

"What's the matter now?"

"You lost your way again."

"You sure are concerned with your ever-lovin' body today."

"Just get on the clit and fool around, Bubba."

"Kind've unsettles me, all these instructions. Looka-here, ole Peter's gone and got all soft on me."

"Why don't we take off all our clothes?"

"Damned good idea."

A couple of quick moves brought me down to bare flesh. But Bubba was having trouble with his boots. "Give us a hand, sister. Put your sweet little rump up where I can get some leverage."

Fool that I was, I bent forward, my ass aimed up at

him. He planted one boot against my right cheek, jammed the other between my legs. "Start tuggin'," he commanded.

I pulled and he pushed. The boot came loose and sent me crashing to the floor. "One more time," he said.

I assumed the desired position. If there was one thing this relationship had, it was dignity. We did it all again.

"There," he said, proud of himself. "Just line 'em up against the wall over there."

When I sat back down he offered me his limp cock the way you might offer a pacifier to an infant. "Sweet-talk Peter, honey, until he gets to runnin' good again. Make us both feel a lot better."

He was right. And from start to finish, I hardly gave Sybil a thought.

twenty-five

Not much you can say about funerals. Never went to a funeral I enjoyed. Last funeral I go to will be my own. The caliber of funeral humor is not very high.

So much for that. Sybil was dead. They put her down in one of those stylish new cemeteries. Long rolling lawns and a select variety of sober plantings.

Weeping at such places is done in good taste, quietly, as privately as possible, with breast-beating, loud wailing, or other Jewish demonstrativeness forbidden. Under a sedate crimson canopy, friends and family collected and listened to a fat-faced rabbi who never knew Sybil hold forth on her many virtues.

Personally I would have welcomed a little sobbing, some crying out loud, maybe even a fainting or two. Instead I kept my knees locked to keep from falling and dug my nails into Walter's strong hand. Solid as the Rock of Ages, my Walter. But chipped here and there.

There we were, the bereaved, sweating under a hot New Jersey sun. Who goes to New Jersey except on business? Or to be buried. What the hell were we doing this far west of Fifth Avenue? Surprise, surprise, Sybil wanted it this way. Sybil had left instructions that she be laid to rest—her exact words—next to her beloved husband, Sam. Always the sentimentalist, my mother. And all that time I thought she owned a vault

211

in the basement of Carnegie Hall. Take that, Lenny Bernstein!

Let me tell you what was on my mind while that plump little rabbi was doing his act over Sybil. I kept worrying about the avocado pit in my kitchen. Sybil's avocado. Either I repotted the damn thing soon or it would surely die.

Two observations about Sybil's death. One: I was profoundly grieved and sorely distressed, more than I ever dreamed I would be. Two: also relieved. Relieved that she no longer drifted in that awful limbo that was neither life nor death, that at last her anguish had been terminated. And my own.

Her passing made me feel as if some essential part of myself had been surgically removed, leaving only a black hole. I had wanted her to die, wanted it all to be finished. Yet I experienced no guilt. That perhaps was the most surprising thing of all.

My son did not attend my mother's funeral. Thanks to Walter. Walter was determined to shield Stevie from the rocks and shoals of life, as he put it, for as long as possible.

"I want him to be there," I insisted.

"Why? Will it do him any good?"

"Death is part of living." Oh, boy. I sounded like a character in a Hemingway novel. One of the early books.

"The last part," Walter shot back.

"Sybil was his grandmother."

"Funerals are depressing at best. He'll have bad dreams."

"Just the services." It seemed to me I was bargaining away bits and pieces of my life, so much junkyard bric-a-brac. "He doesn't have to go to the cemetery."

"No."

"Sooner or later he has to learn that people die."

"Let it be later."

"Sybil was my mother."

"Absolutely not."

"I mean it, Walter!"

"Don't shout, the neighbors will hear."

"I'm not shouting." But I was. "Anyway, nobody can hear us. The walls in this building are two feet thick. They don't build buildings like this anymore. Nobody cares if we're alive or that Sybil's dead."

"I care."

"Then let Stevie go. He should know about such things."

"Tell him about it."

"Tell him?"

"You tell a very good story."

My husband's brain had been corrupted by all those books he reads. "Maybe I can get it published."

"That's not funny."

"I'll call it, *Babar Visits the Graveyard.*"

"Neither is that."

"What's the matter with you, Walter?"

"There's nothing the matter with me. What's the matter with you?"

"My mother is dead is what's the matter with me. Your mother is alive and getting tan in Miami Beach and living high off the hog."

"Fort Lauderdale."

"Same thing."

"Where did you get such expressions—'high off the hog'? Farmers talk that way. Guys I used to know in the army from Alabama and Texas."

Bubba had infiltrated my mind, corrupted my vocabulary. That's what I needed, to have my sinful double life exposed on the same morning my mother was being buried. Think before you speak, I warned myself, or you'll give it all away. And half the fun will be gone.

True, true. Much of the pleasure and satisfaction in the humping and rutting Bubba and I did came out of its forbidden nature. Cheating was the essential condiment that made it all so savory.

All this talk of doing away with marriage. Do your own thing. Anything goes. Make infidelity respectable and socially acceptable and there goes a lot of the fun.

Not to mention putting ninety-nine percent of our novelists out of business. Watch it, guys . . .

I donned my most ingenuous manner. "Did I say that?" A good performance, and Walter went for it. What a flirt I must have been when I was younger. What a dissembling little tease. What a smoldering bundle of passion.

Walter had more pressing matters on his mind. "I do not want my son attending this affair."

An affair was what Bubba and I were doing. A funeral was when they planted your only mother. I continued the argument for a while until Walter and I were able to arrive at an equitable accord. We did it his way. Stevie didn't miss much.

When the rabbi finished his prayers, they lowered Sybil into the hole on a couple of those fancy black plush ropes. I wanted to cry out, "Hold it, boys! Knock it off. Bring her back, it's all a little game and it's over now. Bring her up, open the box, and we'll all get on with our normal, aggravating lives."

But I said nothing. Holding still, neither hot nor cold, crying nor trembling. Just there. Just waiting it out. When it was over, I turned away so as not to see them shoveling dirt on her. My eyes came to rest on Candy. She almost smiled and gave a little shrug.

"Let's ride back together," I said. "Just the two of us."

I explained to Walter that I wanted some time alone with Candy and he said he'd ride back with Mr. Michaels, Sybil's beau.

Big Sister and I climbed into the rented limousine behind a uniformed chauffeur. Gray hair curled out from under his cap like angels' wings and there was a hearing aid behind his right ear.

"You and me," Candy said. "The last of the Marksons."

It seemed to me the chauffeur was leaning our way, so as not to miss a word. It was, after all, a long, dull ride back to town. I tapped him on the shoulder.

"Hey, mister, mind putting that hearing aid on low? My sister and I want some privacy."

He disconnected the device and placed it on the seat beside him. Otherwise no reaction. He was accustomed to people at funerals, they were all a little strange, I guess.

Candy examined me admiringly. "That's very good. I never had nerve enough to do that sort of thing."

"Now that you mention it, neither did I."

She laughed and said that was funny. I sighed and she sighed and neither of us said a word until we reached the entrance to the Lincoln Tunnel.

Candy said, "You've changed since the last time I saw you."

"I don't think so."

"Oh, yes. You seem quite—content. I think you must be having an affair."

I waited for the hot flush of culpability to color my cheeks. For the unpardonable sin to be etched on my face. For my terrible dereliction to make me ashamed.

Instead I felt blameless, unspotted and childlike, my hands clean and the rest of my body undefiled, if not virtuous. The point is, those matinees with Bubba made me feel pretty good.

"Are you?" Candy said, curiosity shining out of those California eyes. "Having an affair with somebody?"

I looked her over. "I am."

"You are!" She was a little disappointed, as if I'd intruded on territory reserved for other, better people. "So am I," she ended, voice trailing off.

There was no precedent for me to talk about fucking with my sister. Sex was taboo, a subject we had never touched on when we were together. We had never exchanged confidences.

"Very long?" she said.

"What?"

"Have you been doing it very long?"

"Not so long."

She pursed her beautiful lips. "I've been at it for

about ten years. With different men, of course. Do you think Sybil fooled around? She and Mr. Michaels, he was around while Sam was alive."

It was a question I'd asked myself. "What do you think?"

"I think Sybil got her share. She loved a good time. I'll bet she didn't do without, especially after Sam died."

"I can't imagine her in bed . . ."

Candy made a face. "All that pushing and pulling, trying to get everything lined up just so. I'll bet Sybil never grunted or groaned. Not our Sybil."

This turn in the conversation made me uneasy. "We never talked about sex before."

"Go on."

"It's true."

"There's always plenty to talk about."

"Remember the summer I spent with you and Moe in Oklahoma? I did a lot of dating that summer."

She raised one brow. "You wild thing."

"All those Oklahoma boys, so different from the kind of boy I grew up with."

"You were used to all those intellectual Jews."

"That's not what I meant."

She gave that shrug again. "I remember the first time I did it with a Christian boy. I'd never seen an uncircumcised cock before. I thought it was pretty odd."

"I never looked in those days."

"Did you sleep with a lot of them?"

"Some."

"How many?"

"More than two."

"What a cozy one you are. And you never said a word. We used to talk a lot."

"We talked but we never said very much. We never confided in each other."

"Why was it that way?"

"You never showed any interest in me. You never volunteered anything about yourself."

"You could have said something."

"No, I couldn't. Big Sister was too intimidating. Married lady. Super-achiever."

When we came out of the tunnel, she said, "You must have known about the abortion?"

"Sybil and Sam talked about it one night. I overheard them."

"I was seventeen. The second time I got laid I got caught. Sybil put up the money and I had it done in Harlem. A very nice black woman, but she hurt me and I cried a lot, bled for days."

"What about the boy?"

"He was a man. Twice my age. I never told him about it. I was too embarrassed, ashamed."

"I didn't know you ever felt shame. About anything."

"A few weeks later I met Moe."

"And got married."

"He was always a fool." She stared straight ahead. "You're lucky, Libby. The same husband, a child, a home. You've got it all."

Then why Bubba, I asked myself. Why the lingering despair, the hunger for rewards not fully realized even in my dreams? If my smart, accomplished, beautiful Big Sister wasn't happy, perhaps there was no happiness to be had. Not by anyone. The circuits in my head cracked and popped as if shorting out and I drew a blank.

We were moving up Eighth Avenue, the limousine barely holding its own against the darting taxis and the buses that lumbered into our path. Candy broke the silence, speaking almost wistfully, "So I've decided to get rid of the bastard. He's got to go."

"Are you talking about Abner?"

"The marriage is kaput."

I blinked once or twice. "You and Abner?"

"I'm going to get a divorce."

"Just like that."

"Just like that. He's loused up everything. The business, my life. Why let him hang around if he can't do me any good?"

"There's never any build-up with you. No warning. You marry them without notice, you get rid of them the same way."

She seemed pleased by the observation. "Yes, I guess that's right."

We made it into West Sixty-ninth Street and I instructed the chauffeur. "The building in the middle of the block." With his hearing aid on the seat, he kept going. We had to circle the block and come back again.

At the apartment door, Candy said, "I've never seen you looking prettier or more relaxed."

It was the first compliment she'd ever paid me. "I guess we'll never take that walk across the George Washington Bridge," I told her with as much cheerfulness as I could muster. "I still don't know anything about the stock market."

She looked at me oddly. "Oh," she said very softly. "I'm sure you'll learn."

part four

1973

twenty-six

At my desk in the Executive Placement Service, I dispatched applicants to some of the best jobs in New York City. Working conditions good. Salaries good. The work challenging. In my first week on the job I began to suspect that I was sending out people who were not nearly as well qualified or as experienced as I was. By the fourth week I was sure of it and resentful. Frustration took hold as day after day I remained anchored to my chair, unable to improve my condition, unable to alter my fate. IFP was the monkey on my back. As long as that situation continued unresolved in my mind, there was nothing I could do to better myself.

My job was pleasant enough, interesting, and it paid well. I was able to take extended lunch periods, to spend time with Bubba, and to stay away from the apartment, away from the heavy tug of wifely duties, away from the tribulations of being a mother. I frequently castigated myself for not measuring up to the conventional perception of what a wife and mother should be, eventually to shrug away the worry, reassuring myself that I needed time on my own to learn to become myself.

It was difficult to define Bubba's role in all this. Sometimes I thought of him as one sizable cock, performing on order. Not that he did. Much of the time our encounters began with me coaxing his passion into being, one way or another. It soon became clear to me that Bubba was hardly the swordsman I had imagined him to be. Or else he had a stable of panting ladies that he wheeled in and out on a tight and precarious schedule. That made me jealous, and at the same time I liked the idea of his coming from another woman to me. In the abstract, that is. Why was everything so damned complicated, contradictory? Life should be smooth and simple. Shouldn't it?

"Are we in love?" I asked Bubba during a break in our playtime.

"We sure do make a lovin' pair," he countered.

"To fuck is not necessarily to love."

"You thinkin' you're in love with me?"

"I don't know. I used to have misty visions of you gleaming in the sunlight, Bubba, pure, committed and beautiful. Sort of a noble savage brought up to date."

"You given that one up?"

"Sort of. I've got the feeling that Bubba Horn is a creature of his own making, with a lot of parts left undone."

"I still think highly of you, Miss Libby. Specially that round fat bottom of yours."

"You're the most anal man I've ever known."

"Like they say, I'd crawl through a mile of broken glass just to kiss your ass. You figure that's what love is?"

Was it love I felt for Bubba? If so, what was it I felt for Walter? Certainly my feelings for him had intensified, and I found myself drawn to him in a variety of ways that I thought had been lost to me. Very few nights passed that I did not become aroused and make overtures toward Walter. I talked lovingly to him, and dirty, I displayed myself to him in soft light, I danced and teased, anything to turn him on. Walter's defenses were magnificent and he managed to hold out against me two out of three nights. But even that was an improvement over past performances.

We made love frequently enough for me to get a pretty good fix on his potential. Though he was decidedly different from Bubba, he didn't always come in second.

Sounds awful, doesn't it? As if I'd lost my bearings. But I loved every minute of it.

Being with Walter in bed was a more tranquil activity than with Bubba. Orchestrated gently, less spectacular initially, but eventually reassuring, with a sweet, satisfying fragrance.

Give Walter a chance, that was the trick of it. He needed time to adjust, to become accustomed to whatever was happening to my spiraling desires. Sudden alterations of mood or intensity put him off. He wanted to do what he'd done before, not take chances, pick his way cautiously over new ground. I decided that Walter had many excellent qualities as a husband and a lover, was a good bet for the long haul.

Then a dangerous thought entered my head. I wanted to tell him about Bubba. Not about sex with Bubba, not directly, anyway. Not about my feelings for Bubba specifically. But what it was like for me to *experience* this other being, this other man, this other person. I wanted Walter to comprehend the mysterious energy being with Bubba provided me. To tell him all about this personal act of human discovery. There was so much I was learning about Bubba, about myself, and about Walter. I tried mightily to shed the urge to reveal any of this to Walter and failed. One night I decided to give it a try. But carefully.

"What are your feelings about adultery, Walter?" It occurred to me that there might have been a better way to begin.

"In the morning," Walter answered, giving one of his best yawns.

"I'm serious."

"It's time to go to sleep. We both have jobs to go to."

"I need to talk."

"You always want to talk when it's time to go to sleep."

"Adultery, Walter?"

"What about it?"

"Are you for it or against it? Or no reaction at all? Choose one of the above."

"Against." He punched his pillow and put his back to me. "Good night."

"I'm not finished. Surely you can visualize a situation where adultery might be justified?"

"No."

"What if the people are incompatible?"

"Cocktail party talk."

"You think people can work out their problems?"

"Everything can be resolved."

"How?"

"An intelligent approach. Imagination. Hard work."

"Practice makes perfect, you mean?"

"Something like that."

I found that encouraging. "But what if one partner in a relationship does sleep with someone else? Can a marriage continue successfully under those circumstances?"

Walter rolled onto his back, his eyes tightly shut. "If a marriage is working, there is no need for any outside sexual activity. Isn't that logical?"

I wasn't concerned with logic, I was after some fundamental functional truth. "Some people require more sex than others."

"There's too much talk about it. Don't believe everything you hear or read. I was in the army, I know. To hear men talk, every one of them could make love all night every night. And every one of them made a hundred thousand dollars a year."

"What about variety? A change of pace. A different face."

He sat up and looked at me, spoke intimately. "I love you, Libby. I am satisfied with everything about you, in bed and out. Being married to you is the natural condition of my existence. There is no room in my life for any other woman. Does that satisfy you?"

At once I grew suspicious. That sounded like some tricky masculine dodge. What was he concealing from me? "Have you ever done it with another woman since we were married?"

He lay back down. "Of course not."

"You've thought about it?"

"Never."

"You've never seen a woman who was so attractive, so exciting, that you wondered what it would be like to be with her? Even if you didn't do anything?"

"Never."

He had to be lying. "Everybody looks, Walter."

"Not me. Oh, maybe in passing, hardly worth discussing."

"Ah," I gloated. "Are there times when we make love that you think about some other woman? Be honest, Walter. How it would be for you with somebody else? Some beautiful young girl with a tight ass and terrific breasts?"

"You must be suffering a moral breakdown, talking this way. I get a great deal of pleasure from all the parts of your body. Your breasts are quite nice."

"I'd never know it, the way you act."

"What is that supposed to mean?"

"You give them a squeeze now and then."

"I'll try to do better in the future."

"You're fixed on the right one," I said. Or was it the left one? Bubba or Walter, whose hand did what to which boob? Adultery was fun, but it put an awful strain on your memory.

I was determined to elicit a satisfactory response from Walter. "Let's say a marriage isn't sufficiently satisfying for one of the partners, as currently constituted."

He closed his eyes again. He kept them closed. "Very well, I'll go along with that."

"Okay, if one or both of them had an extramarital affair, do you think it might improve the conditions of their marriage?"

"My answer is an unequivocal no."

"Why?"

His eyes popped open. "Why?" He sat up. "I'll tell you why. Because inevitably there would be great and lasting psychic damage to them both, a trauma to the marriage that could not be repaired."

I didn't want to believe that. "If . . . what about discretion? Careful arrangements, so that nobody gets hurt."

"Deceit, duplicity, dissembling, the result must be bad."

"What if our hypothetical husband had a lover and his wife never knew about it?"

"She would still be deprived of his total attention."

"Sexually? It's possible that—"

"Emotionally. Spiritually. Sooner or later there would be searing damage done."

"I'm not so sure."

"It's logical."

"It sounds like the plot of an MGM movie. Robert Taylor cheats on Barbara Stanwyck and she senses it. Her faith in love and marriage is shattered. She takes a lover, or at least she tries to, but she can't pull it off. Barbara Stanwyck's too good, too virtuous. After eight reels she returns home and swears to make the best of things. But by then Robert Taylor has had an attack of conscience and has given up his girl friend and returned to the nest, a chastened and wiser man. They kiss, fade out."

"It happens that way."

"Not in life." I was aware of a rising rage and resentment because Walter would not allow for any deviation in human behavior from what he considered right and proper. At that moment I almost babbled about Bubba Horn. All the details. I wanted him to know what Bubba did to me and I to him. I longed to tell him that the reason he and I were having sex three or four times a week instead of once a week was because being with Bubba had triggered a flood of sexuality in me. I said nothing.

Walter looked at me obliquely. "You are referring to someone specific. Who is it?"

An icy shock wave went through me. I'd gone too far, taken too many silly risks. I shivered and hugged myself. "No, this is merely one of those What if discussions."

He didn't buy it. "Who is it?" he said again.

I shook my head.

"Ah," he said, suddenly all-knowing. "It's Cici Willigan. It has to be. Ever since I met her I have been aware of a lack of moral stability in that woman. She was always a little wild for my taste."

A protest came onto my tongue and I suppressed it. Cici could bear the burden of Walter's disapproval without effort.

"I admire that in you," Walter said.

That got my attention.

"The ability to treasure a confidence. Trust. I can see that you know all about Cici's innamorato and don't intend to betray her faith in you. I won't insist."

"Innamorato." That's what he said. I couldn't recall whether or not the word had ever before been spoken aloud in my presence.

"You are a woman of character, Libby. I respect you for it. You are strong, independent, self-sufficient." He patted my arm, closed his eyes, and promptly went to sleep.

The things Walter said, the woman he described. She was a stranger to me. Once he had told me that I was the Girl of His Dreams. His dreams had very little to do with me, I decided. All these years, and my husband didn't know me at all.

twenty-seven

The State Human Rights Commission scheduled my second hearing for ten o'clock in the morning. I told Beth Dooley that I had a doctor's appointment and wouldn't be at work until after lunch. She was properly understanding and I was properly guilty. Why lie? Why did I have to hide what I was doing? The answer troubled me; I didn't want her to think I was a trouble-maker. I wanted people to see me as a cooperative, pleasant woman, to like me. When was I going to grow up?

Since I wasn't going to work that morning, I was able to put Stevie onto the school bus, and that made me feel like an honest-to-God mother in good working order. Stevie had entered kindergarten the previous month and gave every indication of liking it a lot. He had stopped wetting his bed, seemed in a better frame of mind, more playful and more amenable. Apparently, the less time Stevie and I spent together, the more room he had to be himself, to grow. At first I was troubled by that discovery, but then I found that there was more and more pleasure in the time we did have with each other, and more satisfaction.

By the time I returned to the apartment, Pearl Combs had arrived. Pearl was a gaunt black woman with a quiet awareness of herself who had come to work for us two or three weeks earlier. She did the shopping, cleaned, and prepared the evening meal before she departed. Thanks to Pearl the apartment continued to function. No one went without clean socks or a hot meal and I was able to keep working at the agency.

Pearl and I made up a shopping list and then it was time for me to go. She wished me luck at the hearing and locked the door as soon as I left. I was not the only one who recognized the dangers that lurked in the city.

I waved down a cab and climbed in, settled back for the ride uptown. I gave the cabdriver the address on One Hundred Twenty-fifth Street and he let out a moan.

"Whataya nuts going up there?"

New York cabbies are distrustful, rude and rotten drivers. They have this trick, switching off the ignition and claiming the cab won't work, if they don't want to take you where you want to go. I kept my eye on his hand.

We rolled along One Hundred Twenty-fifth Street, windows closed, doors locked. "Got your fare set? I ain't stopping to make change, unnerstand. I pull over, you fork over the dough and hit the sidewalk. Slam the door on your way out so I can lock it fast and get going, okay?"

I agreed that it was a very good plan.

"Lindsay, it's all his fault."

Before I could say anything, we slid over to the curb.

"The dough!" the cabbie rasped.

I handed it through the small opening in the plastic safety panel that separated us.

"Open the goddam door!"

I did.

"Out, out! Get a move on, willya!"

He was moving away, picking up speed, before I was able to straighten up. Horn blaring, tires screeching, just like in the movies. I hurried into the commission office.

There they were, perched around that conference table like fat, satisfied gulls around a garbage dump.

Hard eyes and chilly greetings acknowledged my arrival.

Emil Lieber, glowing with self-contentment, anxious to fling himself into the fray. Jonathan Marras, watchful, uneasy, ready to defend himself. John Hannah, coiled to strike, ominous and mean. On either side of him, two other men. Also lawyers, I found out later. Labor specialists, men with close connections in Washington. Hannah had brought along a pair of carefully groomed killers.

Leon Stephenson put me at the far end of the table again and I accepted his directions without dispute. I tried not to reveal the mounting stress I was under, the fear, the certainty that I was doomed in this quest. These men, their minds were made up. They had no intention of being nice to me.

As if in agreement, John Hannah waved a long, strong finger at me. "You," he snapped off in a voice tinged with malice, "continue to disappoint me, Libby . . ."

twenty-eight

The hearing was a disaster. Hannah, backed by his associate sharks, attacked me. They nibbled away, chewed, sliced, cut, hacked and in general did me no good at all. I became defensive, stammering, contradicting myself, pleading for mercy, pushed all the way back into emotional diapers.

I wet my pants.

And definitely blew the job.

There was no chance of getting a favorable decision from Leon Stephenson. IFP was for me a cause lost and best forgotten. I was no everyday masochist and I decided to give it all up on the bus ride home. The rest of my life stared me in the face like a fright mask; send other people out on jobs, Libby, and that would be that.

Oh, how it hurt.

A subterranean anguish that ripped up my emotional ligaments. I felt like an old-time athlete giving it one last try on bum knees. Gutsy, sure. But outclassed. I needed some adult Teddy Bear to take to bed with me, some furry accomplishment to comfort and console myself with. Nobody can rest with the sharp sting of inferiority and failure cutting up your insides.

To all intents I quit. But not entirely. What kept a

small spark of hope alive was the letter that arrived from the United States of America's Equal Employment Opportunity Commission (EEOC).

Being of reasonably sound mind, and having existed for thirty-years-plus in this world, you give up certain expectations. You don't, for example, expect the U.S. Government to respond to the complaint and the needs of one small citizen.

Surprise; in prose weighted with official gobbledygook, the letter said my worries were over. Uncle Sam was checking things out, would see if that big bad corporation had broken the law. Since Washington had the capability of enforcing the law, I was encouraged. A little bit. After all, Uncle could point a stern finger at IFP and say, Cut the Crap, My Man. Hire the Lady.

I allowed myself to feel better.

My brain zipped out into orbit seeking ways to give the EEOC a helping hand. In a stunning flash of inspiration, I dipped back into Harry Ellenbogen's book. It was more helpful the second time around.

On page 643, in small but readable type, was just what I was after. I studied Ellenbogen's words until I was sure I understood his meaning, then got off a dispatch to the Office of Contract Compliance. According to page 643, it was the responsibility of the OCC to make sure that firms doing business with the Government are in compliance with all federal statutes. I made sure OCC understood how badly IFP had treated me. Here, I told them, in simple but powerful language, is a case worth pursuing. In a stroke of genius, I mailed a copy of the letter to Leon Stephenson and another to the President of International Food Products. Take that, John Hannah.

Next, the letdown. I hit bottom with a thud. I'd gasped my last gasp. IFP had done a thorough job on me. I was whipped and they knew it. Had known it right from the start. Imagine, a silly little girl daring to mix it up with the Big Boys. Give it up. Forget it. No contest. The boys still wouldn't let me play in their game and I had wanted so badly to become a winner. Losing this time really hurt.

I had another idea. If IFP could be harassed a little, why not a lot? I telephoned the *Daily News* and gave my story to a bored man at the city desk.

"If it breaks out," he said finally, "if there's a decision, give us a ring."

I tried the *Post*. Nothing.

The *Times*. More of the same.

I called NBC, CBS, ABC and Channel Thirteen. And got exactly nowhere. All that rejection. I figured it would take at least four visits with St. Xavier and two combat sessions with The Family to make up for lost ground.

I needed someone to talk to, a sympathetic and supportive mien, some smart advice. I sought out Walter. My husband had his attention riveted on *Pentimento*. My tentative queries received grunts and head-bobbings.

Could I measure up to Lillian Hellman?

Contact the People's Advocate, you say. I thought of that. But Bubba Horn was putting on his act in West Scroggins, New Mexico, where a Chicano day laborer had massacred his family: wife, three kids, father, mother and ninety-four-year-old grandmother. Bubba had described the situation as one more insidious example of the dehumanizing results of racist America.

I had asked Bubba if the man was guilty as accused. He had given me a peculiar look, the sunny side of scorn. "What has that got to do with anything?"

Confronted with such moral and legal conviction, I was stumped for a good answer, and so gave none at all. Bubba, I assured myself, was a man of noble purpose and deeply dedicated to justice. In the strong light of his commitment, I was properly ashamed, and confused as I could be.

Which brought me around to Cici. She was on her way to Washington and an interview with Henry Kissinger.

"Can you believe it?" she bubbled. *"New York* Mag has promised me the full cover treatment, my profile superimposed on K's. And the subject, you'll love it— Can a Woman Be Secretary of State? This will make me a star, at least as big as Nora and Gail. You ought to speak to Mae," she said before she clicked off. "Mae's good about things like this."

That sent me into the kitchen for a cup of strong tea to wash down the Valium I needed. All that talk about giving up the battle, about being defeated, finished with IFP, just empty wordplay. I still wanted to play the game. I still craved the action. I longed to win.

But was I ready for Mae Ives? Was I prepared to put my heterosexual purity on the line? I visualized Mae beating me onto my back, performing all sorts of strange, perverted acts on my weak and innocent body. Fear would turn me into a helpless hulk under her depraved and crazed onslaught. What unimagined degradations would I be subjected to? Even worse, what would she make me do?

Palpitating with apprehension and curiosity I dialed her number. Perhaps she wouldn't answer. Where was I headed? What would happen to me? I had thrust myself into a strange and fearful world and it seemed at that moment I was greatly underequipped to make my way in it.

The ringing stopped and Mae said, "Hello," as if that simple response could disguise what a dangerous person she was.

"Libby Pepper here."

She greeted me like a long-lost lover. Or a brand-new one. Actually, she said, "How nice to hear your voice again, Libby." I had expected more.

"I've got a problem."

"The same one?"

"I think I'm being shafted. Cici said you might be able to help."

"If I can. You want to come over?"

I swallowed hard. "Why don't I tell you about it over the phone?"

She laughed without bitterness or great mirth. "Suit yourself."

I began, running down my adventures from start to present. "They had a battery of lawyers up against me," I ended finally.

"Those dirty motherfuckers."

"I was frightened."

"Well, sure you were. Come on over and tell Mae-Mae all about it."

"There's nothing much more to tell."

"We'll review the entire experience. I'm sure I can help. Can you be here in fifteen minutes?"

"Isn't there anything I can do?"

She sighed in resignation. "What does your lawyer say?"

A vision of good ole Bubba drifted into view. He was naked except for tooled boots and a guitar. He was grinning, plucking and singing:

> Roses love sunshine,
> The violets love dew,
> Angels in heaven,
> Know I love you.

"Ah," I said. "I don't really have a lawyer."

"Oh, wow, still no lawyer. Christ on a stick, don't you see how dumb that is? The sonsofbitches will cut your tits off. You've got to get a lawyer."

"How?"

"How? Don't you worry about how. Mae-Mae has the answer to that. Now you just put that pretty little backside of yours into a taxi and when you get here I'll answer all your questions."

"Can't you put me in touch with somebody, Mae?"

"When you get here . . ."

I sighed. "Now . . . please?"

She sighed. "You don't know what you're missing." Her voice grew sprightly and full of familiar drive again. "Okay, what you need is feminist representation. Women who understand women's problems and are strong and ready to fight. Unfortunately that brings us around to a man. Harry Ellenbogen."

"Harry Ellenbogen. I read his book, some of it, anyway."

"Then you realize that he's the ultimate lay authority on Title Seven."

"Title Seven again."

"That's where it's at for you. Talk to Harry. But keep your pants on. He is the worst kind of male chauvinist. I'll give you his number."

I blamed Bubba Horn for much of my trouble. He steered me wrong. And never explained Title VII. I hoped he would lose every case he ever tried. And the water should dry up on Jimmy Guy's farm. The cows should give no more milk, the chickens no more eggs, and all the roosters turn queer.

Why not give Harry Ellenbogen a chance? I called, told him who I was. He didn't remember me at all. I mentioned that we had met at Cici's party. He said, "Who's Cici?" I said I had bought his book.

"Another buck-eighty," he cooed happily. "Just went into its fourth printing. Forty-one thousand copies out. There's talk of a paperback sale and I'm going to do a sequel. What did you say your name was?"

I told him.

"Are you good-looking?"

What did that have to do with my case?

"Pretty women turn me on. I like to look at them, for starters."

"Mae Ives warned me about you."

"Mae Ives, the dyke? Don't tell me you're one of those lesbo freaks. You sound normal."

"I'm a happily married woman," I lied.

"That's a contradiction in terms. Mae told you to call me?"

"Yes."

"Okay, maybe I can work you into my schedule. Next Tuesday okay with you?"

I said Tuesday was perfect. With Bubba on the road, I had nothing better to do with my lunchtimes than eat lunch.

"We go dutch," Ellenbogen said just before he hung up.

"I remember you," Ellenbogen said when he saw me. "We met at Cici's party." He was grinning broadly when he said it.

"I never saw you before in my life," I answered.

"Smartass," he growled. "It don't matter. It's good for me to be around a pretty girl even if it's hard for girls to get around me."

He was a big man with a barrel chest and an even larger belly. He lifted his chin and squinted, as if to see better through those thick glasses.

"Don't belittle yourself." Look who was giving advice.

"I'm not one of those skinny types with no waist and no hips."

"You're not so big."

"You see this body—when I go somewhere I'd like to leave it behind." He began to laugh, a series of truncated gasps, a wheeze or two, as if the effort pained him.

We were drinking Scotch in Charley O's, waiting for lunch to be served. "Mae says you're an expert on Title Seven?"

He shrugged the compliment away. Or perhaps accepted it as his due. "That Mae, would you believe I made a pass at her? How was I to know she wasn't normal? I guess I'm not so up-to-date. To my way of thinking, boys should do it to girls and turnabout's fair play. Not that Mae's bad-looking, she ain't. Also, she had a terrific behind. I have this thing about behinds. My shrink tells me it has to do with my mother. It seems to me everything has to do with my mother."

"My mother died recently . . ." Now why did I have to tell him that?

"Ah, so." He did a bad imitation of a Chinaman. "Alive or dead, they never let go, if you know what I mean." He produced that toothy grin. "What's your way of thinking about boys and girls doing it to each other?"

"It's all right with me."

"I think you're putting me on. That's okay. Maybe I'm not beautiful, but I'm sincere. You mustn't get the idea that I'm trying to get you into bed, or anything like that."

"Nothing like that."

"I mean suppose I was and you said yes and we did. Oh, would that give me a heartburn! I'm practically impotent . . ."

Like a fool, I responded. "Practically?"

"I can only do it with a good-looking woman, which you happen to be." He howled happily, tears running from under those thick glasses. Chest heaving, he gradually brought himself to a halt. "You look worried."

"I am worried, about you, Harry."

"Don't worry. I'm harmless."

"That's the worst kind."

That set him off again and this time he removed his glasses in an attempt to keep them dry. After a while he put them back on and searched the restaurant, finally locating me across a table. "Ah, I know your kind," he said. "You wouldn't want to make it with me anyway."

"I won't deny it."

His face dripped and dropped like melting wax. "I'm not pretty enough for you . . ."

"It's not that."

He perked up. "What then? There's lots of things a determined man can do to change."

"You have a very fine technique. It's hard not to respond."

"Ah-hah, I'm getting to you." He took my hand.

I took it back. Mae was right, he was a male chauvinist, but with an undeniably winning quality. I decided that I liked the way he smiled.

He smiled. "I'm not so sure that I'd want to make it with you . . ."

"No comment, Ellenbogen."

"I haven't even had one good look at your behind yet."

I kept myself firmly fastened to my chair. "Ellenbogen, what about Title Seven?"

"Listen, I can talk about what I want, I'm taking you to lunch."

"You said dutch."

"It's my treat."

He had a way of keeping you off balance, of making you laugh and wonder at the same time. I concluded that he meant everything he said seriously, but not entirely. "You," I said, "are a very tricky man."

"Title Seven," he said in answer. "The Civil Rights Act, 1964. No job discrimination because of religion, race, national origin or sex. Title Seven, the law of the land. That's what you use to get them into court . . ."

"Court!"

"Of course court. When your suit comes up."

"Suit! What suit?"

"You've got to sue them."

I turned icy in a flat second and a half. I rocked back and forth in place, trying to warm up, clenching my thighs in a vain attempt to keep out the cold. Not even a long pull on my drink helped.

"I never sued anybody in my life."

"You hit 'em with Title Seven." He cocked his massive head to one side. "That's if you believe you've got a case."

All of a sudden, no more jokes. No more self-effacement. The Ellenbogen who confronted me now was all business, eyes flat and hard behind those thick glasses, his jaw aggressively angled, a man looking for a fight. But it was my fight.

"I think I've got a case."

"You filed a complaint?"

"The Human Rights Commission found against me. What do I do?"

"Do? You get a lawyer is what you do. A good one."

"Can you recommend somebody?"

"That's what Lonnie does, Lonnie Frieman. Specialization, you know. Lonnie teaches law up at Columbia. Call him, he'll put you onto some legal eagle."

After lunch—he picked up the check—we shook hands on the sidewalk in front of Charley O's. "Thanks for the lunch and the advice."

"My pleasure." He shuffled his feet, no longer aggressive or sure of himself. "Maybe I could call you. We could do it again."

"I told you, I'm married." But it was Bubba I was thinking about.

"Sometimes," he said with a sheepish grin, "it's better not to have been born at all."

Lonnie Frieman had never practiced law. But he taught it. He wrote about it for various law journals. He published books about the law. He dispensed legal advice.

"For a fee," he said without apology.

"This is a capitalistic society."

"If you think lawyers come free under Socialism you've got another think coming. All right. Tell me your troubles and I'll direct you to the correct path. Nobody can do the job better than Lonnie R. Frieman."

Once again I recited my tale of hope, disappointment and defeat. I was getting bored with the sound of my own voice.

"What," he said, when I completed the recital, "are you after?"

"What am I after?" That was the great enigma of my life. It jumped into view from time to time like a grinning jack-in-the-box, taunting me, the answer elusive. "At first, all I wanted was the job."

"But no more?"

"They won't let me have it."

"Given the creation of a suitable climate, companies have been known to change their minds. Sue the bastards, as the saying goes."

"That's what Harry says."

"Ellenbogen is pretty hip, for a layman." He wrote

on a piece of notepaper, handed it over. "Christopher Mallory is the man for you. See him. He's good at what he does and should be able to help. Fifty dollars, please."

A look of sneaky pleasure came onto his face. "Cash, if you can swing it. I'm in a running battle with the IRS. The bastards will tax you out of existence if you give them half a chance."

That night I found Walter curled up behind something entitled *People of Paradox; An Inquiry Concerning the Origin of American Civilization.* I was impressed and said so. Walter grumped an unintelligible answer, annoyed at the interruption.

"I talked to a lawyer," I began.

"What for?"

"It cost me fifty dollars."

He put the book down carefully. It was heavy in more than one way. "Fifty dollars." Now it was Walter's turn to be impressed.

"Walter, up to now it's been sort of a game. But lawyers cost money."

"Lots of money."

"Exactly."

"You think you need a lawyer?"

"Everybody says so."

"I'm sure IFP has a lawyer."

"A small army of them."

"There you are."

"Some people think I should sue the company."

"What for?"

"Back pay at least."

"And you want to do that?"

"I don't know what I want to do."

"You have to be sure."

"That's what the lawyer said. How do I get sure? I thought it was going to be easy, just make a complaint. It keeps dragging along. I've been thinking, Walter, about giving it up."

"They treated you badly."

"I'm not sure I mind anymore."

"I do, I mind. People have no right to treat other people badly."

"You think I ought to go on with this?"

"That's what I think."

"It means hiring a lawyer."

"Then hire one."

"They cost money."

"We're both working now. We can afford to invest a few dollars."

For a beat or two, I believed it meant more to him that I win this small war than it did to me. But then I realized how very important it was to me, perhaps the most important event of my life.

"If you say so, Walter, I'll do it."

"Do it, Libby."

"Fight them all the way? No matter what?"

"No matter what."

"I'll do it."

Walter smiled briefly and went back to *People of Paradox*. As far as he was concerned, it was an accomplished fact. All done. The winner and new champion! . . .

Christopher Mallory was a pleasantly upholstered man in his middle years. He wore a Hopi silver ring and a watch by Piaget. Everything about him was expensive. He rested his chin on the tip of his forefinger and listened to my story.

When I finished, he fingered a Tiffany pen, sheathed in gold. "You want the job?"

"I've got a job."

"You don't want the job?"

"I'm confused."

"Make up your mind, Mrs. Pepper. What are we going after?"

"Yes, it's so hard. Yes, to hell with the job. If they don't want me, I don't want them. Do you think I could get some back salary?"

"How much is involved?"

"Seventeen thousand five hundred was the annual pay."

"That seems within reach. Add costs to that. Legal fees, secretarial services, stationery, stamps, phone calls, transportation. Say in round figures, twenty-five thousand."

"Dollars?"

"Exactly."

"They'll give me that much?"

"Not without a fight."

"Will you represent me, Mr. Mallory?"

He leaned back. "Mrs. Pepper, that's Title Seven."

"I know, I know."

"Just a hair off my normal course."

"Mr. Frieman said . . ."

"Lonnie had his thoughts twisted on this one. Ken Trumpy is the man for you. Right up his alley. You'll get my bill in the mail."

I made an appointment with Ken Trumpy. "Yes," he drawled, "I'm conversant with Title Seven. However you've come at a particularly bad time. My docket's overloaded. Postponements, appeals, so much going on. If you can wait? . . ."

"How long?"

"Oh, you don't want to wait *that* long. Let me put you in contact with someone quite good. Almost the best, I'd say. Louella Cobb is for you. Former Secretary of State of New York State. Former member of the City Council. Former State Representative. Former Assistant Secretary of HEW. Urban League. Executive Board of SANE. VP League of Women Voters. You get the idea."

"PTA?" I said hopefully.

Not even a chuckle. "You and Lolly will hit it off perfectly."

I located Cobb, Mishkin & Nolan on Forty-fourth Street, in a prestigious old building within eyeshot of the Harvard Club and across from *The New Yorker*

Magazine. Gave you a sense of being into something
solid and permanent. Although in New York, any
structure older than twenty years is considered fair
game for the wrecker's ball.

The reception room had French antiques, paneled
walls and no magazines at all. Cobb, Mishkin & Nolan
obviously intended for the individual to develop an
interior existence, at least for a little while.

Louella Cobb's office was richly upholstered in
damask and silk, comfortable and relaxing. She
matched the decor. A plump and solicitous woman of
forty or so with lively intelligent eyes. She encouraged
me to talk, nodding, smiling, saying nothing until I was
finished.

"You seem to have a very good case."

I was immediately cheered.

"The record will undoubtedly show that IFP discriminated against you in clear contravention of the
law. International Food Products, my goodness. All
their business—foodstuffs—is with women. Can they
afford to risk being branded antiwoman? I think not."

"Yet they didn't hire me."

"They hardly expected you to make a cause célèbre.
There is a psychology to all this, the inherent willing-
ness of the ordinary citizen to roll over and play dead
whenever brought into conflict with a large institution.
Cobb, Mishkin & Nolan is one of the two women's law
firms currently handling this kind of litigation. Yes, my
dear, you certainly do have a case."

I almost clapped my hands in joy. "Will you represent me?"

"Did I give that impression? I hope not. We are too
buried in work at this point. Postponements, appeals,
court appearances . . ." She sounded exactly like Ken
Trumpy.

"However, we could take up your situation at a later
date."

"How late?"

"Nine months. Maybe a year."

"I don't think I want to wait."

"Of course you don't. You've waited long enough. You're entitled to justice swiftly. You need action now and I know exactly where you can get it. Hester Trippi . . ."

twenty-nine

It was a long way from the Harvard Club to the blackened old factories of Soho. The street was coated with grime and neglect, the building looking weary and trimmed with nineteenth-century ironwork. Two art galleries were in the street, a health food cafeteria, an auto supply shop and a store that had used military clothing for sale.

I found Number 10 in the middle of the block. The elevator was out of order so I climbed squeaky stairs past graffiti-decorated walls:

> Kill Nixon.
> Free the Attica Seven.
> Che Lives.
> Rockefeller Sucks.
> Grass is Good.
> God is Good.
> God is Good Grass.

On the third-floor landing, a massive metal door the color of ripe cherries. I buckled up my chinstrap, as Bubba would say, and went inside.

A huge space greeted me, running the length of the old building, the ceiling nearly twenty feet high. Pipes of various sizes were brightly painted and made geometric patterns against the white brick walls. Posters insisting on Social Justice, Revolution and Repeal of All Drug Laws were everywhere. One area was masked off by shelves filled with law books.

I found Hester Trippi, long, bony, with frizzy orange hair, sprawled out in a Mexican hammock at the rear of the loft. She was listening to rock 'n' roll on a Zenith Trans-Oceanic and sucking on a joint.

"I'm Libby Pepper."

She offered me a drag.

"No, thanks."

"Cobb filled me in on the phone." She sat up and turned the radio off. "My opinion—they shoved it into you, long and deep."

I agreed.

"You have a very strong case."

"Everyone says so. Does that mean you will take my case? Or are you too busy?"

"You don't know me. I don't know you. Client and lawyer should get acquainted before they team up. It's an intimate relationship, like taking on a new lover, you see what I mean. The point is I want you to be sure you want me."

"I understand."

"Here it is, then. Lucille Goodheart, Fran Bacon and me. At NYU Law, we hit it off right away. A year and a half ago we established this firm. Let's get Lucille and Fran in here." She yelled out their names and soon two young women in overalls and T-shirts appeared. They stared at me while Hester explained why I was there.

"Chauvinist pigs," Fran Bacon growled.

"Fascist bastards," Lucille Goodheart snapped.

"The case is there," Hester said.

"Does that mean you'll take it?" I was weary of rejection.

"Let's rap first." Hester dismissed her colleagues. When we were alone, she looked me over carefully. "We are feminists. One of two feminist law firms operating in this city. We are for women's rights, and privileges. We function within an unyielding philosophical framework, rigorously applied. We stand on principle. We gut it out, down the line. My father was Louis Trippi; you've heard of him?"

I said I wasn't very good with names.

She shook her head in disbelief. "Louis Trippi was one of the best radical lawyers going down. He's the one got the Wichita Sixteen off with life sentences."

I nodded with false enthusiasm. Life in prison; I was not encouraged.

"There's tradition in this office," she said. "Profound, religious beliefs. In a secular sense, that is. We are deeply involved in the Marxist-Leninist struggle and are strongly opposed to feudalism, capitalism, imperialism. Every act taken here is in behalf of the workers against the propertied classes, you dig what I'm saying to you?"

"Oh," I said quickly, "yes."

"We are revolutionaries. Committed to the overthrow of the current order. We make the fight wherever we can. The battlefield extends coast to coast, border to border, around the world. We are in sisterhood with all those who stand up to the oppressors, wherever they may be. Your case is from certain perspectives ideal for our skills, our aims, short-term and long-term. You want us to handle it?"

I was desperate. "Oh yes."

"Okay, you're on. See it through to the end, wherever it may lead. Hit the mothers where they live. Grind their slimy faces into the dirt. Make 'em pay."

Sounded good to me, and I said so.

She offered me her hand. "We're in this together." We shook. She had a grip like a wrestler. "Let's put it all on the table."

"I'd like that." I had no idea what she meant.

"Money," she said, making it a curse. "Shekels. Gelt. Pesos. How much you after?"

"I was thinking about a year's back pay." From the

expression on her face, I could tell I was a disappointment to Hester. I tried to make up lost ground. "Plus expenses?"

"Oh, baby, baby, baby. You get into a fight you go for the jugular. Kill or be killed. It's all the way or no way at all." She tapped her nose with one finger. "By the time we wind things up, two years will have passed from the date of your first interview. Two years' salary alone comes to thirty-five thousand. Add costs, damages, emotional injury and we begin to get into some pretty impressive numbers. What about a shrink?"

I went hot and cold. "Well—"

"Ah." She almost rubbed her hands together. "Psychological harm can be incalculable, not to mention the extravagant prices those lice charge."

"Xavier extends credit."

If she heard, she gave no sign. "Okay, here's the way it is. My addition brings it up to a quarter of a million."

"Dollars!"

"What we do is hit 'em with a half-million-buck suit."

I began to cough.

"You're right," she said. "To ask for too little is a sign of weakness. Let's sock it to 'em—we go for a full million. It has a nice ring to it."

"I was thinking about twenty-five thousand."

She gazed at a poster of Mao on the far wall.

"Fifty?" I said tentatively.

She displayed her fist. I flinched. "Never show uncertainty, Libby. You'll get chopped up. Paid thugs are out there waiting to do you damage. Economic commandos. Hit them first, or they'll hit you."

"All those big numbers . . ."

"Hang tough, lady."

I slumped in my chair. Hester took it for assent. I intended it to be resignation.

"Now here's my strategy. We make it a class action. Demand double the final settlement, to be put into a special fund and distributed to other sisters those bastards have dumped on."

"Is that usual?"

"It's the only way to go. You and me, Libby. We are going to damage those fuckheads. Crack their financial skulls. Bloody their piggish noses and pick their pockets at the same time. One thing you should know, court costs will be your responsibility. You'll have to ante up about twelve hundred. Think you can do it?"

"Oh."

"And five hundred more as a retainer."

"Oh."

She patted me on the back. "After we win, a few hundred bucks will seem like birdfeed."

My head was spinning when I left the office, all circuits sputtering. Nothing made much sense to me.

Along Lafayette Street I went, hunting for a subway station. A man in a doorway clutched his penis in one hand as he slept. Garbage littered the sidewalk. Three men and a woman warmed themselves at a fire in a trash basket, passing a pint of whiskey in a brown paper bag. One of the men muttered something as I passed and I increased my pace, afraid he might follow.

In New York to be paranoid is not a disease, it's an early warning system. I glanced back and, sure enough, there he was, shuffling after me, grinning in anticipation. I looked around for a cop; would I never lose my innocence?

I spotted the subway kiosk ahead and went faster. He was closing in. That was the way they worked, those sickies, isolating a defenseless woman on a deserted subway platform and before you knew it—raped, robbed and dumped on the tracks to die under an onrushing A train.

I ducked into the subway, fishing a token out of my purse. Always prepared, that's me. I hurried to the far end of the platform. Behind me footsteps coming fast.

I took up a position near the flight of stairs. A train thundered into the station across the way, going downtown. Up the steps I went, down the other side. I hurled myself into the train just before the doors closed. The train started to move and I searched the platform for my would-be assailant. He was nowhere in sight.

But what did that prove?

thirty

I was listening to Micha Elman on the stereo when tears began to flow. Why did I weep? For whom? For the disappointed and disappointing Second Fiddler, my father? For Sybil, who never got what she wanted, either? For myself?

I wiped away the tears and vowed to put all that behind me. I intended to go after what I wanted. To get it. All of it. Everything.

I went to Walter and told him I'd hired a lawyer.

"That's a very good idea," he said in measured tones.

"It's going to cost a good deal of money."

"More than fifty dollars?"

"Much more." I told him how much.

He showed no surprise. "In that case, we'd better get the money."

"Where?"

He thought it over. "I'll borrow on my life insurance."

That troubled me and I said so.

He shrugged my doubts away. "What you're doing, it's right. It should be done."

"What if I lose the case?"

"The odds are pretty good that you'll win. Let's take the chance."

"Well," Hester said, when I handed over the retainer,

showing all the enthusiasm of a bourgeois shopkeeper, "we are in business."

Hester bothered me. She spoke continually in the terms of the marketplace. She should have waved the red flag, threatened the system, summoned the Red Army band. She didn't seem to realize we were going up against Corporate Duplicity, Processed Foods and the Military-Industrial Complex. I put it down to bad habits learned early and never completely discarded.

"When do we go to trial?" I asked.

"These things take time."

"What can I do?"

"You? You just wait."

Sit around and wait. Hester would take care of everything. Once I would have been overjoyed, content to place my fate in someone else's strong hands. No more. I grew skittish and unable to sleep well. I dreamed I was Joan of Arc at the Trial of the Century, symbol of oppressed women everywhere. It was terrific, until the burning part.

I went through the motions. I spent time with Stevie. Kept the apartment on an even keel. Made occasional, if futile, attempts to engage Walter in conversation. I did my job. And as soon as Bubba arrived back from New Mexico, I invited myself to his place.

He greeted me with easy country-boy grace. "Jesus, I'm horny. Let's fuck." He began to unbutton my shirt.

"I have to talk to you," I said.

He squeezed one breast and licked the other. "Let it all hang out," he muttered, trying to unzip his pants and work off my skirt at the same time.

I told him about Hester, about the suit she had filed on my behalf.

I took the skirt off while he got out of his jeans. He maneuvered me onto the couch, rubbing, squeezing, pinching.

"That hurts," I complained.

"Off with those panties. I mean to inflict myself on your ever-lovin' body."

"Let's talk first."

He dragged my panties down, cast them aside. "You talk, I'll listen." He put his face between my thighs, muttering about how long it had been.

I gave him time to get adjusted. It became difficult to collect my thoughts. "I'm afraid of what may happen, Bubba."

"Happen?" He looked up, blinking. "Oh, the case. Nothin's goin' to happen. You are the suer, not the suee." He went back to his task.

Ripples of sensation ran into my belly. I shivered and moved to accommodate Bubba; position, angle of adjustment, the correct muscular play. There was so much to think about.

"What," I said, after a certain amount of time had passed, "if the company sues back?"

He never missed a beat. "Never happen."

I studied the top of his head. Busy as he was, ole Bubba was fixed in place. "I would have to say you enjoy what you're up to, Bubba."

"There is nothin' finer in the entire world than a juicy hairy box and you have one of the best."

"Could you possibly cut down on the drooling a little, Bubba? I'm getting a chill."

"Never any complaints up to now."

"Don't tell me about any other women, Bubba."

"No need to be testy. Just give yourself over and enjoy, Miss Libby. You sure do have a unique taste."

"Stop calling me that. It's the vinegar."

That brought his head up. "Vinegar?"

"Vinegar douches."

He shook his head in admiration. "Damn me, ain't that cunnin' of you."

"I'm afraid IFP will find some way of screwing me yet," I said.

"Trust your lawyer."

It seemed to me that all Bubba's advice was bad. "You may as well resume your efforts on my behalf, Bubba."

He glanced down at himself. "It appears I have lost

my manliness, temporarily, of course." It was true. He looked just like Walter felt in the dark, wrinkly and soft, small and cuddly. "Anythin' you can do to help?" he suggested.

"Why not?" I felt no enthusiasm for the task, to my surprise. I decided that I no longer liked Bubba as much as I used to. The Singing Cowboy sounded slightly discordant to me these days. If only Walter would learn some of Bubba's moves, it would make me a lot more tranquil around the house. Not that I expected Walter ever to get into Bubba's league. Which was okay. After all, you needn't be a champion in order to be a winner.

thirty-one

On the same morning that Pearl Combs, my housekeeper, failed to show up for work, Douglas Griffin called. With Pearl not on the scene—she was ordinarily quite punctual—and me unable to leave for the agency, my normal nervous-quotient rose precipitously. I entertained all the awful and colorful possibilities that might have befallen Pearl, striking her down in our glamorous city streets. Further, I envisioned myself being fired by Beth Dooley for my own tardiness. Confidence was not yet my strong point.

The phone rang and I ran to answer. Certainly this would be Pearl. Some minor mishap had detained her and now she was on her way. Not to worry, Mrs. Pepper. Pearl was a good person, concerned, considerate, fond of me and my family, sensitive to our needs and committed to spending the remainder of her working life in our employ. Good ole Pearl.

"Pearl," I screeched into the phone, "are you all right?" I was alarmingly close to the borderline of hysteria.

A man's voice answered. "I'm calling the Pepper household."

"What?"

"Is this—?"

"Yes, yes. Who are you?"

255

"Douglas Griffin."

"I don't know anybody by that name."

"We've never met."

"I don't want to buy anything."

"I'm not selling . . ."

"No magazines, freezer supplies, encyclopedias, cosmetics, nothing. You understand." I started to hang up.

"EEOC," he said.

"How much do I win if I guess what you're talking about? Give me one more hint."

"You don't understand, Mrs. Pepper. Equal Employment Opportunity Commission. From Washington. District of Columbia, you know. You lodged a complaint."

"My God, that was nearly a year ago."

"The wheels of justice grind slowly, but oh, do they grind. Sometimes. Ten months, if you want to be exact. When can I talk to you?"

"Go ahead, talk."

"I mean in person."

"You want to see me?"

"May I come over to your apartment?"

"Now?"

"I can be there in less than an hour."

"But why?"

"I have to get your side of the dispute. Firsthand."

"Half the city knows about me. I've spread the story around indiscriminately. Ask anybody you meet."

"One more time."

If Pearl didn't show up there would be shopping to do, beds to make, vacuuming, Walter's shirts to the Chinese laundry, his shoes to the Italian shoemaker, his suit to the Jewish tailor. My life was becoming a journey into ethnicity.

"I don't know," I said with more certainty than I felt.

"Pretty please."

"Twenty minutes."

"Make it thirty. See you."

I ran from room to room straightening up, kicking Stevie's toys under the beds, couches, into dark corners. I ran a comb through my hair with no discernible results. I made coffee and sat down to wait, mourning poor Pearl's demise. I could visualize her pathetic body battered and bleeding thanks to those human animals loose in the streets. The phone rang. It had to be Pearl.

It was Beth Dooley. "I was worried when you didn't show up."

Oh, my God! I'd forgotten to call. I apologized, a number of times.

"Is something wrong, Libby?"

I explained the situation.

She hesitated and in that brief, terrible millisecond of time the icy clutch of impending disaster set off alarms in my nervous system. Before I could beg her indulgence, plead for a second chance, swear never to let it happen again, she spoke.

"The agency is expanding, Libby, as you know."

I vaguely recalled some mention of it being made.

"They offered me the new office to manage."

"Congratulations," I said automatically, but I was desolated by the news. A new boss would surely disapprove of me and my work, would want to bring in his own people. I was going to be fired. Better quit first and avoid the agony of waiting, avoid the humiliation. Was I losing my mind? Why was I so frightened of losing a job I didn't particularly like or want? What was wrong with me? Make up your own list.

"How," Beth Dooley said with unnerving calmness, "would you like to have my desk?"

I had to struggle not to make a bad joke. "What do you mean?"

"The powers that be want you to take over this office. It means a raise in salary and a percentage of the commissions. Believe me, it's a very nice arrangement."

"I believe you."

"Don't give me an answer now. Think about it."

"I will. I'll think about it."

"When you make up your mind, let me know."

"Yes, I'll let you know." There was an echo on the line, and I was it. I was flattered by the offer, and scared witless. Life was piling up around me like a heap of garbage. Did I want the responsibility of running the agency? Of hiring and firing, of all the paperwork, of ordering people about? What did I want?

Pearl. I wanted Pearl to come walking in the door and take over. First things first. I located Pearl's home phone number and dialed. A man answered.

"May I speak to Pearl Combs, please."

"Who's this?"

"Is this Mr. Combs?"

"Why you want to know?"

I didn't seem to be making much progress. "I'm Libby Pepper. Pearl's been working for me, for us, for a few weeks, nearly two months. She didn't show up this morning and I'm worried . . ."

"Ah, yes. This is Pearl's husband. Pearl . . . she's hurtin'."

I knew it! "What happened?"

"Pearl . . . she's in the hospital."

"Oh, my God!"

"Well, you know how the streets can be. Bad places. Last night, Pearl, she went off visitin' a friend o' hers and she comin' home, mindin' her own business, and some bad dudes climbed up one side o' Pearl and down the other."

A groan dribbled out of me. "She was attacked."

"That's it, attacked."

"Mugged."

"That's it, mugged."

"Was she . . . did they . . . rape? . . ."

He made a choking sound. "Ain't no set o' street cats about to do that to my Pearl lessen they mean to come up against me too."

"Then she's all right?"

"No, Pearl ain't all right. I mean, attacked and mugged. She can't be all right."

"What do the doctors say?"

"You know how doctors talk."

Boy, did I know. "She's going to . . . she's not going to . . . she'll survive?"

"Oh, Pearl's got a few good years left in her. Only she ain't never goin' to be the same, not the old Pearl."

"When can I see her?"

"Oh, not for a long time, the doctor say."

A long time? What did he mean by that? I didn't have a long time.

"Pearl," he went on, "she goin' to make it okay. It just take time."

Time, again. The apartment needed cleaning, the linen, the dinner. My stomach clenched and I thought about throwing up. "You figure Pearl will be back at work by the end of the week?"

"I don't reckon so."

"Next week?"

"More like six months, maybe a year."

Poor woman, I thought. Me, that is. What was I going to do? Stricken by my own selfishness, I again offered to visit Pearl. "I'll bring her some flowers, candy, something to read."

"Oh, Pearl, she don't read much."

"What's the name of the hospital?"

"Can't seem to recollect."

Harlem, it had to be Harlem Hospital. "Harlem?"

"Yeah, but you ain't gonna get to see her. She in that part where they keep the badly wounded peoples . . ."

"Intensive care?"

"That's the one."

"Poor Pearl."

"Yeah, poor Pearl."

I was about to call Harlem Hospital when the doorbell rang. I peeked through the judas-hole and saw a pale, shifty-eyed visage turned my way. With those gray sunken cheeks, that stringy, ratty-colored hair, and no tie, he had to be a dope fiend. If only I had a team of killer Dobermans.

"Go away," I snarled through the door.

"Mrs. Pepper? It's Douglas Griffin."

"The name means nothing to me."

"EEOC."

Oh, *that* Douglas Griffin. I took another peek. "You don't look like a government man to me." They all wore double-breasted suits and cut their hair close.

"I am. I am."

"Prove it."

He flashed a card. "My I.D."

"Slide it under the door."

"Mrs. Pepper, come on . . ."

"And no fancy tricks."

The card came under. There was a photograph on it. "Your hair's too long."

"Next time I'll get a trim. Listen, we're wasting time. I've got other appointments."

"Let's have your driver's license."

He groaned, but sent it along. I compared the signatures on the two cards. "All right," I said, "but be warned. I've got a highly trained guard dog in here. A massive Doberman. One word from me and he'll tear you apart."

"Whatever you say, Mrs. Pepper."

I let him in and he glanced around warily. "Where's the dog?"

"Back there." I made a purposely vague gesture. "All I do is say the secret word and you are his for lunch. Into the living room and no fast moves."

He sat on the couch and looked me over while I looked him over. I was not impressed.

"You don't look like Civil Service to me."

He produced a sneaky smile. "You don't look the way I anticipated you would, either. It's a game I play, trying to visualize what complainants look like. By the sound of them over the phone. By the material in the file."

The *file.* That meant the FBI. Did that mean they knew all about me and Bubba? What we did to each other? By now they probably had movies of us in action. In living color and stereophonic sound. What if they went into general release? Libby Pepper, Porn Queen of West Sixty-ninth Street, Central Park and the grind houses on Eighth Avenue.

"By what right do you have a file on a native-born private citizen with no previous criminal record?"

"I thought you were born in Poland." He checked his notebook.

"Just testing. You're very alert."

"I see." He moved his eyes this way and that, as if searching for something. The dog had him worried; good. "Tell me everything, Mrs. Pepper, right from the beginning."

Once more into the breach. "What do you think?" I said when I finished.

"That's some story."

"What happens now?"

He did a bad imitation of Bogart. "Don' worry about a t'ing, lady, the Feds are here." He laughed, I didn't. "Okay." Suddenly he was all business. "We make a thorough search. Talk to everybody connected with the case. We subpoena all pertinent records. We weigh the information we receive . . ."

"And?"

"And if it's decided you have a justifiable complaint . . ." He stood up.

"What are you doing?" I almost shouted, backing away.

"Just getting ready to leave is all."

"I have a good mind to sic the Doberman on you." The *Doberman*. There was no Doberman. I really was demented.

He hurried to the door. "Please, don't do that." He glanced back. "Federal involvement in these affairs usually results in a great deal of pressure being brought to bear on the company. You may very well see a change in IFP's attitude, Mrs. Pepper."

After he left, I locked, bolted and chained in a hurry. Only then did I remember Pearl, and I went to the phone and called Harlem Hospital. An uninterested voice said that nobody by that name had been admitted that day.

"Try yesterday."

"Not yesterday, either. The name's not on my list."

"Maybe she died?"

She ran a check. "No, no deaths under that listing."

Something was seriously wrong. Mr. Combs had said Harlem Hospital. Had he made a mistake? That wasn't possible. Then what? At once the truth came rushing at me like a runaway locomotive. Mr. Combs had done something terrible to Pearl, my Pearl. Beaten her to death, probably. Yes. Such cases were common in Fun City. He had murdered poor Pearl, the best housekeeper I ever had. I held my face in my hands and wondered where I'd ever find another one like her.

I swore to avenge Pearl's death. But how? Cool and efficient thinking was in order, as well as some help from somebody who knew what he was doing. Someone like Paul Newman or Robert Redford. Since neither of them was handy, I tried Bubba Horn.

"Libby, I'm glad you called. Busy, busy day. I'm goin' to have to cancel out on lunch."

We were scheduled to meet at his apartment. "Lunch," he called it. We confined our eating to each other; I'd lost four pounds in the last couple of weeks. I told him about Pearl. "Her husband's killed her."

"If you really believe that, call the cops."

"Don't you know somebody?" I wasn't ready to unleash the minions of the law; I didn't want to interfere with their coffee breaks.

"There is somebody. A friend of mine is a detective. Let me get back to you."

I stayed close to the telephone and ten minutes later it rang. It was a detective named Johnson who wanted to talk about Pearl.

"You have reason to think she's been done away with?"

"Yes, sir." I told him everything I knew.

"Housekeepers sometimes do that, lady."

"Get murdered, you mean?"

"Not show up for work. No warning, no explanation, no nothing."

"Not my Pearl."

"Well, we can look into it for you. I'll let you know what we find."

The next morning Detective Johnson called back. "About Pearl Combs, Mrs. Pepper. She's okay."

My heart was pounding away. "How can that be?"

"She just didn't want the job anymore."

"Why? Why?"

"Who knows with these people? It happens a lot. She just decided to split."

"You mean it was all a fiction, what her husband told me?"

"Just a lot of—a fiction, yeah."

"Not mugged? No hospital?"

"You got it."

Oh, that hurt. Pearl turning her back on us. On me. Another rejection.

I spent the rest of the week looking for a satisfactory replacement and came up empty. On Friday I told Beth Dooley that I was leaving the agency. Not only was I giving up the job, I was losing the promotion. When I thought about it later that night, I discovered that I wasn't as disturbed as I expected to be. In fact, I rather enjoyed my new-found freedom.

Especially when I came up with this truly super idea . . .

thirty-two

Had I been religious I would have gone to services on
Friday night. But my faith had been constricted, de-
preciated in value by encounters with such as Rabbi
Basketball, the meaningful edges dulled by a lifetime
of temporal Red, White and Blue. I had been con-
verted into a one-hundred-carat Columbia-the-Gem
American, prayerful only for profit, glory and sex.
For such a Jew there's nothing to do on a Friday
night except go to Group Therapy.

The Family welcomed me according to the gospel
of St. Xavier out of S. Freud by C. G. Jung. No
recriminations for missing so many sessions. No resentment at my solo flights into the wide, wide world,
without prior consultation. No initial nastiness.

I had told my idea to Kiernan at my last session
with him. I should have known better. He was a man
without a twinkle in his heart or his hard eyes. There
was no time in his life for humor or laughter, no need
for compassion, convinced as he was of the inviolabil-
ity of his most ephemeral thought. He was a tricky
bastard.

"Libby," he began, in that cool Jesuitical style he'd
developed, "has reached an important decision." All
eyes moved around to me as if I'd committed some
awful social gaffe and now would inevitably repeat it.

I clicked my teeth in despair and they all took it to be a cheerful grin. "Libby," Xavier said, "is about to bring off a major alteration in her life."

"You quit on the lawsuit," Rodrigo said gleefully. "You never did have the belly to go all the way."

Mabel smacked her lips juicily. "You dumped the Lone Star Stud." I was convinced Mabel's clit twitched whenever I mentioned Bubba.

"Nah," Helene, the whore, added. "She's getting rid of the Bookworm."

"Now, now," Xavier murmured, hands folded piously across his belly. "No name-calling. Libby's husband is Walter and so we will refer to him at all times."

"I," I said more aggressively than intended, "am going into business for myself."

A silent period followed, while they digested what I'd told them. Then came considerable hooting and hollering, stamping of feet. A few catcalls.

Frank Rivers punched the air vigorously, as if I'd just scored the winning touchdown. "You can do it, Libby."

"Looka the lover," Rodrigo jeered. "Still thinks he can get it on with Libby."

"Knock it off, Rod," Rivers said.

Rodrigo leaned and made an obscene gesture. "Maybe I punch you out someday."

"Is that how it is, Frank?" Kiernan, from out of his Eames chair, said. "Are you sexually attracted to Libby?"

The possibility seemed to surprise him, as if no man would find me attractive. I almost said something nasty.

Rodrigo did. "Ah, go on, Libby, give the poor sucker a little stuff."

Carla spoke before I could. "I sincerely believe we should get back to Libby's business plans. That's where our priorities lie at the moment, it seems to me. I would like to add that I have been receiving unusually good vibes from Libby. Tonight Libby appears softer

and more accessible than in the past, if you understand what I'm getting at."

"Hold it right there," Rodrigo said. "What the hell,
Libby's givin' it to the farmer, right? All those matinees, right? Why not Rivers, too?"

"For all we know," Mabel the buyer put in, "Libby
could be sleeping with half a dozen men."

Kiernan's eyes were flat and lifeless behind his
glasses. "Are there other men, Libby?"

"My God!" I said. Yahweh, Jehovah, Lord of the
ancient Hebrews. And the Flies. Was I a believer after
all? I kept calling on Him in moments of stress, distress and general emotional disrepair. Somewhere in
one of those impassive, impressive synagogues, there
had to exist Rabbi Human Being, in touch with his
God, himself, with enough left over for the rest of us
poor, benighted souls. Something strange, I told myself, was going on.

"Well?" Seymour the TV-nik insisted.

"Well what?"

"Are there other men in your life besides Bubba
Horn?"

"Who's got the time?"

"Don't be flippant."

Duly chastised, I said, "Nobody. Not now."

"Ah-hah!" they cried collectively, poised to strike.

"Now!" Rodrigo crowed.

"I want the truth," Charley the cop grumped in
his best interrogating manner.

"How come you never told us about the others?"
Helene asked.

"We all love you," Carla said. "We all will understand."

Charley the cop fingered his gun. "How many
other times you cheat on your husband?"

"Never."

"Not even one little time?"

"Well . . ."

"You did cheat!"

"Who?" Seymour stammered. "Who, who, who with? Tell us who?"

"When did it happen, Libby?" Kiernan liked to keep events in order. His mind was an appointment calendar, leatherbound and engraved in gold.

"Tell us the truth."

"It was when I was pregnant . . ."

"Oh, Libby," Frank Rivers said, clearly disappointed in me.

"How revolting," Mabel said.

"You ever think of the kid?" Rodrigo said without his usual ferocity.

"Go on," Kiernan said.

The room grew quiet. "I knew this man and he'd been after me for a long time. I went to lunch with him occasionally and he'd try to seduce me, but it was all in good fun, we laughed about it. He kept trying and I kept saying no. Then I found out I was pregnant.

"After that, Walter wouldn't touch me. He had lots of reasons why and none of them made any sense to me, and I told him so. I told him the doctor said it was all right, but nothing made any difference. All those months, and he never came near me. Never put his hands on me. My breasts were swollen, they were beautiful, and my belly. He never touched my belly. All that time.

"Am I sick or something? I was so sexy while I was pregnant. I never wanted to make love to Walter as much as I did then. But he wouldn't.

"Alex. That was this man's name, Alex. He still kept after me. Said he wanted me more than ever. He never gave up trying until I stopped holding back. I went to his apartment and we did it.

"I needed a man to make love to me then. I wanted it. And Alex was good at it, almost as good as he thought he was. Alex said that any day that went by without having four or five orgasms was for him a wasted day. He could hardly think of anything else.

"He liked to do it in strange places. In different positions. But with my belly getting bigger, I couldn't do everything he wanted. But I would have if I could have. Then the baby came, and when the doctor said it was all right to do it, Walter made love to me again and that was the end of it with Alex. It was only sex, you see. Alex was the most impoverished man I ever knew."

As soon as I stopped, they moved in for the kill. Mabel got there first.

"What about Walter? What about his feelings?"

"Walter never knew about Alex."

"How could you do such a thing?" Helene the whore said, shaking her head. "With the baby in your belly. How can you justify what you did?"

"I'll tell you how," Seymour almost screamed. "She told herself her husband was fooling around, so it was okay to do it too."

"Is that it, Libby?" Kiernan was always there when you needed him. "Did you sleep with Alex because you thought Walter had a mistress? Was that your primary motivation?"

"No. I don't think so. He wouldn't make love to me. I was afraid and sexy, lonesome. Oh, I don't know, maybe it was that."

"Then Walter was unfaithful to you?"

"I don't know. I think so. I'm not sure."

"You should have said something to him."

"I did. I tried."

"You talked to him about fooling around?"

"I tried."

"What happened?"

"I tried to tell him about me and Alex. I thought he must feel rotten because he was probably out doing it with other women and not with his wife. I wanted him to feel better. Not guilty. Not ashamed. But Walter wouldn't talk about it. He put his book down and said, 'Not another word, you hear. Not another word.' He was very angry. Very quiet, low-keyed, but very angry. I'd never seen him like that and I was afraid.

So we never talked about it again. 'Let it alone,' he told me. And I did. From then on."

Carla, all sweetness and dripping encouragement, said, "The way things are, Libby, maybe you should ball Frank here. Frank's got a good head for business and if you're going to go into business for yourself, Frank can be a big help."

Somebody began to clap and the rest of them joined in. They were laughing at me. A good time was had by all.

But that's not why I was there. Not to entertain them. Not to pour out my deepest secrets and make myself naked before them so they could have fun.

I stood up. "You don't care about me. You're not concerned about me."

Xavier made a placating gesture. "Now, Libby . . ."

I waited for the tears to flow, but my eyes remained dry. There was a stillness inside me, lack of focus, everything a little blurred, as if I was seeing with a hooded eye.

"There's only cruelty in this room," I said.

Again that gesture, again Xavier said, "Now, Libby . . ." Was that the eternal answer to all questions, the solution to all problems?

I looked into those cold eyes. "There's got to be respect for people to leaven the pain you give out here. Something must be done to soften the blows, to dull the cutting edge of meanness and this awful failure of humanity."

When nobody spoke, I went to the door and turned around. "To you this is just Friday night fun and games. It could be bingo in the local church basement. Or snooker in the pool room. Kill a couple of hours. Have a few laughs. Let's hear it for Libby the funny lady. But this is my life and not one of you truly gives a damn."

And then I walked out. For good.

thirty-three

I went about it systematically. An assessment of my experience and education, my natural and acquired skills, charting them all, giving each a grade. Add it all up. Divide by fear. Multiply by everlasting dreams of glory. And what did I come up with? Nothing.

What I was was a fish out of my generational waters. The old American dream-fantasy still had me in its clutches. You can do whatever you want to do. Become whatever you want to become. Any mother's son can grow up to be President. Why not a girl?

It struck me as odd that in spite of all shortcomings, defeats and fears, I remained substantially optimistic. In some way Sybil and Sam, that strange and contradictory pairing, had invested me with a certain strength and determination. Let's not talk about weaknesses. How easy it had been to blame them, how long it took to assign credit. How truly American I had become.

Become. That was me—a person in production. Becoming me.

Go into business for myself. It was a laugh. What business? Here I was free to move in whatever way I saw fit, and nothing came to mind. No gleaming Grail to pursue.

I tried to force the issue, breaking down what I

knew into manageable components. What did I enjoy
doing? What did I dislike most? Computers were out
this time around. No way I could be satisfied to be an
extension of a machine. I wanted to work with people, swap ideas, make plans, design grand and noble
schemes.

Still I came up empty. Every idea, every potential
enterprise appeared lame and arid under examination.
Making money mattered, but not so much as not missing out on the other rewards and pleasures of work. I
longed to soar, shake off earthly shackles, attain the
stars. The image delighted me and I clung to it.

One night as I lay in bed, unable to sleep, I turned
on my side and watched Walter read for a while, hardly
an exciting activity. I put my feet against his leg, as
much to prod him into acknowledging my existence
as for warmth.

"You're a piece of ice," he said.

Encouraged, I asked him what he was reading.

"A biography of Henry Luce."

"The _Time_ man?"

"Fascinating individual, Luce. Though I don't care
for his magazines. Who reads them? Why would anyone waste his time when he could read _The New
York Times?_"

A light flickered inside my head, went out and came
back on, gathering strength. I located a pad and pen
and began to write. And for the next two days I ex-
panded on and refined those preliminary notes, that
basic concept, until all that could be done on paper
was done. I had found what I was looking for.

Sunday arrived clear and sunny, the air almost good
enough for a human being to breathe, and I suggested
a walk in the park.

"You hate Central Park," Walter pointed out logic-
ally.

"You've got a fifty-fifty chance of getting out alive
on Sundays—all those bike riders and pot smokers. It
gets too crowded for the killers and weirdos."

Halfway across the Sheep Meadow, Stevie snatched

up a soccer ball and ran, a team of Argentines and a team of Frenchmen in pursuit. He made a sharp turn and reached us before all those foreigners. The Argentines looked me over with lecherous intent while the Frenchmen snarled and demanded back the ball. Walter handed it over and we continued our stroll, Stevie moving out front in search of more trouble.

"I," I declared with a surprising amount of confidence, "am going to go into business for myself."

Walter never batted an eye. "You are? What kind of business?"

I was still riding the emotional high that had carried me for the last forty-eight hours. "You gave me the idea, Walter."

"Did I?"

"Henry Luce, remember? You said who reads *Time* Magazine? Who reads *Cue,* I asked myself? And *Playboy? Atlantic Monthly?* All those magazines."

"Who?"

"That's the point. A research service."

He said nothing.

"Don't you see?" I was begging for approval. Encouragement. Support. "Median income, education, hobbies, sports, other interests, how they spend their time and their money."

"Who are you talking about?"

"The readers."

"What readers?"

"Of the different magazines."

"I see."

"A research service. An advertising and marketing tool. With my service, a magazine can go to a potential advertiser and say, 'Hey, look, we have such-and-such kind of readership. Three years of college on the average. Median age twenty-eight or thirty or whatever. Income pegged at about eighteen thousand. They take skiing holidays at Stowe in the winter and go to the Hamptons in the summer. They snorkel, drive Porsches not Pintos, buy Sonys not RCAs.'"

"Well," Walter said, bringing me back to earth, "we'll see, won't we?" One moment flying high, the next shot down.

"There's more," I started to say, then shut down. For there, not a hundred feet in front of me, was the Singing Cowboy himself, Bubba Horn, boots, jeans and glazed tan leather jacket, Western-style, of course.

There we were on the west side of the sea lions' pool in the zoo. There he was on the east side. With a box of Cracker Jacks in one hand and the Most Beautiful Girl in the World in the other.

Bubba, you prick.

Bubba ate some Cracker Jacks and the Most Beautiful Girl in the World laughed. Maybe to her eating Cracker Jacks was funny, I don't know. When you look as good as she looked, I suppose you automatically laugh a lot. You know the kind, with a super-lean body but curvy and graceful. And a *punim,* as my Yiddish forebears would have said. What a face! One look at that face could send an ordinarily beautiful woman into a deep depression. Me, I felt extra specially bad.

An accelerated filmstrip stuttered through the theater of my mind. Bubba and the Most Beautiful Girl were starring. In living color, Saturday night and Sunday morning, doing disgusting things to each other. No wonder she laughed, Bubba almost always gave satisfaction, for all his shortcomings. Shortcomings? Suddenly Bubba seemed super-perfect to me.

Most Beautiful Girl bumped Bubba a little, gazed longingly up into his face, doing ridiculous things with her marvelous mouth. They kissed. Right in front of the sea lions and all those kids running around. A real kiss on the mouth. That woman had no pride at all.

I watched them disappear, hugging and smooching each other. And it practically ruined my Sunday. Would have, too, had I been an ordinary woman. But ordinariness was behind me, I assured myself, and spent the rest of the day working hard to polish and modify my plan.

On Monday, I began making phone calls to magazines, outlining my service, setting up appointments. I came out of the day with four firm meetings and three expressions of interest. It was, in my opinion, a supremely good day.

Tuesday morning I went to court with Hester Trippi. John Hannah made motions in behalf of IFP and Hester presented arguments against them. Much of what was said was lost on me, legal flim-flam. Hester explained it this way later: IFP contended that I could not sue since I did not represent a class and therefore there could be no class action.

"What if the judge decides in favor of the company?" I wanted to know.

Hester wasn't at all concerned. "Oh, we can always file again, a personal suit. The helpless individual against the heartless corporation. We'll rip 'em up with that old saw."

Over lunch, I told Hester that I was going into business. She frowned and shook her head. "Watch that kind of thing. If we're going to extract any damages from IFP, you can't turn yourself into a fucking capitalist."

That didn't seem likely to happen and I said so. "Speaking of money, we never really talked about your fee."

"Libby, look. This is a labor of love. Unless I'm ideologically involved, I don't take any case. What we are into is the chance to hit the system where it lives. This is a case vital to women wherever they are. I'd make this fight for free."

"That's the right price," I said lightly. Hester didn't crack a smile. Had I been smart, really aware, I would have begun to worry then and there. Instead I paid for lunch.

On Wednesday, I met with Fred Abernathy, Jr., vice-president of Heathcoate, Walters, Jensen, Schwartz and Black. Fourth-biggest ad agency in Manhattan. We had a drink at the St. Regis and Abernathy listened politely while I delivered my sales pitch. When I finished, he stroked my cheek.

"I like you," he murmured. "I really do."

"What about my service?"

"You remind me of a girl back in high school. I was in love with her. Be great working with you, knowing you, but let me level with you, this agency doesn't require the kind of service you're offering."

He touched my cheek. He took my hand. He put the tip of one finger to my mouth. I leaned away.

"If you were my wife . . ." He was grinning without humor. "I'd keep you home, barefoot and behind locked doors."

"Stripped for action, you mean."

"Is that bad? Let's have dinner. Thursdays are good for me."

"What would your wife say?"

"You don't tell her and I won't." He found that funny, I didn't.

"I'm a married woman."

"Let's not confuse the issue."

For the first time in a long time, I was not confused. "I'm looking for business, not sex."

He studied his glass. "If you change your mind, let me know."

That's how it went until I met Lou Rayfield, the publisher of *Showing Off,* the theatrical journal. I made my pitch and he heard me out without saying a word.

"I like it," he said, when I was finished.

"You do?"

"I've been thinking about expansion. Turning the magazine into a more general publication. This may be the way. Let's do it. Draw up a contract, we've got a deal."

I smothered a cry of exultation. I had to keep myself from leaping up, dancing a jig of joy, hugging Lou Rayfield. But I remained in place, staid and proper. Ladylike decorum, that was my new number. Sybil would have been proud.

Once back in the street, my head spinning, my feet

barely skimming the concrete, I had to share the pleasure of my success with somebody. I went looking for a phone booth. For the first time in my life I had set out to do something that was mine alone, had conceived it, planned it, sold my special piece of blue sky to somebody else. I was in business for myself.

The first phone booth I came to smelled of fresh cigar smoke, stale urine and dried vomit. I dialed quickly and talked fast.

"Bubba," I squealed in childish delight. "I'm about to burst. Can I come over?"

He thought it over and I could sense the air oozing out of my balloon. "Why not?" he said finally. By the time I arrived at his apartment, doubts about a lot of things had set in, including my ability to accomplish what I'd set out to do.

Bubba was wearing a short shaving robe when he opened the door. He maneuvered me onto his couch, rubbing and pinching, tugging at my clothes, operating with a kind of remembered mechanical competence. I felt nothing, but I lacked the will to resist. Anyway, I was sure it wouldn't take very long and it didn't.

"There," he said, falling back, brandishing his sexual prowess like a smoking six-gun.

I adjusted my clothing and sat up. "What are you so proud of?"

He laughed. "Did I fail you, pilgrim? Do better next time."

I looked him over. Not a hair on his long, pale body, immaculate, as if he'd just been bathed, oiled and plucked. Fail me? If so it had been an insignificant failure for my expectations were in a minor key where he was concerned.

"I used to believe you were a special man, Bubba."

"I've disappointed you, sorry."

"I used to think you were the greatest lay in town."

"Not hard to get worked up over that pretty little pleasure box of yours, sweet Libby."

I walked across the room and sat in a straight-backed chair. "Tell me about the Most Beautiful Girl in the World, Bubba."

He located his shaving robe and put it on. "What's that you say?"

"The lady in the park on Sunday."

"Oh, oh, you must mean Melinda."

"Melinda, what a darling name."

He laughed. "Melinda, sure. Near forgot all about Melinda. Just a little ole home gal with a legal difficulty or two."

"I'll bet you straightened her out. Cracker Jacks and the fastest tongue in New York."

He found what he was looking for, his boots. "Now, Libby, no need to be petty and mean."

"Vulgarity becomes me, Bubba. I come off the streets of New York."

"You can't be jealous. Ole Melinda, she is nothin' in my life." He put on one boot, posed on the bias. "Melinda's daddy owns a piece of land up the road from Jimmy Guy's itty-bitty place."

"That reminds me, I've been meaning to ask. Just how itty-bitty is Jimmy Guy's farm?"

"Ooh . . ." He drew air in, pumping himself into fighting trim. "Just to the other side of twenty thousand acres."

"A modest little spread?"

"Well—"

"Oh boy, Bubba. I used to think you were King of the Hill, scratching and kicking to do what was right, no matter what. Turns out you're just another Bloomingdale's Bronco-Buster, all style and no substance. You're a fucking rich man, Bubba."

"That's Jimmy Guy's land."

"Which you will inherit one day."

"I reckon so."

"I bet you have toted up the worth of every foot of land, every chicken, every cow. By the way, how many cows does Jimmy Guy have?"

"No more'n a few thousand head, I'd say."

"It's a ranch, not a farm."

He got that other boot on, gave me one of his finest smiles. "Now, Libby, about this time I could sure use a kind word from you."

I had come to share my excitement with him, this so very important victory. No more. Now I wanted only to celebrate what I had done in private. I went into the bathroom and splashed water on my face, ran a comb through my hair. The reflection in the glass might have belonged to a stranger, soft and assured, glowing with inner certainty. It was the first time I liked the way I looked.

Back in the living room, Bubba was sucking Coors from a can. "How about a brew?" he greeted me.

"Got to go, Bubba."

"No need to be put off by Melinda."

"Don't you fret, Bubba. Keep doing what you're doing. You're fine for the short run but over the long haul, you are a lightweight."

"Give us a call soon, Libby."

"I don't think I'll be doing that anymore, Bubba."

"Ah, Libby. I sure do feel fondly about you."

"Goodbye, Bubba."

"Ah," he said again.

I was halfway home before it hit me. Never before had I left somebody. Never had I ended a friendship before it was ended for me. Never had I terminated a romance. Never had I quit a job or turned down one that had been offered to me. Up to now, I was always the one kissed off, cut down, sent packing. It was a lot better this way.

part five

1973

thirty-four

That night I seduced my husband. Deliberately planned and reasonably effective.

I arranged for a babysitter to stay with Stevie and shepherded Walter to Giordano's where we sat in the back room against the brick wall and dined on a superb antipasto and the thinnest veal scallopini in the world, all washed down by a mellow Bardolino that left me feeling warm and pliant, increasingly aggressive.

I directed the conversation. We talked about how well Stevie was developing, about our marriage and our mutual need for each other. We talked for a little while about Sybil, and I explained to Walter how I had come to understand that I liked her very much, respected her much more than I had ever realized.

"Too bad," I said ruefully, "I didn't know it when she was alive."

"She knew it, I'm certain."

"I'd like to believe that. Now I can see what a genuinely moving person she was, how interesting. For so long I tried so hard to put her aside."

"Everybody does, I guess."

"Is that what Stevie will do with us?"

"It's inevitable. If you don't . . . if the grievances of parent-child relationships are allowed to fester—well, it becomes too destructive for everybody."

Walter was looking better and better to me, sounding better. I took his hand and tickled his palm in what I meant to be an indecent suggestion. I'm not sure he got it. "If Sybil came back to life, if she were here tonight, she'd be just as difficult to take as before."

"Of course." Walter squeezed my fingers.

We had an espresso and took a cab back to the apartment, paid the babysitter and went to bed. Walter was about to reach for a book, but I got to the light first.

"What are you doing?" he said in the dark.

"Concentrate, I'm sure you'll catch on."

I made it south of his navel before he put a restraining hand on the back of my head. "Please, Libby. You know how I feel about that."

"The more you hold me off, the more I want to. You might begin to enjoy it and then you might want to return the favor."

"Oh, Libby . . ." My moral inadequacies filled him with sorrow.

"Walter," I assured him. "You won't catch anything."

He removed his hand and I went back to work on his body. But I sensed the tension in him and his silent objections became too much for me to ignore. Too bad, I was getting lost in the effort.

Nevertheless my hopes were raised. Walter had been less strenuous than usual in resisting me. Perhaps I might yet turn Walter on to a normally perverted sex life. Like everybody else.

Hester invited me down to Soho for some Serious Talk about the case. She wore a sweatshirt and jeans, her feet in scuffed bridgeman's boots. A satisfied smile made her look like Raggedy Ann.

"Ready for some good news?"

"Anytime."

"I've squeezed IFP by the nuts. They're ready to give it up."

No elation, only a slowly flowing regret that made

me think I was being deprived of something precious
and rare.

"They want to settle?"

"They do. Did I do a job for you? You've won,
Libby."

Then why did I feel I had lost something? Lost
what? Then I knew and the realization startled me. The
fight, the joy found in the battle itself. Step by slow
step I had moved into it, never throwing out any impressive threats or challenges, always remaining within
the range of my ability to deal with things, yet continuing to struggle, to stand against the enemy, to make
my presence felt. The fight had made me stronger, not
the winning of it. The fight had caused diverse parts
of myself to pull together. Had I finished the project?
Was I now the person I wanted to be, whole, strong,
independent? If so, could I handle it?

"What does it mean, Hester?"

"It means IFP has come across with a solid offer."

"Okay, let's hear it." My voice grated in my ears,
serrated and impatient, not what I was used to.

Even Hester seemed surprised. She blinked and
spoke hesitantly. "Yes. A year's back pay, plus fifty
percent additional for costs, damages, and so on. Comes
up to better than twenty-five thousand."

That set me back on my economic heels. "What happened to all those big numbers we kicked around?"

"This is the real world, Libby."

"Don't they have class actions in the real world anymore?"

"Like the man said, take the money and run. IFP
will make a disclaimer of any wrongdoing, naturally."

"Naturally. Only they did do wrong."

"It's part of the deal."

"I don't like it."

"It's not bad."

"I still don't like it."

"Nobody can guarantee success if we go to trial."

"Hester, I have been *wronged*. Everybody knows that."

"Proving it is something else. Courtrooms are dangerous. Judges are tricky. Juries unreliable."

"You're telling me to take it."

"I'm telling you what in my legal opinion is in your best interests."

At that moment she reminded me very much of every other lawyer I'd ever talked to. They were a cautious breed, afraid to put down a foot without examining the ground first lest they step into something soft and mushy, something that smelled. She reminded me of Bubba.

"Would they make any kind of an offer if they thought they'd win?"

"It's less trouble this way."

"They're afraid of going all the way."

"Nobody wants to go to court. Settlements are not unusual. Makes life easier for everybody."

"You'd take the money?"

"If it were up to me—"

"We were going to teach them a lesson."

"You have to recognize your limits."

" 'Kill the bastards,' you said."

"Pragmatic considerations . . ."

"Wouldn't I be selling out?"

Her face turned hard. "I don't sell out, my clients don't sell out. But you must be practical . . ."

"If I accept, it's over?"

"Exactly, Libby. No more hassling. The worry, the stress, the fighting, all over. I told Hannah I'd call him back with your answer."

"We were shooting for a million. Isn't twenty-five thousand a cheap buy for them?"

"You take what you can get."

"No sale," I said.

Her mouth flattened. "Your decision."

"That's right."

"I hope you won't regret it later on."

"I won't. Put it in legalese, but let Hannah know how I feel. Tell him I intend to kick ass."

Doubt set in fast. By noon the next day I was convinced I'd done a terrible injury to myself, my cause. I looked around for someone to help. Someone able to think clearly, someone sympathetic to my aims, someone able to deal out first-rate advice.

Bubba; he'd have me on my back before I could get a word out. Anyway, I'd written him off.

Walter; take the money, he'd say. Walter was not built for this kind of long-range battle. Especially if it involved getting out there where the big guns were going off.

Which brought me around to Ellenbogen. A phone call and an invitation to lunch took me all the way down to the Lower East Side and Katz's Delicatessen. I ordered a corned beef sandwich and a Coke. Ellenbogen showed his true colors; he had a hot pastrami on a seeded roll, two franks with mustard, kraut and red relish, French fries and a couple of beers. Lots of catsup on the fries.

"Eat now," Ellenbogen said, mouth full of hot dog. "Talk later."

"The way you eat you'll get heartburn and you won't be able to talk."

"The way I eat is a way of life. I grew up on this stuff. Kosher pickles that shrivel your mouth up. Potato knishes, the works. Near Coney Island, the other end of the subway."

"Let's discuss my suit."

Behind his glasses, his eyes rolled. "It's a very nice suit. From where did you get it, Ohrbach's?"

"Not funny."

"You don't like me?"

"I like you, Harry. But you try too hard."

He nodded sagely. "I understand, you're crazy about me, afraid to show it. That's okay."

"Harry, I came for advice, not sex."

"Sex! Who said anything about sex? Why are you

talking to me about sex? You have a very dirty mind, you know that?"

I couldn't help laughing. "Harry, we are not going to have an affair."

"Never?"

"Never."

"What kind of a woman are you? Nobody says 'never' these days. Let it all hang out. Experience everything. Nothing is bad. Try it all. That's life these days. We won't have an affair today, that I understand. Not next Tuesday, you've got another date. Okay. Saturday a month I'll be in *schul* and after there's shopping for my kid's bar mitzvah. Such matters are comprehensible to me. A proper way to talk to a friend. But 'never.' Not 'never.' 'Never' causes friction. It terminates relationships. Creates bad feelings between people, especially men and women. You could change your mind and 'never' turns into 'maybe,' or 'in a couple of days,' or 'what about right now?' People change their minds. 'Never'—that's silly. Yes, yes, you could change your mind. Also, it's polite to wait until you're invited."

"There's more to you than meets the ear, Harry."

"Not good," he muttered into a pastrami sandwich, "but not so bad, either. I was right, you're crazy about me."

"Absolutely crazy."

"That's your second mistake today."

I should've known better, but I asked. "What was the first?"

"Getting out of bed this morning." He waited for his laugh, got it, and was pleased with himself. "You have a nice laugh. A big mouth, good teeth, not too many fillings. Is the rest of you as good?"

"Too small here, too big there, the usual."

"Nobody ever died from the usual."

"You sound like a rebroadcast of my own jokes. I'm getting nervous, Harry."

"Better you than me. Now we'll talk about your case. Go."

I told him about the company's offer, about Hester's advice. When I was through, he took a terrible bite out of that sandwich.

"I'm going to give you my opinion."

"Good."

"A company like IFP makes one offer, they'll make two offers. You got 'em on the run, baby."

"Hester says we might lose in court."

"Hester is an ideological schmuck. Make that schmuckess. The way I read it, you'll never see the inside of a courtroom."

"Nobody says 'never' these days."

He guffawed and wiped grease off his chin. "Probably never, better. IFP can't afford a trial."

"What do you mean?"

"You have got deadly weapons, use them."

"Hester says I've won already. She says there isn't much more to win."

"There are victories and victories. Are you the only one they screwed? Not on your life. Lots of women they didn't hire, the same way. Lots of women they did hire and didn't promote or give raises. What do you think, you're the exception? Everybody gives a shrug and lets it go. IFP, they expect you to do the same."

"You're right."

"Sure I'm right. Make 'em pay, kiddo, right through the nose."

"I'd like that, Harry."

"Now you're acting smart. You agree with me. It's important to read those pissants right. Lemme straighten you out, the guys at the head of those big companies, they're smart, but not as smart as they think they are. It's like they never learned to read the writing on the wall. The world is changing, people are changing, there are new ideas going around. Those guys, they keep trying to do business like it was yesterday. They talk tough, they act tough, but put 'em under the gun and—no guts."

"Maybe I'm not so brave either."

"You're standing up to them. As long as you're willing to pay the price, you can win. Company brass, when they feel the pain and notice it's their blood being spilled—dollar-green blood—they'll quit. No matter what they say, they're men without principles. They care only about profits. You hit 'em hard enough in the profits and they'll quit on you every time."

Listening to him, I forgot that his accent was pure Greenpoint, that he talked too loud and laughed like a herniated goat, that he was pillow soft and myopic, that his table manners were an abomination. I recognized a small but volatile area in Ellenbogen, a fount of power and passion. He played no part, tried to be nothing but what he was by nature and by inclination. You had to judge him by his standards, by his definitions of what a man should be. The Old Definitions. He grew up in a time of frozen Milky Ways and neighborhoods, when the local Loew's movie palace played double features and the program changed twice each week. It was a time that had a friendly cop on the beat, Dixie cups with small wooden spoons, and you paid for what you got and you got what you earned. That was Ellenbogen, all right. He didn't belong anywhere anymore, but he didn't know it, and wouldn't have cared if he did. Ellenbogen, the Fighter.

"You're some tough guy, Ellenbogen."

He let the pastrami sandwich fall out of his hand and reached for me. "Listen, my apartment is your basic New York bachelor pad. An inadequate kitchen, a john that won't always flush, a big mirror in the bedroom. What do you say?"

I retrieved my hand. "Give it up, Harry."

"Ah," he groaned, "it's better not to have been born at all."

I smiled to show I was paying attention. But not enough to encourage him.

He made a swift comeback. "I like you anyway. They wanna talk, those IFP *momsers,* here's how you deal with them . . ."

Lou Rayfield offered me desk space in his office. Free of charge. And just like that, I was in business for myself. All at once work was fun again. Challenging. Exciting. Business lunches, cocktail meetings, conferences, planning sessions, questionnaires to create and mail, calls to make, letters to write. I did it all myself. And managed to very quickly sign up three more clients: *Southern Connecticut* Magazine, *Sunning & Skiing* and *The Bike; Riding and Repairing.*

One morning I received a call from *American Athlete,* the largest weekly sports magazine in the country. Within seventy-two hours I had come up with a marketing research plan and a survey of readership in depth. I suggested a permanent panel of readers to be queried on whatever topics were of interest to the magazine, as to content, length of articles, impact of ads, and so on. Then came a brainstorm. Using the reader panel for source material, I would do a column twice a month free of charge for the magazine: "Readers' Corner." The publisher loved it and we signed a contract for the entire package the following week. I was really on the move, playing with the big boys at last, playing their game. And doing good.

Every Wednesday afternoon after that Ellenbogen phoned to inquire about the suit, my health, and offer to buy me lunch. I kept turning down his invitations until he swore if I met him in a highly public place he would not talk about my body, his body, sex in plant or animal life, beds, sofas, flat areas in general or his apartment in particular. He gave me his word.

And so I met him at Joe Allen's and we ordered drinks, and before they came he broke all the guidelines in one sentence.

"My biggest ambition is to rub my naked body against your naked body and perform other obscene practices as they come to mind."

"You did it." I started to leave.

"What, what, I didn't do a thing. You're too sensitive. Sit down, people will look. You'll be embarrassed."

"You should be embarrassed."

"At least finish your drink."

"It hasn't even come."

"It will, it will." I sat down and he shook his massive head. "So impulsive, it's not nice."

"You gave your word. I trusted you and you broke your word."

"You trusted me? How could you trust me? I'm a spider."

"No stories, Harry."

"This one has a moral. The spider said to the frog, 'Give us a swim to the other side of the river, buddy.' The frog said, 'Whataya, some kind of a nut? You're a spider, you'll sting me and kill me as soon as we get into the water.'

" 'Don't be dumb,' the spider said. 'I'd drown too.'

"The frog bought that and he said, 'Climb on,' and he started swimming to the other side."

"And the spider stung him and he died?" I said.

"Right. As he was drowning, the frog looked over at the spider, who was drowning also, and said, 'How could you do a thing like that?' "

I couldn't restrain myself. "And the spider said, 'How could you trust me? I'm a spider.' "

"Get the picture?" He laughed loudly. "A person's nature—let's go to my apartment."

"Has it occurred to you that I'm not interested in making love to you, Harry?"

"Who said anything about love? Just sex. On that you've got my word."

Harry made me feel good. Alive and youthful, and more attractive than I could remember ever feeling. I wondered what it would be like to be in bed with him. Would the comic routines stop then? Not that I had any intention of finding out. I'd made up my mind that bedhopping from river to river was not my style.

If Harry was in any way deterred by rejection, I didn't notice. A mere no didn't stop him; he was not a man who gave up easily. 'No,' said without anger or bitterness or guilt, made me like myself a lot. 'No,' said simply and effectively, leaving me in control of my life. How nice.

"Ready for some terrific news?" It was Hester Trippi calling me at home.

"Tell me."

"One of the women in the office is shacking up with the clerk of the judge on your case. The word is he's going to hand down his decision day after tomorrow."

Suddenly all strength drained away. This was really the end and I was sorry about it. Had I really enjoyed the process so much? I was discovering aspects of myself I never dreamed existed.

"Is that it?" I said.

"You sound pretty blasé about it all."

"Has John Hannah been told?" I said, trying to think the way Ellenbogen would want me to think.

"I doubt it."

"Tell him. One way or another, make sure he gets the word."

"You think they'll make a better offer? I don't."

"Just give them a little jog, Hester."

"Okay, but I don't like any of it. I still believe you should accept the settlement. Going to that judge, who knows what might happen?"

"They are not going to put it all on the judge."

"IFP, all that bread. They're sneaky, shrewd, they may have bought off the judge."

"Do it my way, Hester."

"What if it doesn't work?"

"Do it."

I spent the time repotting Sybil's avocado. I placed it in a large red pot, giving it plenty of room to take root, to grow, to become the best avocado plant it could be. Something very much alive and successful.

I had just finished when Hester called back. "I spoke to John Hannah. The company's willing to come up to thirty-five thousand dollars. No strings attached."

I began to laugh.

"For Christ's sake, Libby, take the money."

"To hell with it."

"We can't do any better!" she screamed into the phone.

I gave her a quiet moment to think about it, then said, "Tell Hannah I want to talk to him. Right away. Get back to me when it's set up."

I hung up.

thirty-five

The boardroom was on the forty-second floor of the IFP building, an immense elliptical chamber without windows. Soft light glowed from concealed fixtures and carefully conditioned air flowed in scientifically plotted streams. Paneled in polished woods, with a plush gold carpet, it was dominated by a coffin-shaped table hand rubbed to a high gloss. Black leather chairs were spaced at comfortable intervals and at each place there was a ceramic ashtray, a glass and a crystal pitcher filled with ice water, a legal-sized pad of lined paper and three ballpoint pens, red, green and black. There was also a plastic bag filled with a couple of dozen miniatures of IFP packaged foods.

At the head of the table, John Hannah. Next to him an assistant named Alan Maddox. They might have been father and son. Almost identical well-bred but predatory expressions, the same hawkish nose, thin lips and lean, shining, well-shaved cheeks. They wore blue flannel blazers, white shirts with buttoned collars and striped silk ties. Harvard, North Shore, Park Avenue.

Facing Hannah at the far end of the table was Hester Trippi. The frazzled ends of her orange hair waved slightly in the gently moving air. She wore a denim skirt with a clenched fist appliquéd to the thigh. Her sweater, torn at the elbow, was stained and frayed. On her feet, huaraches with soles made from old truck tires. Her feet were filthy.

Some dead air space between me and the opposing legal forces seemed in order and I placed myself halfway up the table.

"Where's Mr. Lieber?" I had the temerity to ask.

Hannah gave me a smarmy smile. "I don't think we require his presence today."

Chalk one up for Ellenbogen. He predicted there would be only lawyers present.

"Shall we begin?" I said.

"For the record," Alan Maddox said in a voice like broken glass, "you've turned down the company's best offer."

Hester replied, a diva hitting a note she knew she couldn't sustain. "That's crap, after what you people put Libby through."

Maddox answered. "It was an adequate settlement." He delivered each word carefully, as if afraid it might break, or that you might not understand. "The offer still stands."

Ellenbogen had said: "In the early going, the prelim fighters will carry the ball. Let 'em talk, clears the air."

"Loss of income," Hester said with feeling. "Emotional anguish, mental distress . . ."

Young Maddox arranged his hands on the table, as if about to pounce. "Your client is currently employed by Executive Placement Service. Excellent salary, commissions. She's suffered no damages."

"They'll know all about you," Ellenbogen had warned me.

Hester said, as if in triumph, "No more. Libby doesn't work there anymore."

Maddox went on scratching. "Your client turned down a promotion, the opportunity for increased income and other benefits. No financial loss has been suffered. If it were up to me, I'd give you nothing, Mrs. Pepper." He showed his teeth in a nasty snarl.

I smiled pleasantly.

"The fervor of youth," John Hannah said to me in a mild manner.

"Not a red cent," Maddox gritted out, giving me the hard eye.

The good cop and the bad cop. They still figured me for a soft touch, unwilling to take me seriously, treating me like an emotional basket case, not able to fend for myself. "Keep your eye on the pot," was Ellenbogen's suggestion. I stood up and walked to the door.

Hannah said, "Libby?"

Hester almost groaned. "Libby . . ."

Maddox toughed it out. "Let her go."

"Alan," Hannah said politely. "Please be quiet. You've had your chance. Mrs. Pepper, Libby, won't you please come back and sit down?"

"What for?"

Hannah was on his feet, holding my chair for me. He was very smooth. "So we can discuss this matter. Bargain, if you will. Settle our differences."

Hester spoke. "If my client wants to break this off, okay. I mean, you guys are trying to dump all over us." Hester was very strong. After the fact.

"I'll listen," I said, and sat back down.

For a long time nobody said anything. They sat without moving, watching me. All that silence, all those staring eyes. I began to get a little antsy. Until I understood that they were antsy, too. More than that, scared. Scared of me. I was a creature unexpected. Smarter, meaner, and they didn't know what to do about it.

"The company takes the position that it has done nothing wrong," Hannah said finally.

"The company screwed me," I replied.

"Naturally that would be your position."

"Are we at an impasse, Mr. Hannah?"

He actually shuddered. "Compromise between adversaries is the only way to prevent bloodshed. We are both reasonable people, Mrs. Pepper."

"How reasonable?" Hester said.

Nobody paid any attention to her. Hannah kept me in his sights; dumb he wasn't. "We want to do right by you, Mrs. Pepper. We also want the company done right by. We're facing what is essentially a simple problem. Consider this—you will receive thirty-five thousand dollars. That will cover any salary you might have earned, costs, et cetera. And as evidence of our good will, I am empowered to offer you the same job you applied for at a salary of twenty-one thousand five hundred dollars per annum. Four thousand more than the original salary."

Hester shot me a glance.

"There is no way I would work for IFP after what's happened."

Hester shriveled up in place. The Soho revolutionary was not much of a threat to the System. Any system.

Hannah fingered his old school tie. "Suppose we make it fifty thousand?"

"Ah," Hester said, coming back to life.

"What does it come to," I said, "after taxes?"

Hannah thought he saw light at the end of the tunnel. "In the interests of harmony, IFP will absorb the tax bill. That means a full fifty thousand dollars to you, less your attorney's fee, of course." He got a big grin out of Hester on that one. They had a lot in common, those two, and it was money.

"That," Hester said, full of radical enthusiasm, "is a generous offer."

"No," I said.

Hannah's smooth Presbyterian face flushed and his lips worked soundlessly. At the other end of the table, Hester chewed on her thumb.

Alan Maddox began shooting off his mouth. "That's it, then. We go to court and win, win, win." He must've been on the pep squad at Groton.

Hannah ignored him. "The company would prefer to avoid a trial," he said to me. "A long, terribly expensive and debilitating court case can do nobody any good. A settlement is in the interest of both sides.

No matter who wins, there will be appeals. More litigation. More legal fees to meet and no payment to you, even should you win. IFP can well afford it, since I am on a yearly retainer and am paid in any case."

"Let's go to trial."

Hester groaned. "He's got a point, Libby. It can drag on for years. Be practical."

" 'Hit the mothers where they live,' you said. 'Make 'em pay.' What happened to the revolution, Hester?"

She grimaced. "For God's sake, take the money."

I addressed John Hannah. "You must know by now the EEOC is waiting to move in. The Feds know I've been discriminated against. With the case in federal court, the EEOC is holding back until a decision is reached. When that happens, look out."

I imagined a flash of admiration lit up Hannah's eyes. "You are a difficult woman to deal with."

"At last you noticed."

"What do you want?"

"Everything, Mr. Hannah. Everything." My temperature shot up and there was a pounding between my eyes. But no palpitations. *That* was what it was all about; I wanted everything. At least a shot at it. Whatever the rewards. Whatever the price. I was willing to chance it now.

"Everything." Hannah shook his head. "You leave us no choice. We will go to trial. There is nothing more to lose."

"Give them some room!" Hester shrieked.

I kept my eyes on John Hannah and reached back to my conversation with Ellenbogen, struggling to recover everything he had said. "You have a great deal to lose, Mr. Hannah."

That supercilious air that Hannah utilized so effectively failed him now. His shoulders seemed to go slack and much of the steel left his expression. He was too smart not to anticipate where I was headed.

"Here it is," I said. "IFP does business with the women of America. Not some of its business, but all of it business. Go to court and those women will discover the miserable way you treated one of them. Women will learn what IFP thinks of women in general."

"Nobody has to know anything." Maddox was determined but dumb. He was not another John Hannah.

"Everybody has to know. Everybody will know. I will make sure of that. Check out my résumé, gentlemen, and see my experience in communications, public relations, advertising. I've got the media contacts. Women across the country will hear of this case and they will follow it closely. I'll see to it. Can IFP afford that kind of notoriety? That kind of adverse publicity? If the answer is yes, then let's go to court."

Hannah checked me out as if I were some rather dangerous and unrecognizable creature. For so long I had felt myself to be a stranger everywhere, out of joint, out of step. Suddenly it was different. I was at ease with myself, in charge, belonging wherever I happened to be.

"It's got to be my way, John," I said pleasantly.

"As long as the numbers are revised downward," he answered conversationally. "A million is too far afield."

"One hundred thousand," I told him. "That's the bottom of it."

Hester held her breath.

Maddox held his head.

"Plus the tax bill," I added on.

Hannah doodled briefly. "The class action, it must be withdrawn."

Hester was on her feet. "It's been a good fight and we can all be satisfied with the outcome. I see no reason why the class action cannot be withdrawn."

"No," I said.

"Then no deal." Hannah planted his feet.

Hester pleaded. "Libby . . ." The sharp stench of gold made her quiver with desire.

"If I give up the class action, I want something in exchange."

Hannah, smart as he was, misunderstood. He grinned. "So you do want the job after all."

"What I want is for IFP to end its discriminatory practices against women."

"Without admitting anything," Hannah said, too slickly for my taste, "of course."

"There must be a way to make sure. For two years I want the company records made available to the Equal Employment Opportunity Commission."

"An affirmative-action plan." Hester made it sound as if it had been her idea.

"That can be arranged," Hannah said.

"Trust nobody" was Ellenbogen's watchword. For all I knew, IFP had a pipeline into Washington. They probably catered all affairs at the White House. Free of charge.

"Here's what I want," I said. "For the next two years, the right to examine company records, employment policies, salary schedules, promotion lists. If any of it fails to measure up, it must be changed . . . penalties will have to be worked out, written into the agreement . . ."

Hannah leaned back and looked me over. With approval, I'd say. He very nearly smiled, and said, "You win."

thirty-six

I was a heroine. Goddam, I really was. No more playing games. No more perceiving myself in terms of somebody else. No longer a victim. Just me, and feeling good. So very good. I'd traveled into the deep, dark places; the only places where you can find the deep, important answers, and now I was back out in the light, having survived all the abuse, the fear, the absence of personal power.

No more waiting for my prince to come, to do it for me. No more playing hide-and-seek with myself. I'd located my center, and I was ready to be taken seriously.

Going along the crowded streets, surrounded by people and oblivious to them. They must have noticed me. Perceived the differences in me. After all, how many real live heroines go floating down Fifth Avenue? I glowed. I shimmered. I felt absolutely beautiful. I longed to share this incredible golden moment with somebody. I phoned Walter. He was in a business meeting and could not be disturbed. The glow began to fade.

I started to dial Sybil's number until I remembered that she was dead. I never missed her as much as I did at that moment.

Bubba. A vision of his hard lean body pressed against my own unloosed circles of passion behind my navel. But that would be a step backward and I intended never to take a backward step again.

I called Ellenbogen. A secretary informed me he was working at home. I almost headed back uptown to the apartment to wait for Stevie's return from daycare. But I needed someone to talk to, to celebrate with. I dropped a dime in the slot and dialed.

"Come out and I'll buy you champagne," I told him. "We'll have a party."

"You come over here. No champagne, but I've got some good booze and we'll drink to the winner and new champion."

If I went, he would expect to make love to me. And I—charged with the thrill of victory, tingling with excitement—would not be able to stop him.

"I better not." The words were without force.

"Listen," he growled like a lecherous Groucho Marx, "you had one good thing happen today. Why not try for two?"

"Is that a guarantee?"

"Double your money back."

He was waiting for my answer. I hardly hesitated. "I'm on my way, Harry . . ."

thirty-seven

I was at my desk in Lou Rayfield's office when Hester Trippi called. "It came," she announced on a rising note. "The settlement check from IFP. I've never had so much money in my hands before—a hundred grand."

"Send it over." I heard a new authority in my voice, full of assurance and command. I liked it.

"It'll take a few days to clear the bank," she answered. "Then you'll get your share."

Hester made it sound as if I were working for her, as if the money were hers. "Why didn't the check come to me directly?"

"The lawyer always gets it. That's the custom."

A custom created by lawyers, dealing with each other for their mutual benefit. Trust a lawyer, you've got to be crazy . . .

"When the check passes," Hester said, "I'll get your share to you."

"My share," I said slowly. "How much is that?"

"Sixty thousand. That's a great deal of money and . . ."

"There's some mistake."

"No, no mistake. The litigation was long and complicated, expensive. I put in a lot of time, my partners. Research, briefs, talking to—"

"Forget it," I said in a low, clear voice.

301

She giggled. My radical revolutionary feminist hotshot counselor-at-law giggled like a schoolgirl about to wet her pants. I, Libby Pepper, frightened her. That did no harm to my ego.

"Send it over," I said. "Now."

"Libby. You don't understand . . ."

"Now. Forty thousand is out of the question."

"Libby, come on. We have to live, too. We owe five months' back rent. There are other costs. We really need the money, Libby."

"No."

"I've got the check, I'm going to deposit it."

"No," I said again.

"There's nothing you can do about it."

"I can sue."

part six

1974

thirty-eight

After the check arrived in the mail, Walter and I went on holiday, as Sybil might have put it. To St. Thomas, in the Virgin Islands.

The flight was smooth and uneventful, the taxi ride to the Lime Tree Hotel was slow, hot and frustrating. We inched along the waterfront highway in a noisome traffic jam reminiscent of the East River Drive. The driver—Samson was his name and he had a wife and seven children, though two years shy of being forty—placed the blame on the influx of sailors off the aircraft carrier *Saratoga,* which floated at anchor behind an island in the harbor. I knew better; stateside civilization had trailed after us determined to spoil our vacation. I decided to ignore all inconveniences and intrusions and enjoy myself greatly.

Lime Tree was situated on a small curved private beach. There were coconut palms and cacti, iguanas and mongooses, and a lame duck, all living on the grounds in apparent harmony. A lone pelican dived repeatedly into the soft green water, catching a fish each time.

At night Lime Tree served up steel bands, limbo dancers and a man dressed up like a character in an early Tarzan movie; he ate fire and danced on broken glass. None of them was going to become a star, but I kept the news to myself.

We spent the first morning getting tan. At least I did. At rest on a lounge on the beach, thoroughly greased and changing positions every twenty minutes or so. I spread my arms and legs so that my armpits and thighs would match the rest of me and allowed my mind to go blank under that hot, penetrating sun.

As for Walter, he sought out a safe spot in the shade of a palm tree, complete with a wide-brimmed straw hat, dark glasses and a Hawaiian-type shirt. He was reading *All the President's Men*.

After a couple of hours of this, I began to get antsy. I located Walter behind his book and said his name. He looked up reluctantly. "All this sun is making me sexy," I announced in a throaty caress.

Walter clung hard to Woodward and Bernstein. "Sun and sex," he mumbled. "You must be obsessed."

I couldn't deny it. "It's all these naked bodies. Have you noticed, some of them are very attractive bodies."

Ever the precise thinker, Walter said, "Nobody's naked. They're all properly clothed, considering the surroundings."

"That would be nice, to be surrounded by lots of naked people. Have you ever been to a nude beach, Walter?"

That got him out of the book. "You know better than that. What a question."

"What a kick, being naked in public. Everybody inspecting everybody else."

"You have some very strange ideas."

"You still look good in a bathing suit. You have a very fine figure. It would be fun to see you naked once in a while."

"I'm your husband."

"That's what I mean. I can't remember the last time I saw you without anything on. And I'd like you to see me naked, too."

He turned back to the book. "I know exactly what your body looks like."

"Oh, Walter . . ."

He held up a hand for silence and got it.

The next morning we went shopping in Charlotte Amalie. Walter was concerned that he might get too much sun, though not one ray had managed to reach his skin as yet. He explained that the incidence of skin cancer was on the rise and sunbathing was frequently the cause. He warned me against overdoing it. I kissed him on the cheek and promised to be careful and thanked him for worrying about me.

Charlotte Amalie is a free port and so reputed to be the Emerald City of consumer delights. In such a place you expect bargains, right? Forget it. Cigarettes, perfume and liquor were the loss leaders. All the rest was offered up at inflated prices: jewelry, linen, clothes, watches. But all public markets are addictive and I constructed a mental list of things to buy that never quit; and ended up with a delicate silk scarf of many colors.

We found a French restaurant, called L'Escargot, in Creques Alley West, and stopped for lunch. Behind thick, cool brick and stone walls, we had excellent omelets and green salads. I drank chilled white wine with my meal. Walter had water.

I lifted my glass in a toast. "Here's to IFP for making it all possible."

"You must be glad it's over."

"To tell the truth, I miss it. A lot, some of the time."

Walter was surprised and said so. "It's over. You got all that money. Seventy thousand dollars, that's a great deal of money."

"At the end, I didn't want it to end. I was caught up in the flow of action, all my senses, my intelligence, operating at a high competitive plane. It was very exciting."

"You really liked it?"

"Yes. You encouraged me to make the fight."

"I'm not sure why I did."

"It doesn't matter now. But you did and that was very, very important to me at the time." He turned away as if embarrassed by what I'd said. "You're right about the money, having it is good. But there were better things . . ."

"Your business?"

"Yes." Libby Pepper, Inc., was growing, adding new clients. When we got back to New York, I was going to have to find larger quarters and hire a number of people on a full-time basis. "I never believed it would turn out this way."

"One step at a time." Another of Walter's truisms.

But life wasn't like that. The life I knew came at you without plan or purpose, unfolding in its own good time for its own murky reasons. There was pain to be had, and pleasure, if you were lucky. One thing was clear to me, nobody gave you a damned thing.

"You have your work," Walter said. "I have mine. I've never seen Stevie happier. Our lives couldn't be better. Everything is in order."

In order. There was some truth to that. What had gone before had been chaotic, empty, and without direction. Now there was discipline and purpose. I was getting what I wanted by going after what I wanted.

My war against IFP had caused changes in me, in my personality, my character, changes subtle and imperceptible to most people. Changes greater than anyone would ever know.

So much had happened since that first interview at IFP, events large and small. I tried to evaluate the gains and the losses, to separate them. But I couldn't be entirely sure that the gains were pure profit or the losses were all debit.

One thing was certain, I wanted to improve my marriage to extract bigger and better benefits from it for us both. Somehow I had to break through Walter's rigidity, his unwillingness to experiment, to participate in new experiences. There had to be a way to win him over, establish an *entente cordiale,* perhaps not a perfect union but the best we could put together.

The days passed comfortably, lazily, and as my

energy level rose I began to realize how worn down
and weary I had been. I could almost feel the tension
draining away.

One morning we took a motor launch over to St.
John Island and I went snorkeling at Trunk Bay, exploring the coral reef and watching the fish in such
great variety and color. On the beach, Walter sat with
his back to a tree and read.

Another day we toured St. Thomas and went swimming in Magen's Bay, perhaps the most beautiful beach
on the island. So it went.

And at night in the dark of our room, we made
love. I began to receive new vibrations, deeper feelings,
as if Walter was giving himself over to the experience
with intensified enthusiasm and passion. Not that he
was any less meticulous in the way he utilized my
body. Or less judicious in what he said, or when he
said it, or *if* he said anything at all.

Once or twice, I offered an indecent proposal, suggested some obscene practice, only to be rebuffed and
rebuked as before. Nevertheless, I sensed a certain
slackness in his opposition, as if his grip on those
damned puritanical convictions was loosening.

Those nights were good. Slow, warm, without conflict, without pressure to perform; but also without the
kind of flashy physicality ole Bubba brought to the
bedroom. Absent also was the stormy huffing and
puffing of an Ellenbogen. But good nights, so very satisfying and friendly in a still, deep, lasting way.

In the slow moments, I remembered how it had
been with Bubba. His lean and lovely body, his athletic gyrations, the satisfaction he got and gave. How
much fun he had been. For a while.

And now Ellenbogen. What a great leaping whale he
was, powerful and passionate, adventuresome, possessed
of a truly dirty mind. He hardly appeared to be the pro-
totype of your Manhattan wife-servicing bachelor.
But I doubted anyone could do any better.

How soon would I give up on him? Or he on me? It

was inevitable, I supposed. These sexual lunchtimes that fed lust and ego but offered few nutrients to the spirit. After Ellenbogen what?

Another man. Sooner or later someone would come along. Someone different and therefore exciting in his newness. I needed that. I wanted it. Everything the world had to offer.

What about Walter? My home, my family? My investment in them was too great to risk losing, and I was dedicated to the safety and well-being of us all. But without neglecting myself.

Yes, I wanted it both ways. All ways. In my private life, in my professional life, in bed and out. Are you any different? Is anyone? I had discovered it could be that way. If the correct prescription was written and the instructions on the label carefully followed.

Contradictory? Of course. So much of life is, isn't it?

Hypocritical? Perhaps, by some lights. Or had I finally become more honest in dealing with the reality of my existence?

All my moves were going to be thought out from now on. Carefully planned, competently executed. This meant playing a part, but most people projected an image in order to compete and succeed.

I would, too. I would do it right, have it all eventually, everything I wanted.

Everything.

thirty-nine

Two nights before our vacation was to end, we had dinner at Harbor View. A fine old house set high on a hill in back of the town. We drank planter's punch on the wide terrace over the pool and watched the lights of the boats in the harbor skitter around in the dark like nervous fireflies.

A waiter announced that our dinner was ready and escorted us to a table in a gracious Victorian room. We had a superb gazpacho served in a pewter bowl, a really fine veal piccata, and a good Chablis. For dessert, a sinfully rich chocolate pie, and espresso.

The meal put Walter in a surprisingly romantic mood and as soon as we got back to our room at Lime Tree I got out of my clothes. Later, in the darkness and suspended in a warm state of acute satisfaction, I began to plot a change of life for Walter and me.

The following morning I went shopping. There was booze from Sparky's to be delivered directly to the airport; a Baume & Mercier watch at H. Stern's for Walter, outrageously expensive; Joy by Jean Patou for me, billed as the costliest perfume in the world, bought at Tropicana, the World's Largest Perfumerie. For Stevie, a snorkeling outfit, fins, snorkel and face mask, some finger puppets and a few toys. And for

Ellenbogen, a stainless steel Rolex, courtesy of Little Switzerland, costing much less than Walter's present; everything in its place, yes.

After a light lunch, Walter and I sunned ourselves at the side of the pool. I swam some laps before we went to the room for an afternoon nap.

I took off my bikini in the dressing alcove and draped the silk scraf over myself. In the mirror I could see my body, prettily veiled and made more sensuous for being so, I thought. I went into the bedroom.

Walter was already in bed, sheet drawn pristinely to his waist. I placed myself where he could get an unobstructed view and did a slow, provocative dance behind the scarf. Walter averted his glance.

"You said you wanted to take a nap."

"Look at me, Walter." I danced nearer to him.

He watched my face.

"Here," I said. "Look at me here. Do you find this so revolting?"

"Don't be silly. It's just that—I can't help the way I am."

I took a step or two closer. "Of course you can. I'll help you."

He lay back down, eyes closed. "Come to bed."

"My pleasure." I took the sheet away. He was half-hard and I was encouraged. I lay down next to him, spreading the scarf across us both. "Look, darling, it's very pretty, exotic, exciting . . ."

He took one quick look and fell back on the pillow. He was all hard now and I hadn't even touched him.

"I love your body," I said softly, moving my lips across his chest. He was stiff and tense, braced against whatever I might do. I put the tip of my tongue in his navel and he reacted as if in pain. His knees rose up, the rigidity gone suddenly. I bent over him and kissed his penis through the scarf, nibbled lightly.

"Libby," he protested feebly.

I continued to kiss him, gently, lovingly, going everywhere. He moaned and sat up. I lay back down and directed his attention to the scarf. "Now you do me, Walter."

He shook his head, eyes flicking back and forth.

"Haven't you ever?"

"No."

I put his hand on me. "Not with anyone? Even before you met me?"

"Never."

"Have you thought about it?"

"Libby . . . please."

"Have you?"

"Once in a while."

"Don't you want to see what it's like?"

"No."

"You might enjoy it."

"I don't think so."

"Some men do." I touched him lightly, stroked him gently and he stiffened in place. "Look at me, Walter. Down there."

"I can't."

"Yes, you can. Nothing bad will happen."

His jaw flexed. His mouth tightened. His eyes rolled shut. And finally he looked. But not for long.

"There. Are you satisfied?"

"Was it so bad?"

"I'm past forty, Libby. In all this time, I never really looked at a woman before."

"Look again."

"I don't think so."

But he looked.

"Closer, Walter."

He swayed and leaned.

"Rest your face on me, Walter."

"We better stop."

"I want us to share this . . . everything, Walter."

"I can't."

"The scarf is a screen. Kiss me, Walter. Once."

"Once?"

"Kiss me."

"Must you have your own way?"

He bent over me and I pulled the scarf away. His mouth pressed between my legs, lips hard and tightly shut. For a stopped moment of time it seemed that he would rise up enraged and humiliated. Instead his lips grew soft and he kissed me again. And then again.

"Ah, Walter, do . . . to me. Do . . ."

He hesitated only briefly. I opened myself to him and the sap began to run thick and deep, warming me out to the edges.

A vague uneasiness came over me. For someone with no prior experience, Walter was exhibiting a high degree of Yankee know-how. A rising enthusiasm, you might say. I chose to mark it down to love. To his desire to please. Even to an innate talent.

I put my suspicions aside. Why look for trouble when everything is coming your way? Everything you ever wanted. There is, after all, such a thing as a happy ending.

Isn't there?

ABOUT THE AUTHOR

BURT HIRSCHFELD is best known for his bestselling novels, *Fire Island* and *Aspen*. A native New Yorker, Mr. Hirschfeld was born in Manhattan and raised in the Bronx. He left school at the age of seventeen and took a series of menial jobs. Immediately after Pearl Harbor he enlisted, and spent three of his four years in service overseas. After the war, he attended a southern college for several years. For the next fifteen years he worked on and off for movie companies and also did some radio and acting work. Burt Hirschfeld did not write his first novel until he was in his early thirties. He worked on it for three years and, when it only earned $1,500, he abandoned writing for several years. At thirty-seven, he decided to find out for once and all whether he had the makings of a successful writer and began to freelance. He wrote everything—from comic books to movie reviews. He also wrote numerous paperback novels under various pseudonyms and eleven nonfiction books for teenagers which were very well received. *Fire Island* was his first major success. *Aspen* was made into a mini-series presentation for national television. Burt Hirschfeld lives in Westport, Connecticut, with his wife and two sons.